CORRUPTION

'My . . . my bosom hurts,' she said softly, in a feeble whisper. 'Here.' She grabbed Patricia's salve-stained hand and pressed it against her chest. Her skin was hot, her nipple a stiff warm poker against her fingers. The tingle in her hand seemed like a red flame – the sudden fire travelled up her arm, through her suddenly erect, full nipples, down her belly, finally finding a home in between her legs.

'Mother Superior . . . Mother Superior wants me to rub the medicine on her bosom?' asked the beautiful slender novice, her eyes dazed with the fiery sensations coursing through her womanhood.

'Yes!' cried Elsbeth. 'Please rub my . . . rub it.' She clasped her fingers around Patricia's hand and forcefully rubbed the girl's fingers against her naked heaving bosom. 'Yes . . . like that. Like that.'

Patricia rubbed the Mother Superior's tits with her hands. She vaguely realised the salve on her hand had been used up already, but she couldn't seem to stop fondling the nun's shapely breasts. The nipples were so erect, so nice in between her fingers. Her skin was soft, warm, inviting. She was fondling Elsbeth's quivering tits, abandoning all pretence of simply applying medication.

'Yes . . .' moaned Elsbeth. 'Suck on my nipples, Patricia.'

CORRUPTION

Virginia Crowley

This book is a work of fiction.
In real life, make sure you practise safe, sane and consensual sex.

First published in 2006 by
Nexus
Thames Wharf Studios
Rainville Rd
London W6 9HA

www.nexus-books.co.uk

Typeset by TW Typesetting, Plymouth, Devon

Printed and bound by Clays Ltd, St Ives PLC

ISBN 0 352 34073 8
ISBN 978 0 352 34073 3

One

'Lord Peabody used to be the heart and soul of this congregation. Without his kindness and generosity, our good works in Redfork would never have succeeded. When this Priory was founded less than thirty years ago, we monks struggled mightily every single day of the year just to survive. Lord Peabody made it possible for us to pray for the souls of this congregation, as it is our sacred duty, without the constant spectre of starvation staring us in the face. Lord Peabody came to our aid and lifted our spirits when they were at their lowest. He did not permit the seeds of doubt – seeds sent by the devil himself, no doubt – to take root. When Mother Elsbeth came to Redfork with the two orphans who sought refuge at the Convent, it was Lord Peabody who generously donated his manor house near the convent at Mount Eleanor as the site of the new orphanage. He was a devout, honest, Christian man, a man of great generosity and spartan asceticism –' and here Prior Steven paused, grimly, for he hated having to add this last – 'for the greater part of his life.'

Laura Peabody, the Lord's sole surviving issue, sat behind a black veil in the back row, surrounded by sympathetic villagers. Her weeping had already interrupted the service once. At least the young sombre woman had the grace to mourn. She had not been seen in Redfork much over the last five years, as she had been learning her letters, etiquette, needlepoint and other arts of high-born ladies with a distant aunt in the far north. It was a double tragedy for the poor orphan that several weeks before the news of Lord Peabody's death, her aunt had succumbed to some kind of a pox, effectively leaving the budding beauty at the mercy of her stepmother. Laura had seen to her aunt's funeral arrangements and hurried home immediately, receiving news of her father's death with a majestic, solemn grief that was in such sharp contrast to her stepmother's behaviour.

The Prior glared at Lord Peabody's downfall, Laura's stepmother, the strumpet sitting in the front aisle. The honest villagers who made up the bulk of the congregation spurned the company of the pretty widow. The harlot did not even wear a proper dress to her husband's funeral. Stephanie Peabody's dress was nearly transparent, expensive black lace imported from the continent at horrifying cost, enough for the upkeep of perhaps the entire orphanage for a year. At least she was sitting now, and those whore's spiked stiletto heels were no longer gouging the simple wooden floorboards of his church. He took grim satisfaction from his next announcement. 'Lord Peabody, the day before he died, came to me.' His announcement generated a frenzied avalanche of excited whispers. He was not the only one to glance over at Stephanie.

The tawdry blonde harlot's vapid blue eyes were suddenly sharp and attentive. She was waiting for him to get to the crux of the matter, he knew.

'He came to me and told me he knew he was dying . . .' here he took a deep breath, 'and he told me he knew his conduct over the last few months had damned his soul for all eternity.' The congregation exploded anew, a few animated whispers rising to a tumult in the nave. Stephanie sat stiffly, a gilded alabaster statue of rage and fury.

A scant week after the death of his wife, Lord Peabody had married her former upstairs maid. The death of Lady Jane Peabody was a scandal in its own right – people whispered that she died of a broken heart, the direct result of Lord Peabody's cruelly blatant fornication with her own maidservant. Others spoke of poison, or criminal neglect. The weeks leading up to her death had seen a general deterioration in the religious devotion of the late Lord. Some of the villagers began to whisper about a sordid affair between Lord Peabody and this haughty, coldly beautiful maidservant, a scandalous young woman named Stephanie Hayes. Fuelling the rumours was the estate's gardener – drunk, the man claimed to have seen the Lord and the upstairs maid committing adultery in the castle rose garden while Lady Jane lay helpless in her sickbed. The rumours were apparently confirmed when Lord Peabody asked – no, the late lord *demanded* – that he consecrate his union with the maidservant, not even waiting for a few months to mourn the passing of his wife, the mother of his only daughter. As soon as Stephanie Hayes became Lady Peabody, the castle's new mistress began to place orders for expensive wines, foods, fabrics and all sorts of fripperies. Lord Peabody's lifestyle changed drastically upon succumbing to Stephanie's charms – overnight, he went from an ascetic exemplary family man into a wine-guzzling gluttonous fornicator, a drooling pitiful shambles of a man, wrapped around the perfectly manicured finger of his manipulative gold-digging wife.

'Lord Peabody, like I said, came to me.' Steven held up his hand, asking for silence. The congregation slowly quietened down.

'He said he was concerned for the state of his soul – and the direction he had taken, and the Priory with it, before his illness. I need not remind every one of you that without Lord Peabody's generosity, the Priory has fallen on hard times. This, at least, Lord Peabody has been able to solve for us in death, may God grant him peace.' He quoted the Gospel of Matthew: 'If thou wilt be perfect, go and sell all that thou hast and give to the poor and thou shalt find treasure in heaven.'

Steven stared directly at Stephanie as he delivered the words of the Gospel. She was glaring at him, her eyes blue, icy daggers. If a look could kill, Steven knew he would be a thousand times dead already. He gripped the bible with both hands, gaining a measure of comfort from the protection of the Good Book.

'Lord Peabody executed a new will three days ago, just before he died. It was witnessed by Mother Superior Elsbeth, Bishop Warener and myself. It is available for inspection by any who so desire.' He allowed himself a small satisfied smile.

The congregation was abuzz. He had to ask for silence again. 'The Priory shall gain direct title to Lord Peabody's accounts, without exception. This includes all accounts receivable and the jewellery . . .' here he allowed himself an indulgent gentle smile, 'including, of course, the family's ancestral jewels. The Priory shall also act as custodian of Lord Peabody's assets, to use them in a charitable and just manner, until Lady Laura Peabody reaches the age of nineteen, or until she is married. This includes the castle, the cottage, the forest and the livestock. The late Lord bequeathed the town house in Salisbury to the Priory, to be used as an orphanage.'

Stephanie stood up, apoplectic with rage. Her hiss was louder than any scream. 'You want to turn me into a pauper! You can't do this!'

He nearly stepped back from the chilling waves of naked fury radiating from her face. 'I most certainly can, Miss Hayes,' he said with calculated brutality. She gasped aloud as if slapped; the insult was open and deliberate. Not only did Steven fail to address her as befitting the widow of a Lord, he addressed her by her maiden name, as if the marriage had never taken place. The echo of unabashed sniggering rang throughout the church. She was being treated like a common whore! Her lips were tightly pressed together, a lurid pink line of painted hatred.

The Prior waved the will in the air. 'Take off all that jewellery and go in peace, young woman, or I will have it taken off of you.'

He closed his eyes to pray for God's divine grace in this uncomfortable situation. There was some expectant sniggering from the congregation. A young man chuckled, his voice carrying loud across the breadth of the nave. 'I will strip the harlot for free.' The sniggering grew into mocking laughter.

Stephanie caught his gaze, her eyes blazing, icy blue stars of unabashed hatred. She took off the earrings, her obscenely long painted fingernails sliding the shiny gold jewellery from her pierced ears. She slowly and reluctantly unclasped the Peabody necklace, the diamonds sliding against the flawless skin of her ample bosom. The Prior found his eyes lingering on that alabaster skin – surely an accident, he chided himself, he was just looking at the unwholesome site where she rested the jewellery she was surrendering. Still, he was momentarily unnerved by the calculating cold smirk that flitted across her shallow beautiful face.

She walked out of the ceremony without another glance at her late husband's bloated sad-looking corpse, her stiletto heels leaving tiny stab wounds in the church floorboards.

Steven noticed several of the young men in the congregation stare lustily at the harlot's swaying hips and her nearly exposed bosom. He made a mental note to address the corruption of the flesh during his next sermon.

He had the Sub-Prior place the jewels in the Priory treasure chest, next to several holy relics. Since taking over as Prior, he had managed to improve the finances of the monastery through the imposition of thrifty Christian discipline and the practice of honest Christian values. Lord Peabody was instrumental in this process with regular large cash donations. The donations dried up as soon as he became infatuated with his whorish wife – but he has seen the light in the end, thank the Virgin. Now Steven could continue to build the monastery's library with precious expensive books. He would not have to sell the sacred golden chalices consecrated to various saints, the jewelled golden platter depicting the Immaculate Conception, and other less precious but just as sacred treasures, just to meet the expenses of the orphanage.

It has been a long and fruitful day despite – or perhaps, because of – Lord Peabody's funeral. He felt a pang of shame at the uncharitable thought. At least the late Lord's gold-digger widow seemed to have accepted her imminent poverty without any further uncomfortable fuss. He had already decided to turn the town house into an extension of the orphanage in Salisbury. Perhaps he would let the harlot stay in a barn on the Peabody estate, or even in the guesthouse. Surely, to allow her to stay in the late Lord's small modest cottage during the winter, as well as receive a small supply of firewood and food to see her to spring, would be Christian charity. He had promised to look after the late Lord's family in any event – technically, the painted harlot was a member of the Peabody clan. He felt good about this generous charitable impulse. In fact, he felt so good about the day's events, he allowed himself the modest luxury of a fresh pastry, a strangely exotic-tasting gift that an anonymous parishioner had left on his doorstep for him before he'd returned home. He fell into an exhausted slumber, gratified and emotionally drained.

He found himself inside a wedding chapel – the altar was a cross-shaped table with a beautiful pure-white three-tier wedding cake in its centre. He smiled at the wedding cake, pleased at its simplicity, its beautiful lines, the holy matrimony it signified. Thoughts of marriage made him think of the last ceremony he had conducted. He frowned. It was a lurid distasteful affair. Lord Peabody insisted. The Prior had been forced to marry the enfeebled Lord to that tawdry wench Stephanie. She came to her wedding dressed like the Whore of Babylon, in brazen nearly transparent lace, her slender naked ankles covered in gold chains. Her feet were clad in hot-pink pointy shoes, the heels, stiletto daggers, gouging the soft wooden floorboards of his beautiful church. Lord Peabody, red faced, drooling, had spent a fortune on expensive wines and food – he gorged himself and degraded the institution of marriage with his lurid behaviour. The besotted Lord kept staring at his harlot bride's temptingly luscious, practically naked bosom and pretty ankles with unabashed lust, his saintly old mother's diamond necklace already adorning the upstairs maid's slender neck. For some reason, the vision of the ceremony tugged at the Prior. He shook his head, surprised. He felt a more insistent, faint tug on his member, as if whisper-light fingers were caressing the shaft. Surprised, he felt the beginning of a lustful stirring. He frowned and spoke the Lord's Prayer in quick fervent tones, trying to will away the sinful impulse.

It was no good – the stroking on his member seemed to grow more tangible, quietly insistent.

He felt eyes upon him. When he looked up, he saw Stephanie had magically appeared on the altar table. She was reclining, luridly exposed, luscious, her supple young body and large quivering tits glistening with oil. Her feet and back were seductively arched, making her long pretty legs appear even longer and her breasts look even bigger. She wore the same pink whore shoes she wore at the wedding. Her eyes were huge, outlined with kohl, her lips painted a lurid hot pink. She gave him a lazy cold calculating smile, her long manicured nails slowly stroking her nipples.

Her gaze on him did not waver as she traced a perfectly manicured nail on the icing of the wedding cake. She began to suck on the rich creamy stuff. Her finger left a careless ugly furrow on the smooth white confection.

Steven tried to look away, his face suffused with a confused mixture of lust and moral foreboding. His virgin member, ignored and disregarded for so many years, was a quivering eager iron-hard sceptre of confused and aching desire.

Stephanie gave a knowing bitchy smile as she pointedly stared at Steven's massive erection, obvious against the coarse brown fabric of his robe. She giggled and extended a prettily arched foot, prodding his robe where his member turned the fabric into a tent of base lust. She slid the pointy toes of her slutty pink shoes up and down, up and down, up and down, rubbing the coarse cloth against his raging erection. His eyes were drawn to the hot pink of the leather, the stiletto heels. Inexorably, his gaze travelled up her long slender naked legs, dazed with unfamiliar lustful cravings.

She maliciously clawed into the pure smooth white of the cake, her fingernails long pink claws, leaving a jagged ugly crater in the beautiful confection. She smeared the sweet mess on top of her wantonly displayed, naked sex. The rich cake sat on top of her brazenly displayed womanhood, the icing oozing into the exposed yawning pink, yellow crumbs forming tiny little islands on the glistening lurid surface. She gave him an indolent sleazy smile, her voice dripping with condescension.

'Puppy is hungry, no?' she cooed, her voice soft, lazy, insistent. She continued to rub his erection with her shoes, up and down, up and down. The pointed slender heels poked into his stomach.

He groaned, her condescending bitchy tone somehow worming its way through his ears, directly into his twitching responding member.

'Puppy wants to eat cake . . . puppy wants to eat cake . . .' she giggled and he felt his lips part and drool dribbled onto his monastic robes. She slid her finger into the centre of the cake on her pussy, sliding it up and down, up and down, matching the motion of her high heels on his robe, her busy digit sliding into the creamy crumbling mess in between her legs. She took her finger out of her cunt after a few strokes and slowly shoved the sticky filthy digit into Steven's stunned helpless mouth.

'Puppy has to be fed . . .' She smirked, sitting up, her long naked legs prettily folded to the side, her feet still prettily arched. Her tits jiggled with the motion, arresting his gaze, while she slipped her pink talons underneath his robe, her long fingers triumphantly latching around his quivering rock-hard cock. She fingered his mouth and manipulated his cock at the same time.

The cake was incredibly sweet, cloying. Steven had never tasted anything like it in his entire life. Without knowing what he was doing, he found himself suckling on Stephanie's outstretched beautiful finger. Each sweet taste made his erection harder and harder, until he felt nothing but Stephanie's degrading manipulation, his cock eagerly leaning into each filthy caress. He licked her finger clean.

His lust-crazed member drooled at the tip as Stephanie's hot-pink manicured nails, so sharp and long, slid along the shaft. He felt a momentary pang of pain. The sensation of the slight cut was immediately replaced by a phenomenal wave of filthy pleasure, an addictive insistent explosion in his mind. His balls contracted and he felt great gobs of cum spurt from his tortured cock. Spent, he moaned out loud, the gasp of fornication immediately overcome by a wave of guilt.

He woke up, sobbing and ashamed. To his horror, he felt a sticky cold puddle in between his legs. He raised his nightclothes and stared at his offending exhausted member, still dribbling his seed as it contracted. To his surprise, he felt a tiny pang of pain – he took his penis in his hands and examined it like some kind of alien beast. Near the top of the shaft, he discovered a tiny cut. He gasped in superstitious fear, then thought better of it. He must have dreamed it all in a heartbeat after his penis was scratched by something on the bed. It was still sinful, of course, and he would have to seek absolution for his impure thoughts, but dreams of this nature were not unknown in the monastery, albeit almost always experienced by the younger monks, particularly novices, certainly not the Prior. He considered the possible effect of any confession on his authority. There would certainly be a lot of sniggering – it might even jeopardise his plans for the expansion of the orphanage. He could see in his mind's eye how Laura, Lord Peabody's young bright daughter, would shudder with revulsion as she learned of his carnal dream with her wicked stepmother. He made a mental note to see to her welfare after his return. She had gone through enough.

He would seek absolution from the Bishop in Salisbury, a week's journey at most by foot. He had to send someone to town anyway – the orphanage needed warm coats for the winter, and the garments could only be acquired in such quantity in town.

He summoned the Sub-Prior. Anders was competent, still young and vigorous, he could be relied upon to see to the monastery for a week or two. The young man also had a sharp clear head on his shoulders – he acted as the monastery's cellarer, keeping track of the Priory's business. He would be a fine stand-in.

'How long will you be gone, Prior Steven?'

Steven considered carefully before he replied. 'Two weeks, perhaps three at most.'

He gave Anders the key to the treasury. 'I shall have no more need of this – I believe you have earned the right to safeguard the key to the treasury. If some ill fortune should befall me on the road, I would rather not carry this key upon my person.'

Despite the considerable amount of silver he was bringing with him to purchase the coats for the orphanage, he decided to go alone. No robbers would attack a monk. There was no point – most monks were men of no material means. Saint Francis insisted that his followers carry no purse, wear no shoes, and wear a triple-knotted rope instead of a belt. Steven followed those rules to the letter. He wore only his monastic robes, coarse brown wool that would never tempt a bandit. He wore his triple-knotted rope belt. He had no purse. Of course, in these modern times, many monasteries dispensed with the proscriptions of Saint Francis, but Steven was a throwback, a true ascetic. He procured an oak strongbox for the silver, putting the ungainly container inside a burlap sack. He supposed the heavy sack could be construed as a purse, but as long as it was not worn on his rope belt and used for his personal needs, he was not in violation of the Saint's wise restrictions. Money, readily available, only leads to temptation.

He set out at daybreak, walking briskly. He could have taken a horse: the monastery was fairly well off, particularly with the Peabody bequest, but he felt the need to do penance. He broke into a merry hymn as he hurried along the path, his eyes gleaming with holy fervour. He carried only a jug of water and the precious burden of silver to purchase the winter coats. He brought very little food – a small sack of turnips. He knew he would starve, but he welcomed the deprivation of his body after his sordid experience. 'Rich food is a gateway to corruption' – he remembered his own words, one of his favourite themes this past Easter. He had admonished the congregation with exceptional severity, his ardour fanned by the late Lord's refusal to contribute to a modest Easter feast at the orphanage. The besotted noble had sent him away empty handed while he feasted on capon and sturgeon with his painted tawdry mistress.

The only other item on him was the key to Lord Peabody's town house. He intended to inventory the valuables inside. The place was well furnished, a gilded elegant mansion in the best part of town. Steven planned to purchase the coats and store them there until he could send a cart for them from the Priory. The mansion was too luxurious for a simple monk such as himself to sleep at, of course – he would seek simple spartan accommodations at the Bishop's palace, perhaps a servant's chambers. The small oak cash box was heavy – he carried the burlap sack slung over his shoulder, its humble material disguising its valuable nature from greedy eyes. By dinnertime, he was famished and exhausted, his back sore with the weight. He drank some water and ate some turnips.

He made steady progress. His hunger grew greater and greater, and he welcomed it. The stars were bright in the heavens and his spirits lifted somewhat. He prayed to Saint Christopher to keep him safe and to the Virgin to help him with his mission in Salisbury. On the fourth night, he came upon some travellers.

A family was about to sit down to dinner, he could smell the scent of roasting meat. When they saw him, the man of the family, a craftsman of some sort judging from the box of tools to the side, bowed deeply. 'Please join us, Father,' he said, properly deferential.

'Thank you, my son – God shall repay your kindness.' He found it hard not to drool as his nostrils widened to admit the wonderful smell of freshly roasted meat. He reminded himself of the reason for his self-imposed penance as he sat by the fire. He usually made do with a mere handful of fitful flames at night. So long without a good hearty fire, he felt it was not inappropriate to enjoy a moment of comfort.

The woman boiled water in a pot. 'Some sweet tea, Prior?'

'That will be most welcome, thank you for your kindness.' He lowered himself next to the warming blaze. The firelight played on each member of the man's family. Steven sipped on the tea. It was indeed sweet, an unusual pleasant flavour mingling with the berries and leaves of the forest that had been added to the mixture. His eyes lingered on the man's wife, on her bright blonde hair. She was most comely. He found himself smiling, entranced by the way that the fire made shadows in between her large heavy breasts. The woman seemed to feel his eyes on her and smiled back at him.

'Please share our humble fare with us tonight. Where is your monastery?' She handed him a bowl full of succulent freshly roasted meat.

'Prior Steven. I am Prior Steven of Redfork.' He stared at the savoury offering. His stomach rumbled.

'We have seen you before.' Her voice was a velvet purr. 'We just came from Redfork ourselves. We left right after Lord Peabody's funeral . . . Have some more tea, Prior.'

He frowned in confusion – if they just came from Redfork, why did they ask who he was? He sipped his tea. The heavy mix of herbs and berries made the water cloudy. The meat in the bowl smelled wonderful. His fingers wrapped around a juicy mouthwatering portion of roasted fowl. He raised it to his mouth, only to drop the meat in sudden shame. He recalled his penance, his crime, and the need to cleanse his body. Even the sweet tea seemed like a sin, a sybaritic luxury, now.

The comely woman yawned aloud, stretching her shapely arms over her head. Her breasts seemed to swell in her linen shift.

Steven felt a no-longer unfamiliar, filthy yearning below his rope belt. He stood abruptly, thrusting the untouched bowl into the woman's lap. 'I am fasting, and I must get to Salisbury by the day after tomorrow,' he babbled, keeping his gaze centred on the flames.

He was hungry, but not for roast meat – as his eyes avoided looking at the craftsman's comely wife, his tongue recalled the sweet cloying taste of the cake in his dream. It was sweet like this tea, this wonderful tea. His member remembered as well – the sweet flavour was intense on his tongue as his cock began to twitch expectantly beneath his robe. He practically ran out of the campsite, carrying his heavy burden of silver in his hands. The woman's surprised laughter seemed to chase him. Somehow, her tinkling soprano voice excited him even more. His erect member slapped against his thigh as he ran.

He finally reached Salisbury. He smelled the town well before he saw it – the smell of refuse and garbage was a stale and unwelcome reminder of city life. His feet and back were incredibly sore; his belly ached with hunger. The great gates were open wide, with peasants from the countryside carting vegetables, chickens, eggs, barley, flour into the open market. Other, less savoury business was also conducted here, near the gates – painted whores sauntered through the streets, their eyes openly assessing the potential of his purse. He carefully wrapped his robe around his heavy sack, scanning the crowd for pickpockets.

One of the whores caught his eye, a brazen sultry wench with long unruly brown curls, wearing a flimsy bright red robe. She smiled at him, weighing the unlikely interest of a monk and the even less likely possibility that he had coin. He was too surprised to look away. Her eyes never breaking contact, the young woman arched her back, parting the full-length slit in her robe. She exposed her supple naked body beneath, her long pale legs luridly visible against the red background. He saw her breasts were not quite as full as Stephanie's in his dream, and her dark bush still had hair on it. She pushed her tits together, fondling her breasts in a tawdry invitation of lustful pleasures. Suddenly he realised he was ogling her naked body, as if he was one of her fornicating customers!

Smirking, she deemed him interested in her wares, and was walking over to him, her robe still halfway parted, a greedy calculating smile on her pretty painted face.

‘Sinful harlot!’ he blustered, his face bright red. He hurried past the amused whore, shoving her aside as he brushed past. She laughed mockingly as he fled. His hand burned with the incidental contact of her soft warm flesh. The Prior’s manhood rose eagerly at the contact. His walk turned into a near run, directly to the Cathedral. The great church was already closed. He considered banging on the immense doors, but decided against it. It was not becoming of a Prior, a humble man of God. Nevertheless, he felt he could not seek rest until he at least made an effort at penance and absolution. It was obvious that the devil had sent Stephanie, the pretty wife of the craftsman, and this other whore to tempt him. He felt compelled to seek purification – the feeling of being sullied was overwhelming.

He remembered there was a small chapel at the Peabody town house. He made his way past the market, heading north. The street became narrow, turning into a maze of dark alleys.

‘You don’t want to go in there, Brother,’ a jolly fat man in a baker’s apron warned him with a smile. ‘That is the Whores’ Quarter. It is dangerous at night, and a man of God has no business there anyway. You can go around it by going three streets west and then take Goldsmith Lane north again.’

‘Blessings of the Lord upon you, my son. Thank you for your courtesy. I have not been to Salisbury in quite some time.’

The man waved him goodbye as he turned west, the cluster of sinister alleys receding behind him. As he made his way north on Goldsmith Lane, the shops went from respectable to downright prosperous. Salisbury seemed even busier and richer than the last time Steven had been here. At the end of Goldsmith Lane, an elegant row of town houses – homes for rich local gentry, and residences for great Lords of the land while they were in town to visit the Cathedral – adorned the wide avenue. The Peabody town house was off the main artery, in a small, even more distinguished little street near the north wall.

It was near dusk by the time he found the town house. His feet hurt. He wanted to go inside, find the chapel and pray before he sought out the Bishop tomorrow morning. He fished through the sack for the sizeable cast iron key of the town house. Steven inserted the key in the huge lock and began to fiddle with it. The long weeks of non-use had made the lock uncooperative – or perhaps he was just unfamiliar with it.

'You! You in those . . . monk's robes!'

He turned around to see a thin bald man bearing down on him. He wore a disagreeable angry scowl and the mantle of a master merchant of some kind, in bright hues of blue and green.

'Who are you? What are you doing at Lord Peabody's town house?' His suspicion cut like a knife.

'I am Prior Steven of Redfork,' he answered patiently. 'Lord Peabody bequeathed the town house to my care. What is your name and interest in this, milord?'

The man threw up his hands defensively. 'I am no Lord! My name is Tisdale. I am a wool merchant. Master Tisdale, if you will, my Lord Prior. What . . . What are your plans here, Prior Steven?'

Steven sighed. 'I intend to go inside and pray inside the chapel until sunrise.'

'I understand, I understand . . . so when you are done praying, what then?'

Steven began to get exasperated. 'Thereafter I shall visit the Lord Bishop.'

The man had the temerity to make the sign of the cross, as if Warener was some kind of a saint. 'Good for you, Prior, so . . .'

'I really must go and meditate, my son.'

The man blushed and made as if to open his mouth but he was interrupted by a shrill demanding voice coming from the other side of the street. 'Is it some beggar, Master Tisdale?'

'My wife . . .' said the merchant in a low voice.

Steven finally managed to turn the key. He opened the door and waved the merchant goodbye, shutting him out.

He fumbled through the ill lit antechamber and the solar before he found a candle and flint. Once he was able to see, he gawked like the country monk that he was. The town house was beautiful – it was richly appointed and furnished in an elaborate manner. He even found a small library full of precious books. A good half of the books concerned theology. For the first time since his arrival in Salisbury, he felt safe and happy. Not without regret, he left the library room to look for the chapel. When he found it, he put the candle on the altar and took out his rosary. He recited the rosary all night until he saw the red light of the sun striking the windows high within the chapel.

He hurried over to the Bishop's palace. A guard admitted him to the Bishop's office, where a young deacon, Robert, met him in short order. Robert was a short pious man, well known for his beautiful voice in chorus throughout the county.

'You look tired, Father,' said Robert. 'Can I offer you a goblet of wine?'

'I've come to see the Bishop,' said Steven. 'It is a matter of urgency.'

'I fear I have some bad news.' Robert paused delicately. 'Bishop Warener has been summoned to Rome.'

Steven was not surprised. He had seen few high-born visitors around the palace, and had anticipated something like this. He sighed heavily.

Robert smiled. 'The good news is that he is expected back soon – any day now.'

Steven immediately felt better. 'That is good.'

Robert fell silent and studied Prior Steven for a moment. 'Prior . . .' he began.

'Yes?'

'I am sure Bishop Warener would be honoured if you lodged at the palace while you waited.'

Steven considered – it was not at all unusual and, in his present state, some privacy was called for.

'It would be I who would be honoured,' he said, gratified.

A servant led him to a small, but well appointed room. A clean small bed, a bed stand, a table, a chair – it was all he needed and more. He gave silent thanks to the Lord and sat down on the bed. He felt the tiny cut pull on the skin of his member, an annoying reminder of his current spiritual crisis. He motioned to the servant.

'I need some kind of salve for a small cut.'

The man bowed. 'I will bring it right up, Prior. Will there be anything else?'

'No, that should do.'

Prior Steven stoked the fire and was reading his bible by the light of the flames when the servant returned with an earthenware jar. It was full of a creamy white salve with a strong sweet flowery odour, very pleasant. Steven dismissed him and latched the door. He treasured his privacy, the silence in which he could commune with the Lord. He sighed and uncovered his sinful member, looking for the cut. He put his finger into the creamy salve; the stuff felt cool and soothing. He smeared some salve on the cut. Almost at once, he realised he had far too much of the stuff on his hand for such a small non-injury. As he applied the thick grease upon the tiny, yet irritatingly painful cut, the miniature wound seemed to soak the salve in. A pleasurable tingle spread from the base to the rest of his member.

He hesitated with the heavy dose of sweet-smelling grease on his hand. *Why waste such powerful medication . . . I can feel it working on the cut already* . . . Fingers trembling a little, he smeared the rest over his member. The sensation reminded him of Stephanie's filthy caresses in his dream. It was just like this. He became confused for a moment, the sweet scent of flowers strong in his nostrils. His hand slid over his cock, applying more salve. It was just like this. He began to rub his rapidly hardening member, working the stuff into his skin, the ointment still remaining in his hand not quite enough for proper lubrication. His penis seemed to soak the tingling salve in faster than he could apply it, instantly absorbing it, hungry for more. He dipped his hand in the jar again and smeared his prick thickly with the stuff. He closed his eyes, visions of Stephanie's hot pink heels rubbing up against his swollen member dancing in his head, her pouting lips smiling with condescension. His hand slipped on his salve-drenched greasy cock, the initial tentative fumbling turning into a single obscene stroke of obvious masturbation. A flash of Stephanie's luscious tits, the nipples huge and pink, intruded into his consciousness. Another stroke followed. Suddenly, his hand was moving up and down on his erect penis, stroke following stroke of his engorged well greased cock. He imagined Stephanie's hot pink nails sliding up and down his shaft, manipulating him through his mindless erection. He stumbled onto the bed, his hands checking the crumpled fall, smearing the sheets with the salve on his fingers. His fingers resumed their labour of filthy obscene degradation. He closed his eyes and saw Stephanie's naked bare pink cunt, the yellow crumbs of the wedding cake waiting for his drooling mouth. Endless echoes of Stephanie's filthy cooing seemed to add their own unique caress to those of his fingers. 'Puppy is hungry, no?'

His engorged greedy cock couldn't take any more of the seductive insistent images – with a final convulsive stroke of his greasy salve-stained fingers, he climaxed inside the lurid vision of Stephanie Peabody's yawning pink pussy. He fell back on the crumpled sheets, sweat-drenched, overcome by a guilt-ridden, fitful, shameful sleep.

He woke up late. Bright sunlight shone on his crumpled stained bedding. Guilt-ridden, he realised that he must have missed morning mass. The jar of salve lay on the floor, the lid missing, the sadly plundered contents mocking him. There was barely anything left in the fat earthenware container. Overcome with angry remorse, he picked it up and violently threw it against the wall. It shattered into dozens of shards, the sound brutally loud in the quiet serene atmosphere of the Bishop's palace. Ashamed of his anger, he collected the pieces. He donned his coarse brown robes and went to find the servant who had brought him the soothing concoction, put to such filthy use by his unworthy lustful fingers.

He found the man in the kitchens. He was mixing eggs in a gigantic wooden bowl, a large sack of flour waiting on the stout oak table. To his shock, there was a jar on the table beside it, an intact twin of the one he destroyed this morning. The servant looked up when Steven entered.

'Father,' he nodded. He did not look surprised when he saw the shards in Steven's hands.

'I broke the jar,' said Steven, simply. He was vaguely irritated by the non-specific nature of his sentence. He did not want to lie, not even by omission.

The servant smiled. 'We all get clumsy sometimes, father. Slipped out of your hand?'

'. . . Uh . . . Yes.' The lie burned like lye in his mouth.

'Here.' The servant smoothly slipped the new jar into his trembling hands. 'It's a wonderful ointment.'

Steven wanted to refuse, but the man's manner was so disarming, and his uncharacteristic lying so shameful, that he could not bring himself to open his mouth. He carried the jar back to his room and latched the door shut behind him. He wanted to pray alone, more than ever. He set the jar down on the table and collected his stained sheets, a crumpled heap in his hands. He would have to wash them somehow, without involving the staff. Dried gobs of semen adorned the coarse wool. It would have to be a vigorous thorough scrubbing. He sighed, distressed. The Bishop's return was becoming increasingly imperative. Steven sensed that his immortal soul was in danger. His anguished musings were interrupted by someone at the door, trying the latch.

'Father?' He heard a woman's voice, vaguely familiar. He shoved the shameful heap underneath the bed and opened the door, composing himself. He saw the comely wife of the craftsman on the road, her linen shift replaced by the purple and white livery of the diocese. She carried a bucket and a rag. His eyes grew wide, lingering on her ample bosom, her new uniform a shade too tight, or perhaps her bosom a size or so too large. The skin of her exposed cleavage was a healthy creamy white, luscious, tinged with pink. His manhood stirred, eagerly straining against his monastic robes. His eyes snapped back to her face when she addressed him again.

'My name is Sylvia, my lord Prior.' He blushed as he realised she knew what he had been looking at. How long had he been ogling this woman's breasts?

'What can I do for you, my child?' he asked, dry-mouthed.

'Like I said, I found employment here.' She smiled at him and curtsied, her breasts jiggling with the motion. 'I am to see to your every need while you are a guest here.' She smiled prettily, her large brown eyes doe-like on her young attractive face.

'Thank you, my child,' he said, exhausted by his ill fortune and by the devil's cunning to place such temptation in the path of righteousness.

The young woman squeezed past him to enter the room, her chest inadvertently rubbing against his own. Her breasts were firm, tight, like melons. She did not seem to notice his anxiety. She squeezed water from the rag and got on all fours, mopping the floor. Her shapely bottom gently swayed from side to side as she worked, collecting the fragments of pottery into a heap. She scrubbed the stains of the salve from the floor. He watched her open-mouthed, his cock straining against his robe. Her breasts looked immense, hanging down the way she was on all fours, her new shift barely able to contain them.

As she got to the bed she frowned prettily, puzzled. 'Where is the bedding?' she inquired.

'Uh . . . I will wash it myself,' he said, lamely. He realised his mistake immediately.

'I can't let you do that, Prior Steven,' she chided him gamely. 'It's my job, you know.' She leaned low, looking under the bed. Her ass rose up in the air, the purple linen skirt hugging each tempting curve as she pulled out the tangled mess of bedding. He tried to take the heap from her hand, but she turned to the side, the tangled fabric unfolding to reveal the filthy stained mess on its sullied surface.

She raised a pretty eyebrow, mock furious. 'This will have to be thoroughly washed, Prior,' she said softly, her eyes slowly taking in the huge obscene cum stains and the places where his exhausted salve-stained hand rested after his cock spurted his sinful seed. She gently patted his tonsure with her hand, understanding mixed with a sort of amused sympathy. Steven nearly swooned: her touch and fresh young scent fed his eager member plenty of reasons to rise to the occasion.

'It's all right, Prior. You are not the first, or the last.' She giggled, her throaty contralto stiffening his member further with desire. 'I will wash it myself, don't worry.' She gathered the sheets and left, winking at him. 'Nobody has to know . . .' She giggled softly in farewell.

He forced himself to return to the room without obeying his base instinct to stare at her retreating swaying bottom. He kneeled on the wet floor and prayed until sundown. He was exhausted, physically as well as spiritually. He decided to retire early, to regain his strength. Before he retired, he gazed upon the crucifix on his wall and begged the Lord for strength, for the courage to face up to his incessant evil lust, to quiet his demons. He fell asleep on the bare cot, wearing a contended weary smile.

Sylvia was suddenly inside his room. She was luscious, naked, her huge heavy tits glistening with salve. She dipped two fingers into his new jar and smeared the dribbly goo over her nipples.

She cooed as she petted him on his reeling head. 'It's OK, Prior . . .' She peeled off his nightclothes, freeing his eager throbbing cock. Her nails were hot pink, the same as Stephanie's. He watched her long fingers as if mesmerised. She caught his gaze and slid her fingers over her thick blonde bush, spreading her pussy lips with one hand while softly manipulating her clit with the other. She moaned and arched her back, making her gigantic breasts even more prominent.

His eyes snapped up from the tawdry spectacle of wanton masturbation to resume their worshipful gaze of her immense glistening tits. The spectacle of her masturbation goaded him on to touch her breasts.

Her fingers, glistening with her juices, slowly travelled back to her breasts, pushing them together, the massive fleshy globes offered tantalisingly close to his drooling lips. 'Puppy want to lick pretty titties, no?' she smirked. 'Or maybe Puppy want to hump pretty titties?'

Prior Steven moaned as he nodded, frantic with the need for release. His cock strained to reach the tempting offering. She smiled knowingly as she heard his eager whimpering, sliding his unresisting quivering organ in between her breasts. Her tits were warm, slick with the salve.

And he woke up. He was alone, his cock painfully hard, the afterglow of Sylvia's lickable tits an insistent corrosive tug on his cock.

Sobbing pathetically, with trembling fingers he uncorked the jar. The Prior dipped his hand all the way to the bottom, then spread great fat globs of flower-scented grease on his rock-hard cock. He fondled himself to the edge of a filthy obscene climax, rubbing his greasy prick in his hand, imagining Sylvia's big heavy tits sliding against his cock, her lips wide open, awaiting his member in a kind of filthy alluring invitation. He leaned back on the cot, trembling, his hand a blur on his salve-drenched, rock-hard cock, about to cum, when his door opened. It was Sylvia – she had a lit candle in one hand. In the other, she carried a wicker basket with his laundry. She gasped when she saw him on the cot, exposed, his hand wrapped around his oozing erect member.

She dropped the basket and ran out of the room, leaving him ashamed, terrified, guilt-ridden . . . and still painfully erect. Even in his moment of shame, he could not help but notice that Sylvia's tits were more exposed than usual, her linen shift damp with the perspiration of a long day at work, the thin fabric too skimpy to shield the sight of her hard pink nipples. He let go of his member, his guilt overcoming a debased reluctance to continue his frantic masturbation. He donned his robes. He had barely finished putting on his clothes when the young woman returned. She wore a strict expression as she marched towards him, her tits jiggling in her shift.

'Prior, this has to stop,' she sighed. 'I only know of one way to chase away your demons.' She looked at him solemnly. He tried to look her in the eye, but a filthy lustful hope entered his mind, and he could only nod as she spoke. Her breasts kept intruding on his consciousness.

'You must do a good work, a great work, in the face of temptation,' she intoned.

He was somehow disappointed, yet at the same time relieved, seized by an impulse to obey her, to cleanse himself, to purify his increasingly sullied soul. 'What must I do?' he asked weakly, desperation evident in his voice.

'Come with me,' she commanded. He followed her silently, praying, resolutely keeping his eyes on the flag-stones. It was a cold night. She was taking him to the Cathedral. The wondrous soaring stone edifice gave him hope. Surely, if there ever was a symbol of God's divine grace, it was this place.

Before they went through the side door, Sylvia turned to face him. 'Prior. A sinner will come to you. You are to listen to this creature, give penance, and grant absolution.' She led him inside and took him to the confessional. He heard her receding footsteps, and silence filled the church. It did not take long to examine his surroundings. There was a simple crucifix on the wall of the confessional. There was a bible and a rosary on the priest's side. The partition was composed of a carved lattice of wooden bars in the shape of crosses. You could see into the other side without too much difficulty. That was unusual. There was also a larger opening, also in the shape of a cross, in the exact center of the partition. He took his customary place on the bench and composed himself. He was to be the epitome of Christian virtue – strict, unyielding, but merciless in the war against sin. He knew he would give this sinner a harsh, harsh penance – and he would perform each act alongside him, doing penance for his own sin at the same time. He welcomed the harsh punishment. After what felt like hours, he heard a sound – the characteristic hard tap tap tap sounds of high heels against the wooden floorboards. He steeled himself.

'It doesn't matter,' he told himself. The mumbled reassurance felt lacking, even to himself. He heard the other door open, then close. The scent of a heavy sweet perfume flooded the confessional, and a throaty, all too familiar contralto voice shredded his hard-earned calm.

Two

‘Bless me, Father, for I have sinned.’ Her voice remained the haughty prideful contralto he knew so well from his dream.

His voice stumbled as he blessed her.

She giggled. ‘Prior Steven . . .’ Her voice seemed to caress his name. ‘It has been years since my last confession.’ Steven paled as his member responded to her voice. His heart beat frantically against his chest.

The gold-digging harlot continued, her manipulative dulcet tone dripping with contempt. ‘I am here to confess how I turned a kind charitable man into my drooling . . . fornicating . . . cunt-lapping puppy dog.’ The widow’s pretty manicured fingers gripped the bars of the cross forming the small window inside the confessional. Her long hot-pink fingernails slid up and down upon the consecrated wood. He was unable to look away from the sacrilegious repetitive insistent motions of her hand. Her voice matched the rhythm of her hand movements, a constant seductive insistent purr percolating through the layers of his soul.

‘I made him watch my beautiful naked body while his wife lay sick in her chambers. The image remained in his heart, a hungry maggot eating away at his virtue.’ She giggled softly, her oozing silky voice rich with a sort of amused contempt. ‘I made him watch while I fingered my shaved slutty little pussy in the Peabody family chapel.’

The Prior’s erection was obscenely hard; he felt each mocking word as a tingling caress on his member. He desperately wanted to touch himself, but his will was still strong. He managed an angry gasp. 'Desist, harlot. Confess your sins and be done with it.'

'Oh, I've barely begun . . .' She giggled. 'Like I said . . . I turned him into my cunt-lapping dog. Second . . . I turned him into my personal cash vault . . . He couldn't get enough of my luscious firm tits and my young gorgeous body . . . He couldn't stop himself, the poor little Lord . . . His wife kept calling out for him on her sickbed . . . You know, he heard every plea, Prior Steven . . . But he was too busy worshipping my pretty body.' She giggled and put her slutty pink heels in the cross-shaped partition, the pointy tip of her pink shoes and the stiletto heel making it across to the side of the confessor. 'Later, he kept licking my pretty heels, up and down, like a dog, while I went through his wife's jewellery box.'

Steven stared at her pink shoes, the same ones in his dream, the same ones the shameless adulteress wore at her wedding.

'You like the pretty shoes, don't you, Prior Steven?' cooed Stephanie. 'Can you blame Lord Peabody for licking them?' She removed her foot from the partition and leaned forward. The cross-shaped hole in the partition was wide enough to allow her arm to snake through – her other hand maintained her filthy caressing grip on the vertical bar forming the main section of the cross-shaped hole. She extended a long manicured finger, her painted nails like talons dipped in lurid pink blood.

Steven was shocked into immobility. It was less the result of being distracted by his intense rock-hard erection, than the shock over her brazen attempt at seducing a monk, a Prior, a man of God. He watched her finger approach his lips with sheer disbelief.

She pushed her finger inside his stunned unnerved mouth. He tasted an intense sweet flavour, cloying, sticky like glue. Her fingernail tasted like the cake in his dream, just much more concentrated. He was lost for a moment trying to identify the flavour – the impulse to spit it out disappeared with the first wave of intense sweetness. The taste made his mouth water, saliva dribbling from the corner of his lips onto his coarse brown robe.

She withdrew her finger from his mouth and continued her tawdry confession as if she hadn't done anything. 'Third . . . I made him stop supporting the monastery, the convent and the orphanage. He needed all his gold to keep me happy. When I was not happy, he did not get to worship my beautiful pussy.'

'I have heard enough,' he said, anger overriding his lust, his member softening. 'This is no confession.' He felt betrayed by Sylvia. Sylvia, blonde-haired, comely Sylvia . . . Sylvia with the immense luscious tits, the curvaceous bottom, so readily on display as she scrubbed the stains in his room . . . Suddenly, the sweet taste in his mouth mixed with the invoked image of the treasonous serving wench. He thought of his corrupt sin-filled dream, and his lust rose gleefully, smothering his righteous anger.

'Oh, it's a confession . . . An honest, true confession . . . Look at me, Prior Steven . . .' Stephanie's voice was a velvet-tipped wicked hook, worming its way deep into his soul. 'I am naked before God.'

He tried to look away, but a barely perceived, smooth, seductive motion drew his gaze in. His vision was inadvertently sucked through the partition into the smoky tiny chamber occupied by the harlot widow. Once his eyes focused on the sordid scene in the candlelit gloom, he was no longer able to look away.

Stephanie sat on the tiny bench. She was wearing those obscene pink harlot's heels, her long slender legs spread as wide as the small confessional allowed, exposing her shaved smooth pink sex. Her eyes were full of calculated loathsome confidence, her mouth frozen in an amused contemptuous smirk.

'For these sins and all the sins of my past life, especially the sins against purity . . . honesty . . . and charity, I ask absolution and penance from you, Father . . .'

Steven looked at the shameless creature on the other side of the confessional, aghast. 'You are asking me to absolve you of these crimes?!'

'I did confess . . .' purred Stephanie, luscious, naked, a lurid vision of temptation.

'You – you are a creature of evil. Put your clothes back on and I will give you penance. I will give you penance for your foul attempt at seducing a man of God.'

Stephanie put her robe back on. She did not bother to lace it up properly – her breasts were naked full globes of tempting flesh as she impudently met Prior Steven's eyes. 'I did not offer my flesh. My naked beautiful body . . . I did not offer it.'

His eyes were still locked on her skin, on her exposed breasts, on her prettily arched feet. The words imposed by the duties of his office fled his lips with unseemly haste. 'Your penance . . . Your penance shall be: You must go on a pilgrimage to – to Mount Eleanor, for ten days and nights with nothing but bread and water to keep your flesh. You must recite the rosary a hundred times every day of your penance . . . and meditate on your crimes. You shall give half of all you own to charity.'

'Is that all?' she asked, amused.

Her impertinence fazed him. Mount Eleanor was a harsh brutal place – cold and unforgiving even in the springtime. The late autumn weather made the windy rocky cliff a dangerous destination. 'For now.' He absolved her, hastily and with a sour taste in his mouth.

She bowed her head – her breasts jiggled with the motion. 'O my God, I am heartily sorry . . .' Stephanie's seductive purr sullied the Act of Contrition.

'Stop!' he said, angry, desperation ruining his effort at maintaining a degree of formality to this sordid proceeding. 'Say it in silence, if you must!'

She nodded. Without another word she exited the confessional. He composed himself as best he could and left as well. The Cathedral was dark except for the customary candle burning on the altar. Stephanie was kneeling before it, the white of her perfect round bosom, lusciously exposed, reflecting the flickering flame.

He walked back to his chamber with trembling knees. The nerve of that woman! Everyone, of course, thought she committed adultery with Lord Peabody, but to hear it told in such brazen fashion . . . She did not sound repentant at all – in fact, he suspected she was just trying to get to him with the obscene story. He shut the door. The jar of salve on the cot seemed to mock him. The glimpse of the salve sent faint tingles through his painfully erect member. He picked it up and put it on the table. He sighed and began to pray on his knees before the window, asking the Virgin to lend him strength in these days of temptation. He prayed for hours on end, his fingers seeking solace and comfort from the rosary. He fell into an exhausted haunted slumber.

He knew he was dreaming – he felt the touch of a ring on his finger – he raised his hand and saw the characteristic griffin and sword of the Peabody clan on a heavy gold signet. He glanced in the mirror – sure enough, his reflection showed Lord Peabody in his sombre black wool coat. His face did not bear the bloated red marks of lust and gluttony that so marred his countenance over the last few months of his life. He was a passive observer of his progress through the elaborate marble staircase of his castle. The Lord was making his way upstairs. The Lord's thoughts became intertwined with Steven's own – he seemed to become more and more aware of every notion, every worry. Jane was upstairs, ill with some kind of a pox. The new maid, Stephanie, claimed it was due to noxious fumes – she had been scenting their chambers with a sweet potpourri. He passed by the tiny room of the new maid. The door was open. The sweet scent of potpourri was overwhelming. He breathed in deeply, stopping for a moment. A movement caught his eye in the maid's room and he glanced inside. The girl did not have her hair up in a bun like she did when she interviewed for the position with Lady Jane earlier this week. Her hair was a tangle of lustrous golden curls. She was wearing her maid's uniform, but she seemed to have altered it – the skirt was indecently short, exposing long slender legs all the way to the swell of a shapely bottom. The cut of her livery was altogether too daring, displaying the new maid's ample bosom nearly completely. The tawdry blonde vixen was putting on a new pair of shoes, straight out of an expensive-looking velvet box. Her legs looked impossibly long in the six-inch heels. Impudently, she met his eyes, arching her feet, leaning back slightly, her full firm tits accented by the movement.

'My Lord . . . I do not feel well . . .' He heard Jane's plea from their bedroom.

'Won't you come in, Lord Peabody?' the maid's voice was petulant, demanding. 'I can't seem to get my new shoes on . . .'

He was so surprised by the request that he found himself responding – he was inside the small room before he knew what was happening.

The maid giggled. She arched one of her feet, the sleazy stiletto heels dangling from her perfect toes. 'You like my new shoes, Lord Peabody?' she asked, her voice a throaty vapid purr.

His lips felt dry. He licked them. The cloying sweet scent in the tiny room was even stronger than in the hallway. His eyes were locked on the beautiful blonde maidservant. His manhood was a rock-hard sceptre; he had never felt this hard in his entire life. He couldn't seem to tear his eyes away from the seductive offering before him. He felt his head nod. 'Yes . . .' he whispered.

'Are you there, my Lord? Have you seen the new maid? I've been calling for water all day . . .' Lady Jane's voice no longer reached Lord Peabody – with a cruel smile, Stephanie unlaced her blouse, her red-tipped talons unwrapping her luscious full breasts.

'You like my tits, don't you, Lord Peabody?'

'Yes . . .' he whimpered, his eyes locked on her wares.

'Please someone help! Dearest, are you there?' Lady Jane's voice was becoming hysterical, weak. With an annoyed raised eyebrow, Stephanie stood up and walked to the door, her bottom swaying rhythmically with each click-click of her sleazy shoes. She slammed the door shut and turned around. 'I don't want us to get interrupted.'

* * *

Suddenly, his eyes snapped open – it was still dark. He heard a sound – someone had just entered the chamber. His dream was still vivid in his mind – his cock was so hard, he guessed it was exactly what it felt like for Lord Peabody.

'Prior!'

He recognised Sylvia's voice. Anger rose within him, fuelled by the guilt of his arousal. 'You sent that harlot to "confess"?'

She sounded scared. 'Did I do something wrong, Prior? I thought it was the right of anyone to seek penance and absolution.'

He paused – technically, she was right. 'Well . . . yes.' Suddenly, he felt ashamed. 'You haven't done anything wrong. What can I do for you?'

'Stephanie Peabody sends her regrets for her unwholesome behaviour. She wishes to beg your forgiveness and humbly begs for another chance to confess – all her sins, this time.'

Steven considered – his arousal was nearly driving him insane. He could not possibly confess someone as tempting as the late Lord's widow without – without – He sighed. 'When does she want to confess?'

'As soon as possible, my Lord Prior.'

'Give me an hour to . . . meditate.'

As soon as Sylvia left he barred the door. He practically ran back to the table and uncorked the jar of grease. The sweet smell of flowers filled the room. He sat on the cot and raised his robe. 'Penance and absolution . . . Penance and absolution . . .' he whispered to himself. Surely, it was his sacred duty to give penance and absolution. He could not do his sacred duty if he was sullied by desire. He had to expunge the desire from his soul. He put his fingers in the jar. Surely, this was a lesser sin than to take the risk of temptation inside the confessional. 'Penance and absolution.' He smeared the salve on his fingers. 'Penance and absolution.' He put his hand over his rock-hard erect member. He leaned back on the cot, his hand a blur on his greased cock. 'Stephanie . . .' He moaned lustily as image after image from his dreams gleefully took residence in his soul.

By the end of the hour the jar of salve was exhausted and he still had not gained release. He was trembling with pent-up lust.

Someone knocked on the door.

'Yes?' He frantically dressed himself.

'It is time, Prior Steven. Are you ready?'

He nearly laughed with bitterness. He had never been more ready in his life! 'Yes, child, I am.' He would just have to withstand the devil with his lust unabated.

She was already inside the confessional – he could smell her sweet cloying heavy perfume.

'Bless me, Father, for I have sinned.'

'Blessings of the Lord unto you, my child,' said Steven, woodenly. Her voice sent shivers down his back.

'I . . . I am not sure if what I am about to confess is really a sin, Prior Steven.'

Steven had heard this sort of thing a hundred times. 'If you are in doubt . . . Just tell me, I shall levy penance or dispense advice if needed.' He felt ashamed of his arousal. Every time she uttered a word it felt like Stephanie's long fingernails caressed his member.

'Very well . . . I desire to do something in the future. It will be a sin.'

'You do not have to be a slave to your desires. To sin is a choice – a choice between Heaven and Hell. Only past sins are sins.'

She giggled.

He opened his lips to admonish her, to remind her that this was a place of sombre contrition, but the vapid high-pitched sound of her laughter felt as if it was a tangible touch upon his erect member. A dribble of pre-cum oozed from the tip of his cock. Steven whimpered softly.

'I will light an extra candle or two, Prior Steven . . . I wish to see the bible while I speak to you.'

He nodded and said in a weak voice. 'Of course . . .'

She lit a few more candles. He could see her clearly now on the other side. She wore an expensive ermine coat, full length. Her cleavage was deep, daring, her nipples nearly visible. His gaze travelled down to her feet, seeking the telltale pink of her harlot's shoes. Her white fur coat blocked his view.

She smirked as she watched his gaze travel down her body.

'I want to turn you ... Prior Steven ... into my fornicating pussy-licking lapdog ... That would not be a sin, then?'

He gasped. 'But – but I was told you were truly penitent –'

'I am ... I am sorry you didn't succumb the first time ... Don't you like me?' she cooed, her voice oozing like tainted honey.

'No! You are a whore of the devil!'

'Look at me, Prior Steven ... would a whore of the devil have the courage to touch a crucifix?'

He peered through to the other side. With contemptuous sinuous grace, Stephanie opened her full-length coat to display the wares that caused Lord Peabody's fall from grace. She wore the same hot-pink high-heeled shoes. She had spread her legs, displaying the lure of her naked womanhood. His grease-stained pre-cum oozing member seemed to pull him forward, through the partition, to certain damnation.

'Doesn't Puppy want to play with Puppy's cock?' she cooed, slowly stroking her naked pussy with a manicured finger. She maliciously stared at Steven's raging erection through the partition. 'I think Puppy wants to play with Puppy's prick!' she said with pretend-surprise. 'Take out your cock and rub it, Prior Steven!' she commanded, her bitchy contralto demanding obedience.

'No ... Confess your sins ...' he whimpered as his cock raged against his crumbling principles. He saw Stephanie's smirk. The manipulative beauty smoothly kneeled before the cross-shaped central hole. He felt a fleeting hope that perhaps she felt the need for contrition, kneeling to do penance. His hopes were dispelled in short order as Stephanie pressed her rouge-stained lips against the cross-shaped hole of the partition, that gorgeous full fleshed mouth becoming a gateway to some barely imagined, filthy paradise.

'You don't have to do anything, Prior Steven . . .' cooed Stephanie. 'Just let your cock slide into my mouth . . . You won't be doing anything, practically, just letting it happen . . .' She leaned back a little to let her arm through – the vision of her painted pink lips was replaced for a brief instant by a brief view of her luscious full tits – and her hand once again snaked through the partition, those useless elegant fingers skilfully undoing the sacred knots of his rope belt.

He knew he should run away, he should yell for help, he should . . . he should . . . He felt her fingers caress his exposed prick. He moaned softly. His cock practically sprung upwards, straining eagerly.

'There is a good Puppy,' smirked the beautiful manipulative widow. 'Stand and let pretty Stephanie turn Puppy into a proper fornicator.'

He wanted to sit, to disobey, but her tongue began to luridly trace the outline of her rouge-stained lips. He found his cock straining towards her wide open glistening mouth. His body seemed to rise of its own accord, following his cock like a mindless herd follows the lead bull. His quivering member tentatively brushed against her warm wet flesh. Her lips immediately fastened around the head of his cock, sucking in his member until she held it completely imprisoned. Her mouth was filthy warm, her skilled tongue the caress of hellfire around his engorged prick. She milked him with her mouth, slowly, the taste of her nail polish cloying sweet on his tongue.

His moral agony disappeared as she manipulated his trapped swollen erection. He felt his balls begin to contract. He moaned softly, leaning forward even further. Just as he was about to climax, she released his cock. Her mouth remained partly open, permitting his feverish gaze to lock on her pretty pink tongue nestled teasingly between those luscious fleshy lips.

He was sobbing with pent-up lust. 'Please . . .' he cried.

'Please what?' she giggled cruelly.

'Please . . . Lady Peabody . . .' he finished, sobbing.

'That's better. But not good enough. I should be a princess, shouldn't I?' she said with amusement in her bitchy sultry voice.

'Yes . . . yes, princess,' he said quickly.

'Obey princess. Take out your cock and stroke it, Prior Steven!' giggled Stephanie, reclining on the confessional bench. She rested the tip of her high heels on the cross-shaped hole, feet arched, her long naked legs leading Steven's stricken gaze to her cruelly exposed shaved pink cunt. He stumbled to his knees before the partition as his desperate fingers latched around his engorged prick, stroking, stroking, stroking.

He kneeled on the confessional floor, his face pressed against the cross-shaped opening in the partition, his eyes soaking in the lurid vision of Stephanie's naked flesh. His fingers smeared her pink rouge into his cock, the colour mixing with the grease he had rubbed into it during his obscene bout of masturbation. She rested her stiletto heels on his flushed sweaty face as his abused rouge-stained member finally surrendered to his ministrations, spurting a near avalanche of seed against the partition wall, cum dripping from cross to cross in the lattice work. He collapsed in a heap, whimpering as he lay there, in a cooling puddle of his own filth.

He vaguely heard Stephanie's heels click-click on the floorboards, and his door opened. She stood there, her long curly blonde hair framing her beautiful face, wearing a contemptuous sneer. She walked inside, pulling his head away from the partition by his ear. She stood over him, legs spread, her high-heeled pink whore shoes on both sides, her pussy bare, pink, naked. Steven's cock stirred again, his eyes locked on the pretty widow's blatantly displayed shaved womanhood.

'Like I said, Prior Puppy.' She stood over his red whimpering face. 'First, I will turn you into my cunt-lapping dog.' She prodded his member with the tip of her sleazy high-heeled shoes.

Steven was mortally ashamed as his member responded to the contemptuous gesture. His embarrassment instantly turned into lust, overriding his resistance. He hesitantly extended his tongue, not knowing what to do. He has never tasted a woman before – this was his first time. He tasted perfume, sweet, cloying – pussy-perfume, he thought, and the thought excited him. His tongue rasped up and down on the harlot's exposed slit, mindlessly licking her obscene shaved cunt.

'Tastes good, doesn't it?' cooed Stephanie. 'Puppy like?' She ground her cunt into Steven's face. 'Puppy suck on Stephanie's pretty pussy.'

Steven felt his mouth latch onto her pussy lips. He was sucking on her cunt with obscene abandon, slurping down her juices, her pussy-perfume soaking into the scalp of his defenceless tonsured head.

'Good doggie . . .' She giggled as she straddled his face. She came on top of him, grinding her sex into his mouth. His erection was as if he had never cum before, much less a few minutes ago. Stephanie's pussy-perfume scent made him light headed, greedy for more. He thought of what it would be like to be allowed to slide his cock inside of her. He was certain he would climax, he would gain release. This new ambition pervaded his body and soul. Steven's tongue redoubled its efforts, servicing the gold-digging slut's womanhood. She waited until she climaxed, and then, with calculated cruelty, she pushed his drooling face away.

'I am leaving, Puppy.' She stepped over him, her tight delectable bottom swaying from side to side.

'Please don't go . . .' he whimpered, his member twitching in anticipation.

'You want more, Puppy?' Her condescending voice matched the look on her face – both were suffused with a smirking calculating greed.

'Yes, please . . .' he sobbed.

'Bring me all the Peabody jewels . . . and a new fur coat. Mink will do. You will stock the Peabody mansion for me in town. I only eat the best, drink the best, wear the best.

Then I will see if I deem you worthy of a little reward . . .' She laughed cruelly and sauntered away, her naked form disappearing in the shadows of the Cathedral. Despite his orgasm, he was nearly crazy with pent-up lust. He stroked his rouge-stained member over and over, but he gained no release. He began to sob, frantic with unmet need.

He collected his fallen robe about himself, hastily tying a slipshod knot on his rope belt. He practically ran back to his room, his trembling fingers seeking the oak chest with the silver he brought to buy the orphanage winter coats. His hand hesitated over the open chest – he needed a purse. Another problem occurred to him: he had no idea how much a whore cost. He picked up the burlap sack and poured the contents of the box inside, the coins an avalanche of clinking hard-earned money, the result of months of collections, of kind-hearted charity. Sobbing, he dropped the sack, overcome with moral anguish. He weakly leaned against the table, trembling. His erect member rubbed up against the plain honest wool of his undergarments. He could not seem to stop thinking about Stephanie's scented sex in his face, the texture, her seductive flavour. The Prior was filled with debased lust. With a final whimpering sound escaping his throat, he picked up the bag and tied it on his rope belt, a huge heavy purse, crammed with silver.

His new purse was awkwardly heavy. He practically ran towards the Whores' Quarter, coins jingling mockingly against one another. The leather of the sack slapped against his thigh every time he took a step. It was dark outside, but the Whores' Quarter always had traffic. Steven's eyes were desperately scanning the shadowy figures for the telltale voluptuous outlines of the painted harlots he so detested upon his arrival. It did not take long for one of them to spot the jingling heavy money bag and the monk attached to it. She looked familiar – a brazen sultry wench with long unruly brown curls in a bright red robe. Her legs were long, slender, her bosom shadowy, luscious mounds under that crimson robe. His mouth was dry as he saw her catch his desperate gaze. She broke out in a sudden greedy smile, looking at his fat bag of silver. He knew she was naked under that red robe, and his gaze was already trapped, awaiting her lewd advertisement.

'I knew you would come back,' she smirked in a throaty, sultry voice.

'Can I see you naked?' he asked pathetically.

She looked him over, her eyes resting on the heavy jingling bag of coins. The monk was drooling, his erection forming a small obscene tent under that monastic robe. He had a dazed look about him, as if he would do anything for play.

'I will let you see me naked . . . and more . . .' she cooed. 'Take me somewhere nice, a good inn . . .' she purred seductively, stepping closer, putting her hand on the monk's robe, right over his rock-hard erection. 'I will let you fuck me anywhere you like, if you take me to a really nice place . . .'

Steven groaned; her offer opened a delicious cesspool of possibilities to his inexperienced lust-crazed mind. He was frantic with the need for release. 'I have a town house we can use,' he sobbed.

The whore's cold eyes grew large – Lords had town houses, not monks. 'You must be very rich.' Her voice was breathless with avarice, shallow cunning mixed with ambition. 'I love to let rich men fuck my pussy.' Her voice became a sultry calculated purr: 'A rich man can slide his cock into me anytime he wants . . .' She raised the monk's robe with her hand and slid her fingers over his engorged shaft, stroking it.

'Yes, I am very rich,' moaned Steven. He led the whore to the town house, fondling her ass and tits when he could not stand it anymore. She teased him with her flesh, carefully, wary he would cum on the street without rendering payment. By now, it was dark; otherwise, his business would have been obvious. The town house was in the richest part of town, an imposing, three-storey structure, normally staffed by eight servants, but at the moment, by grace, empty. It would make a splendid orphanage.

Right now, all he could think about was the pussy he bought for the winter coats of his orphans. He opened the door, fumbling with the key – the whore gasped with greedy delight as her eyes took in the rich décor, the gilded tapestries, the gold candelabra.

'Oh yes, my horny little monk, you can have my pretty pussy for . . . ten silver pennies.' She named ten times the going rate, hoping he was too addled to realise. Steven nodded frantically, fished out a fistful of coins and pressed her fingers around them.

She let her red robe slide to the marble floor, displaying her luscious naked body. She rubbed her clit with her fingers, watching his transfixed eyes. She purred softly, seductively, 'Is this what you want?'

He tried to turn away, to shake his head, to say no . . . Instead, he felt his head nod eagerly.

She got on all fours on the marble tiles of the foyer, her naked ass raised high up in the air. The pretty brunette wore heels similar to Stephanie's, except these were black. 'Fuck my whore pussy, Father . . .' she cooed as his coarse brown robes joined the fiery red ones on the floor. She did not apply any of her lubricants – all that silver in her purse turned her sex into a sopping wet mess.

His virgin member oozed with anticipation as he thrust inside the wet greedy whore he bought for the winter coats of the orphans under his care. He fucked her like a dog in heat, his member sliding in and out of her wet cunt. He was making satisfied doglike noises with each thrust, his face red, drooling with lust. He came inside her, but the perverse satisfaction lasted only a few seconds. He tried to collect himself while his member's exhaustion kept the lust at bay, but the greedy whore's mouth rapidly brought his erection back to iron hardness. He set out to mount her again.

'You want seconds?' She laughed at him, cruelly, stroking her naked tempting slit. 'That's another ten silvers.'

He counted out ten coins, five less good winter coats for the orphans of the monastery, stacking the pile of money on the whore's irresistible swaying bottom, coins jingling with each stroke of his pussy-crazed member. She was laughing at him, the sound exciting him even more.

Her sex was sore and she was exhausted, but the opportunity to milk the addled cunt-crazed monk's purse dry was too tempting to pass up. She fingered his balls and he spurted cum all over her legs – and still he wasn't satisfied. There was a drooling frantic need in his eyes. 'Stephanie ...' he whimpered as her fingers wrapped around his twitching cock.

'Please find me Stephanie ...' he begged the naked smirking whore.

She put on her red robe while Steven lay in a crumpled heap below her, sobbing Stephanie's name. Her purse has swallowed most of the monk's silver. From what he said about this slut Stephanie's hot-pink high heels, her luscious tits and the curve of her ass, drool oozing down his face, she must have been the whore of his dreams. She would find this woman and they would work in shifts, milking the pussy-addicted monk dry.

She did not have to wait long; as she exited the town house, she ran into a self-possessed smirking beauty in hot-pink stiletto heels. She had long curly blonde hair framing a beautiful haughty face. The woman was examining the town house as if she owned it. She carried a large basket in one lace-gloved hand. She looked her up and down, from her black stiletto heels to the top of her skimpy red robe, and smiled knowingly.

Her voice was amused. 'I see little Puppy couldn't wait anymore.'

The whore smiled back – she could see they would get along splendidly. 'You must be Stephanie.'

Stephanie smiled back. 'And you are ...?'

'I am Heather ... I have never seen a more pussy-whipped little boy.'

Stephanie chuckled, her slender arm taking Heather's. Arm-in-arm they went inside the town house. They found Steven trying to sate his lust on the foyer carpet. He was lying on his stomach, his cock a happy trapped worm between his belly and a priceless Turkish silk prayer rug. When he saw Stephanie, he let out a filthy needy groan of welcome, rubbing his erection against the knotted silk. His cock left an oozing trail of pre-cum like a slimy serpent. Stephanie examined the cum-stained pussy-addled monk and giggled. 'No need to get up, Puppy.'

As she walked closer, Steven's eyes slavishly followed the movement of her stiletto heels, his tongue licking his lips with anticipation. He was masturbating against the Hereke silk, his eyes glazed, expression fawning and mindless. When she finally reached him, he was once again at the edge of climax.

Stephanie smirked, prodding him on the chin. 'You may lick my pretty shoes clean, Puppy.' As he tongued her slutty pink shoes like a dog, he felt his balls contract, and finally thick white gobs of cum stained the sacred prayer rug. With the release, the sex-inspired daze lifted from his mind. Stunned, guilt-ridden, he stared at Stephanie's spittle-shined pink shoes as if seeing them for the first time. He stood up, weakly, his naked body wracked with guilt. He picked up his discarded monastic robe and saw the plundered sack of silver lying by the door on the marble floor.

Heather laughed, her voice rich with contempt. 'I will think of you next time I attend mass, *Father*.' She smirked.

'That money was meant to keep the children warm . . .' he whispered, frozen by the enormity of his crime.

'It looks like that money was meant to rent Heather's cunt,' laughed Stephanie.

Heather leaned closer to the widow and began to whisper in her ear, occasionally glancing in Steven's direction.

Steven's cock was exhausted, his balls completely empty, spent. He had never felt so weak, so hungry. He was too weak to feel the stir of desire, and that finally gave him strength. 'Go away!' he ordered the two temptresses, angry.

The women ignored him. He stomped his foot, the gesture appearing pathetic, even to himself. The women finally stopped whispering, naked calculating greed momentarily transforming the beauty of their features.

'All this cum, Prior Steven . . .' cooed Stephanie, condescension dripping from each syllable. 'You must be positively spent.' She uncovered her basket and took out a perfectly round white cake, the fresh icing filling the sex-drenched air of the house with a delicious sweet aroma. The scent was cloying, flowery, familiar. Steven swallowed hard, his nostrils soaked with the smell. He suddenly felt like he was dying of hunger. Stephanie emptied the basket. She removed two bottles of rich red wine, a roast chicken and a glass jar with a honeycomb. The scent of the rich tempting food was overwhelming, mouthwatering. Stephanie carefully set the food down on the floor, her luscious tits nearly popping out of her lace dress as she bent over. Finally, she took out a dog's bowl, a faded wooden thing, chipped, adorned with crudely drawn figures of little pink puppies.

Steven was livid with rage, but too hungry to do anything but stare at the food. Stephanie uncorked a bottle of wine. She whispered in Heather's ear and looked at Steven.

'You sure you want our pretty pussies out of the house, Puppy?' she cooed, mockingly.

'Get out, harlot!' he gasped with ascetic conviction. His hunger and physical weakness robbed his cock of desire.

'Harlot?' She giggled with undisguised contempt. 'Are you sure?'

'You are both painted Jezebels, witches who shall burn in eternal hellfire!' he gasped.

'In that case . . .' She paused. 'Let us leave, Heather.' She cruelly laughed at Steven as she turned to face the smirking brunette. 'But if we are harlots . . . let us act like harlots.' She slipped her hand underneath Heather's red robe and allowed it to slide all the way down to her waist, exposing her entire upper body. She gently teased the whore's large erect nipples with her manicured useless long fingernails. Stephanie leaned close in, her pretty blonde locks mixing with Heather's silky dark hair. She slowly began to tease

Heather's nipples with her mouth. The widow felt the brunette respond, her nipples hardening inside Stephanie's warm wet mouth. She began sucking, teasing with the tip of her tongue.

Heather moaned softly, her hands roving over Stephanie's gorgeous body, caressing the flesh of her beautiful seductress.

Steven felt filthy perverted lust creep into his soul as he watched the two giggling whispering young women manipulate him, but as spent and as hungry as he was, for the moment, lust had no power over him. His mind absorbed the spectacle, helplessly memorising the corrosive seductive images, but his member was too exhausted to rise to the occasion.

The women turned in unison, their tight shapely bottoms swaying, high heels clicking on marble. Unhurried, they walked to the door and left.

Steven was surprised by this unexpected turn of events – his enfeebled cock twitched with the pang of a lost opportunity. He managed to stop his hand from seeking out his member and ran towards the door, only stopping to scoop up his nearly empty purse in his hand. He had to get out of here, to seek solace in the woods, to cleanse himself. Stopping to pick up the money proved to have devastating consequences – just as he got to the door, he heard the contemptuous giggle of the two painted Jezebels. Stephanie locked him inside, the sharp metallic sound of the key turning in the lock sounding like the creaking of Heaven's gates, locked forever before his sullied soul.

He banged on the door, but there was no answer. The wood was so thick, he did not think much besides a dull thudding sound would reach the street. His hunger was a living thing, a painful wound in his belly. Only now did he remember the Gospel of Matthew: 'The Kingdom of Heaven is at hand . . . Take no gold, nor silver, nor copper in your belts, nor bag for your journey, nor two tunics, nor sandals, nor a staff for the labourer is worthy of his food.'

His greed, the bag of money, was his downfall – he was trapped in this House of Sin.

He walked through the town house, seeking an alternate exit. He knew all too well there was none. The place was constructed to double as a fortress in case the town was raided. It would not stand up to a determined siege, or fire, but unless he wanted to set fire to himself, there was no way out. The windows were steel barred, the few that were large enough to admit a man's body. The main door was thick, made of stout oak. The lock was heavy, nearly five pounds in weight. He was trapped.

The smell of the cake was all-pervasive, a wonderful flowery sweetness. He finally remembered where he last smelled such odour – it was just like the smell of the salve in those jars he put to such unbecoming use. His cock was still weak, but now that it was so used to attention, it once again began to make its needs felt. Steven tried to ignore the stirrings and began to pray to Saint Anthony, to deliver him from temptation. He thought of all the hermits who had reputedly forsaken food, all the saints who had given up the delights of the flesh, in all its forms. It was no good. He knew he had to eat something. Maybe if he just had a chicken leg, just a single drumstick . . .

Steven sobbed and tore off a chicken leg, devouring the meat in an instant, sucking the grease with his famished pussy-glazed lips. The meat only made him hungrier. He picked up the entire chicken, telling himself he would stay away from the cake. He gorged himself, taking greedy massive bites of the rich flavourful meat, fry grease joining the cum stains on his robe. Each bite seemed to make him hungrier – and thirsty. Without thinking about it, he raised the open bottle of wine and took a great gulp of it. The smoky heavy red was sweet, fortified, a pleasant fire in his aching limbs. Suddenly, his whole situation did not look so bad. He could just clean himself up, and yell from the upstairs window for help! Why didn't he think of that before? He took another swig of wine, then another. He felt much better. He finished the entire chicken and looked for more. He opened the glass jar and suckled on the honeycomb. The sticky yellow honey had an odd consistency, a flowery intense flavour. He did not want to add sticky stains of honey to his robe's dubious decorations, so he looked for a bowl. Without thinking much about it, he picked up the bowl with the pink puppies on it, cradling it in his lap, and sucked on the honeycomb. Wine dribbled from his lips.

'Dessert ...' he drooled as he noticed the cake. He spooned cake into his bowl with his hands. Without an actual spoon, he just lowered his mouth and gobbled down the sweet stuff, slurping greedily on the white icing, the yellow crumbs. Each taste made him think of Stephanie and Heather, locked in their filthy dance of manipulative fornication. His member grew gleefully hard beneath his monastic robes. Steven broke off the neck of the second bottle of wine and poured the fortified spirit in his mouth, staining his holy garment even more.

Three

He woke up with the hot flesh of two young women pressed against him. He had never seen them before. One of them had long silky blonde hair, the other, curly red. They wore frilly expensive Belgian lace garters, hose and pushup bras, white stiletto heels and glittering cheap glass earrings. When they saw his eyes open the blonde with the vapid blue eyes giggled and shamelessly crawled over him, her tits rubbing against his member. She smiled at him, her painted lips an open filthy gateway to tempting damnation. She brazenly lowered her mouth to his aching cock, slowly trailing the tip of her tongue over his exposed manhood. The redhead giggled softly and followed her lead. In a moment they were fully engaged in the coy manipulation of his obedient erect member, their tongues teasing, lingering on his shaft. He moaned, helpless, his eyes trapped by their intertwined lingerie-clad bodies, the milking of his organ a mere sideshow to the drooling gluttonous lust-crazed damnation of his soul.

Suddenly, he realised this had to be a dream – every time something like this happened, it was a dream. This could not possibly be real. These women . . . These wanton beautiful nymphs were simply the products of his imagination. He groaned as one of the seductive dreamlike temptresses pulled his cock all the way into her hot wet lips. It felt so real, so good . . . If it was real, he was fornicating . . . This could not possibly be real, of course. It had to be a dream . . . Yes, it had to be a dream . . .

The redhead raised her beautiful face from over his crotch and pressed her painted lips over his own. He felt her push her tongue past his lips. She tasted like fresh strawberries. His own lips felt unwilling to combat the intrusion. If this wasn't real, he might as well enjoy himself, that would not really be fornication. The pretty woman's tongue sought out his own, teasing him with warm wet caresses. Yes, this would not be a sin. The gorgeous redhead rubbed her stiff pink nipples against his chest as she tongued his unresisting mouth. Steven felt so much better after he worked it all out. He was not really fornicating. He moaned as the blonde milked his shaft, fondling his balls with her long graceful fingers. The monk surrendered to the hot young flesh surrounding him in a cocoon of manipulative fornication.

Steven leaned into the filthy caresses surrounding his manhood, desperate for release. As before, he came to the very edge of climax. He just needed a touch more stimulation . . . He thrust his cock into the pretty lips, obscenely fucking the luscious red lips, losing all pretensions of passive non-participation. Nevertheless, complete release eluded him. The pretty red-haired harlot cruelly pushed his drooling head downward, until his dazed eyes came level with the tempting smooth pink flesh of her womanhood. He licked his lips, overcome with a base hunger. His tongue seemed to acquire a life of its own; he began to lick, moaning with helpless unmet need. The leash of his flesh prodded him with new ideas: perhaps this latest humiliation would finally gain him release. His well fed cock rewarded each successively sordid act of debasement with more and more intense almost-moments of a never quite complete release.

Stephanie walked in, Heather in tow. The two women looked satisfied as they beheld the sordid scene.

'He is a pussy-addict, Lady Stephanie,' giggled the beautiful redhead riding his prick.

'I know, Amber,' smirked Stephanie. 'But remember to call him by his name and title.'

'Puppy Steven?' said the other young woman with amused condescension.

'Friar Slut,' giggled Amber.

'Not a bad name,' smiled Stephanie. She came over to Steven's prone body and prodded his cheek with the pointy toe of her shoe. 'You like your new name, Friar Slut?' she cooed.

His stunned realisation that this was not a dream, that he had willingly fornicated with two young women for the past few hours, had not dampened his filthy perverted desire. His cock was a twitching greedy monster, demanding more and more. Somehow, only Stephanie's permission allowed him release, only her pink shaved womanhood had been able to give his member a moment's peace. Despite being ridden by a pretty, young slut, he craved Stephanie's filthy caresses on his cock, Stephanie's hot pink mouth bringing him to orgasm, Stephanie's cunt drenching his lips with pussy juice.

'Yes . . . Yes . . .' he whimpered. 'I am Friar Slut.'

'Yes *what*?' she asked firmly, prodding his flushed wine-stained lips with her newly bought slutty red heels.

'Yes, Lady Peabody . . .' he answered quickly, eager to please, his voice made muffled and nearly unintelligible by a sudden drooling need to lick her feet.

She recognised his obscene desire and moved her foot away from his face. She pouted prettily. 'Just Lady Peabody?' Her voice was whiny, bitchy, full of mockery. She watched his tongue try to slavishly follow her retreating foot.

'No . . . Not just Lady Peabody,' he gibbered. 'Princess, princess . . .'

'A princess should have jewels, and a pretty mink coat . . .' she cooed with calculated contempt.

'Yes, yes . . .' he whimpered. 'A princess should have jewels, and a mink coat.' The only organs in his world were his throbbing aching cock inside Amber's warm tight cunt, and his yearning tongue, an infinitely distant half-inch from Stephanie's six-inch stiletto heels.

'You bring me the jewels . . . and you go and pay for my coat. It has been finished already, at Garode's.' Stephanie named the posh French clothier's exclusive shop. 'You do that, and I will let you cum in Amber's pussy while you lick my new shoes clean.'

'Yes, princess. Yes, princess!' He moaned with ecstasy as the corrosive filthy picture of this new degradation invaded his lust-crazed mind. She rewarded his pathetic surrender with the prodding touch of her harlot's shoes on his lips. His tongue resumed licking the bright red six-inch heel, up and down. He looked exactly like a dog on heat.

She arched her foot prettily, letting his tongue cleanse the leather where the street's filth stained it. Amber, the pretty redheaded young woman riding him, giggled. 'He is getting so hard licking your shoes, Lady Stephanie.'

'Of course he is.' Stephanie smirked. 'He is Friar Slut.'

His mindless subservience was finally rewarded by his contracting balls; his helpless rigid prick shot his seed into Amber, her perfumed pink sex a private slit-shaped gateway to damnation.

The pretty young women finger-fed him venison, chocolates, rich pastries and more cake. The blonde, Stacey, kept his eyes trapped, fingering herself while he ate. Every single dish, even the meat, was laced with the thick sweet flowery spice. The vague thought occurred to him that maybe he was being drugged. He tried to spit out the first bite, but just then Heather's skilful lips clamped around his arousal, her back arched, manipulating him with the swaying motion of her curvaceous bottom. He drooled and the cloying sweet pastry slid down his throat whole, the flavour sending tentacles of pleasure through his quivering body. Each bite seemed to make him hungrier than the last. He was craving the rich sweet food now; he needed it. His well nourished engorged prick was sliding in and out of Heather's painted lips.

Amber gave him instructions, her sultry voice a gloating contemptuous prod. 'Go get some water and clean yourself up. You can't go outside like this.'

He was confused. Like what? He glanced around and noticed his reflection in the gilded wall mirror. He did not recognise the sad sight before him. This man was wearing the tattered remnants of monastic robes. The rope meant to tie around the waist was missing. The coarse wool was covered with the stains of countless orgasms, spattered, dried seed covering the sacred cloth. A huge wine stain dominated the fabric stretching over what used to be a flat, now a somewhat bulging stomach.

He opened his mouth with an angry retort. 'Who are you to give me orders?' he meant to say, but his eyes chanced upon her crotchless white lace panties. His sudden erection was a cruel sudden reminder of his addiction, robbing his lips of the power of speech.

Amber giggled as she noticed his arousal. She pointedly stared at his straining cock, the shameful attention exciting him even more. His wine-stained fingers sought out his stiff cock, stroking himself. She held his gaze, reclining even further on the couch, torturing him with a blatant display of pussy play. He stepped closer, his need to fornicate a living goad around his mindless cock, but Amber pushed him away with her slut shoes. 'No, Friar Slut,' she said, giggling. 'No more pussy for you until you bring Lady Stephanie her pretties.'

'I think our holy man needs a reminder of what he will be missing if he doesn't bring me what I want from his monastery,' smirked Stephanie, reclining in an easy chair. She was naked, except for her high heels. Heather, in perfect make-up and white lace lingerie, was standing behind her, braiding Stephanie's gorgeous blonde curls. She was putting pretty pink silk ribbons in her hair. Stephanie undid a braid. 'Cut a lock of my hair, Heather.'

The sultry brunette cut a lock of hair from Stephanie's head. A pink ribbon was still tied to it. 'Come here, Friar Slut.' Stephanie beckoned with a perfectly manicured finger.

Steven came closer, his cock twitching. Each act of fornication made his craving worse. His tormentors, naked or clad in lingerie, wearing harlot's stiletto heels, kept him in a state of perpetual arousal. Every time his mind approached the level of mental clarity needed for true contrition, the whores would engage in lewd calculated play, skilfully manipulating his lust, putting his shiny tingling pussy-soaked member firmly back in control.

He obeyed her command, desperate for some reward, like a drooling pitiful dog.

Stephanie rolled the lock of her hair on his erect member. She smirked contemptuously as he moaned in response to her touch. The blonde lock of hair smoothly tightened around the base of his member. Stephanie tugged on the pink ribbon, a shameless pink silk leash on a cock-collar of pretty blonde hair.

'Friar Slut looks sooooo pretty . . .' giggled Stacey.

'Friar Slut has a pretty ribbon.' Stephanie petted his head. 'Now . . . I have another little gift for you.' She handed him an earthenware jar. 'You liked the salve, didn't you . . . Good Puppy . . .' She scratched the Prior behind the ear. 'This jar is special . . . it is very . . . nice.' The widow laughed, a cruel, teasing sound. She giggled as she mockingly used her pink lip-rouge to write MEDICINE in block letters on the glazed surface of the jar. 'Now get my jewels, Friar Slut.' She began to apply powders to her face, dismissing the Prior with a wave of her hand.

Already, his need to fornicate was nearly all-consuming. He looked at each whore in turn, desperate, pleading, his need for release twisting his once gentle saintly features into a mask of drooling lust. Amber prodded him with her feet, kicking his prone side as he scuttled on all fours from harlot to harlot. 'Go get.'

Steven, sobbing, ran outside. Maybe he could hire a whore in town. He saw one, her features sharp, calculating.

'Please let me fuck your pussy . . .' he begged her, his erection straining. His voice was pleading, whining, desperate.

She laughed. 'Have you coin?' she asked, mockingly.

Steven automatically reached for his sack of silver – his trembling fingers slid on his bare rope belt. The bag was long gone, plundered by the greedy women in the town house. He sobbed. 'I have no silver with me. But I am the

Prior of a rich monastery. I have more silver, gold . . .' he babbled.

The whore looked him up and down, her eyes full of contempt. 'And I am the Queen of England,' she smirked. 'Get lost, monk.'

He ran to the Bishop's palace. It was late, the gate was locked. He yelled for admittance, his voice hoarse with his need. A surprised servant let him in. He walked briskly to the stables, his erection constantly rubbing the coarse wool, making each step into a kind of thankless masturbation. The women in his own town house did not allow him undergarments. Stephanie's cockring of hair on his swinging rock-hard cock kept him at an excruciating level of filthy arousal.

'I am Prior Steven,' he told the groom. 'I need a fast horse, at once.'

The groom looked him over. He saw a monk after a massive bender, obviously – his rope belt haphazardly tied, his tonsure needing a good shave. With carefully hidden distaste, he smelled the sour odour of wine on the man's lips. The Prior even had the beginning of a bloated little gut, a most unbecoming sight on a man of God. Nevertheless, the man's haughty manner suggested he exercise some caution. 'Prior Steven, right?' asked the groom. He knew the Prior was in town – when he did not return, it was assumed he had taken lodgings in more modest surroundings, perhaps with a poor family in a bad part of town. Steven's flight from the Bishop's palace in the direction of the less reputable section of Salisbury supported this hypothesis. The Prior's preference for spartan simple accommodations was well known. The groom sniffed loudly – he smelled perfume, sweat, wine on the monk. Obviously, the Prior was out seeking a different kind of accommodation. The groom was looking forward to spreading the exciting news about holier-than-thou Steven's whoremongering.

'Get a move on, man, this is a matter of life and death,' snarled Steven. He stood behind a stool to hide his unsightly arousal. The groom nodded and saddled a horse, a great dappled stallion. 'Boots and spurs, quickly,' ordered Steven, eager to be off. The groom obeyed silently. 'Help me with these boots!' yelled Steven, suppressing the impulse to slap the slow incompetent fool. His feet were callused, honest implements for slow stately processions, not used to wearing riding boots. The feeling on his feet was warm, luxurious. He stretched his toes inside, enjoying the sensation. He ordered the groom to help him mount the tall stallion. He carelessly stepped on the man's feet, the sharp spurs leaving an ugly bleeding wound on the man's hands. He yelped in pain, but Steven was too busy to notice – mounting the horse reminded him of the first time he fucked Heather, her pretty curvy ass bumping into him. As soon as he was outside the Bishop's stables, he applied the spurs, the heavy horse wildly scattering the few pilgrims on their way to prayer. It was time for vespers. He rode the stallion hard. He was forced to slow down a mere hour out of town, as it was too dark to ride at such a pace. His horse would be sure to break a leg, and he would have to travel on foot. He struck the pommel of his saddle with his fist, frustrated. The pain distracted him from his obscene need for a moment. His cock was a stiff hungry goad in between his legs, a collared, leashed pet. He slowed down to a steady trot and moved due south through the warm evening, the full moon allowing his horse to find a path through the glades. The beauty of the scenery was lost on Steven; his mind was a cesspool of filthy images: Stephanie's luscious naked body goading him in the confessional, her painted lips wrapped around his cock, her harlot's pink heels prodding his cheek, his tongue buried in her sweet-perfumed sex; Stephanie and Heather, locked in their teasing manipulative embrace. He had to get those jewels back to Stephanie, to earn his reward, sweet perfumed addictive pussy play. He kept hearing Amber's vapid throaty purr: 'No more pretty pussy for you until you bring Lady Stephanie the Peabody jewels.' The filthy visions felt so real, he practically swooned. His right hand snaked below his robe, pulling on the pink ribbon. The little pull tightened Stephanie's special cockring – it felt like a subtle pinprick orgasm. He pulled again, and again, and again, moaning on top of the horse, tugging on his pussy-leash.

To his horror, he realised he had pulled too hard; the knot on Stephanie's precious hair came undone – it slid off his worthless stiff prick. He saw the full length of the pink ribbon in his hand, the ringlet of hair lost in the gloom of the coming night. He practically jumped off the horse, landing in a heap on the ground. He searched the tufts of grass on the path for at least an hour, scrabbling from bush to weed to molehill. He couldn't find it! He began to cry. In the pitch dark, as he scrambled from thicket to thicket, he ran into the unyielding cold trunk of a tree. He fell backwards on a pile of yellow leaves, his eyes open.

Overhead, the stars burned, the moon shone, the night spun clockwise, crystal clear. It was beautiful – his mouth gaped open, eyes lost in wonder. The air was cool and fresh and clean. The purpose of his search slowly faded under the light of those cool-burning stars, and an exhausted dreamless sleep finally claimed him.

He woke up shivering in the autumn chill. His head hurt – his fingers came away with blood when he touched the back of his head. He was confused. The events of the last few days – or was it weeks? – seemed like a hazy strange nightmare. He took off the riding boots and saw that the spurs glistened with blood. Did he ride here? He couldn't have – he would have a horse, then. He was incredibly disoriented, hungry and thirsty. He felt like there was a fiery hole in his belly. He touched his stomach – to his surprise, he found a gut. He thought of water, but his thirst did not seem to find solace in the idea. What was he craving?

He began to walk, carrying the boots. He would give them to a man who had need of them. A monk such as himself would never need such grand footwear. Spurs! The idea that he wore them – and that they were covered in blood – troubled him. Perhaps the rider forced him to put it on? He yearned to know – yet his mind cowered away from the knowledge, a silent terrified observer on a seaside bluff, on the shores of an ocean of bubbling filth. Disoriented, he searched himself. He found a sack attached to his rope belt. It was not a purse – he shook it and did not hear the sound of coppers or worse. He was relieved about the lack of coinage. Such would violate the teachings of Saint Matthew, defy the word of God. It was bad enough that he carried a sack – he was hoping the contents, whatever they were, did not incriminate him even further. Inside was an earthenware jar, MEDICINE written in pink ink on the shiny glaze. Steven stared at the jar. It looked familiar, somehow, but he couldn't place it. Certainly, carrying medicine was not much of an offence in the eyes of God. Perhaps he was visiting an invalid, bringing aid and comfort in an hour of need. He felt a gentle satisfied glow. That made sense. He pulled his robes closer about him – it was getting quite cold. He had to get to some form of shelter or he would catch his death out here in the woods. Steven followed the vague path in the brush, trying to orient himself by the light of the moon. After an hour of walking, he came across a well travelled wide trail. After a moment's indecision, he turned right. One direction was as good as any, and he somehow felt the need to be on the right path – he laughed quietly at his own silly pun.

He walked until the trail ended. He found himself in a moonlit sheltered valley. In the centre of the green oak-studded expanse, the white buildings of the Convent of Saint Eleanor shone in the moonlight. He was pleased to remember this bit of information. The sight of the valley was enough to jar his memory. He remembered certain bits of information now. He knew that he was a Franciscan monk, his name was Steven, and he was the Prior of Redfork, a monastery not far from here. He felt a vague sense of foreboding as he tried to force his mind to recall more. Exhausted, he abandoned the effort. He walked to the visitors' gate, a heavy door within a simple graceful arch of white pine. He used the knocker and kneeled, occupying himself with humble prayer while a nun clothed herself and saw to his admittance.

A young woman in a nun's habit opened the small window within the door. She had sleep-filled worried eyes. The nun stared at him, taken aback.

He must have looked a sorrowful sight before the gate.

'Who are you, traveller, and why do you seek admittance at such a late hour?'

For a terrible moment Steven searched through the recesses of his mind. He felt sudden fear – without being aware of it, he skipped across the memories of his recent past, memories like a dark pulsating cesspool, a barely glimpsed taint of corruption. He reached further back, past the stain.

'I am Steven. Prior Steven of Redfork.'

'Oh! Let me unbar the door at once, Prior. We did not expect your visit. Is everything all right?'

He opened his mouth to assure the young woman that everything was indeed all right, but a sudden stabbing pain in his head made him wince.

She unbarred the gate. Her concern was evident. She gently touched his head and he sighed with the pain.

'You are wounded! Were you attacked by bandits?'

'I . . . I am not sure. I fear my memories are scrambled.' He felt vaguely nauseated. What was wrong with him? He felt an unfocused craving, a strange need for something. Was he hungry?

'It is highly unusual to allow a man to stay at the convent. In your case I am sure Mother Elsbeth would make an exception. I shall awaken the Mistress of Novices. Please wait here, Prior Steven.'

He nodded, grateful. 'God shall bless your kindness, Sister . . .'

'Oh, I am still a novice.' She flashed her hand – she had no ring on it, her unadorned hand signifying that she had not yet taken her vows and become a full-fledged Bride of the Lord. 'My name is Livia.' She rushed off, leaving him no less confused. Why was she not summoning Mother Superior Elsbeth? Surely his arrival was unusual enough to warrant the attention of the Mother Superior. In a few minutes the novice returned and led him deeper into the convent. The Convent of Saint Eleanor was relatively new – it had been built less than two decades ago, shortly after Steven ascended to his office as Prior. The newness of the place could not hide the nearly fanatical, sombre devotion of the nuns inhabiting these walls. They walked by a number of cells. Peeking through the open archways, Steven noticed several young women – novices, Steven noticed by their lack of rings – scrubbing floors, carrying laundry, baking bread. Livia sighed. 'Mistress Emma is a harsh taskmistress.' She coloured and touched her lips with her hand. 'Harsh but fair.' She sounded frightened.

Steven smiled with understanding. These women were to become Brides of the Lord. He has done much the same with the young men who sought to learn what it meant to be a monk under his tutelage at the monastery. 'Hard work builds character.'

She nodded dutifully. 'Yes, Prior. We have arrived.' She pointed at a dark oak door. 'The visitors' hall. This is where we receive the occasional male . . .'

He knocked on the door.

'Come!' The voice was quick, energetic. He entered to find the Mistress of Novices standing behind a long table, critically examining the wooden surface with her hand. She was old, her countenance like that of a withered proud oak. Her head was unbent by age. She slammed her hand against the table. 'Dust and grime!' she barked. 'I shall have to assign even more penance to these novices. Obviously they are not doing their assigned chores, idling away their days with daydreams and wishing for luxuries.' She glared at Steven. 'I am Sister Emma. We have met before. Normally, we do not allow men here – but a man of God, such as yourself, is welcome.' She stared at his head as if it personally offended her. 'Please allow me to touch your head with my hands, to see the nature of your injury.'

He bowed his head, remaining silent. Sister Emma made him feel unwelcome. He prayed silently for her understanding. He would not have chosen to interrupt the sacred workings of the Convent with his male intrusion if he had any choice in the matter.

The Mistress of Novices examined Steven's wound with grave attention, her obvious concern giving way to relief. 'It could have been much worse,' she said, shaking her head. 'It should heal with no trouble in a few days. You say you don't remember how you came to be in the forest?' she asked.

'No . . .' He tried to think back, to remember, but a wave of foreboding came cascading down upon him, and he shuddered. 'The last thing I remember is . . .' he trailed off and shrugged. He pulled out the earthenware MEDICINE jar. 'Perhaps I was going to see to a sick man's welfare?' he asked, plaintively showing her the odd container.

The old woman's mask of annoyed irritation seemed to melt away – suddenly, her face was suffused by a warm friendly smile. It was a welcome transformation. 'Of course! Although, not entirely accurate.' She hugged the startled Prior. 'You must have been on your way here to treat a woman – our Mother Superior. Her fever seems unabating, and we fear she may have contracted some illness for which there is no cure. We have been praying non-stop for deliverance – and here you are!' The old woman was positively beaming.

This definitely sounded plausible. 'What is the nature of her illness?' asked Steven.

'She went on a brief pilgrimage to the sacred peak of Saint Eleanor, just a day's journey to the south of here,' said the nun. 'Each year, as you well know, the Mother Superior must perform penance in a more . . . arduous . . . fashion than is customary for ordinary sisters.'

Steven nodded – he always felt those in charge had to show the most humility.

Sister Emma continued: 'She fell in the night, spraining her ankle and hurting her shoulder under the heavy weight of the cross. She spent the night in the chill, and by the time she found her way to the Convent, she was running a fever. She is weak, and we fear her condition is getting worse.'

* * *

The Mother Superior was a woman in her late thirties, by now attractive rather than beautiful, strict, with burning dark eyes of fanatical devotion. In her youth, she had been a famous beauty, the daughter of a proud renegade baron. Upon his arrest for high treason, she fled to the Convent, demanding sanctuary from the raping pillaging men-at-arms devastating the countryside around her imprisoned father's castle. Within the Convent, she found Christ, divine love she did not know existed until her world came crashing down around her. She did not respect men of God much – Steven was an exception to her low regard for the sex. There was no hypocrisy at the Monastery. The Priory did not run on gold or indulgences, it did not fleece the villages it owned, it punished adultery severely, and Prior Steven was a just and honest ruler. She trusted Steven.

'Mother Superior! Are you awake?'

Emma has been at the convent ever since Elsbeth's arrival. The old nun was a trusted confidante, an honest true friend. Elsbeth coughed. 'Yes – I am awake.'

'May I come in?'

She was exhausted. Why did she ask this question? 'Yes, of course. You don't have to ask for permission, you know that.'

Mistress Emma walked in. She checked her forehead. 'You still have a fever, Mother Superior. Perhaps you should take some wine with your evening meal, or at least eat some cheese to give you strength. I do not believe fasting is good for your body at this point. The soul must have a house to live in.'

Elsbeth sighed. No matter how many times she told the senior nun not to insist on the formalities when they were alone, inevitably, she used the title. Emma did everything with fanatical rigorous dedication. Still, her concern was obvious and touching. 'A clean body houses a clean spirit. A clean spirit, by God's grace, shall infuse the vessel with purity. But you are not here just to check up on me.'

'No, Mother Superior. We have a visitor. Brother – Prior Steven of Redfork arrived a short time ago. Some ill fortune seemed to have befallen him in the forest. He struck his head –'

The gentle smile of genuine pleasure over hearing of the Prior's arrival was replaced by a look of concern. 'Oh no! Is he gravely injured?'

'He struggles with his memory, but is otherwise fairly hale, Mother Superior. With some rest and minor care he should recover without any ill effects.'

'That is good news.'

'Yes, Mother Superior. Even better, the Prior must have been coming to see you. He carried upon his person a jar of medicine, no doubt to assist in your care.'

Elsbeth smiled, excited. 'I sense a touch of providence in Prior Steven's fortunate arrival. I am concerned for his welfare. Please see to it that he is comfortable. Lately, I have been praying for divine wisdom – not for me, but for my successor. Perhaps I have been too hasty. I may yet hope for my own recovery, however unworthy my own flesh may be of God's grace.'

Emma nodded with gentle love. 'Perhaps so, Mother Superior.'

Sister Emma ordered a novice, a buxom young brunette named Mary, to take the Prior to the cell of the Mother Superior. 'She is not well,' gossiped the young woman. 'They say she caught a cold while lying on her back in the woods, unable to move – they say there were wolves and bears, it was only by divine miracle that she survived.' She smiled at him, her pretty white teeth perfect pearls in the treasure box of her chattering red lips.

He smiled back, unable to stop himself.

'Here we are!' she declared, pointing at a stout plain door of treated pine. Her voice acquired a petulant resentful tone. 'Sister Emma has a novice with the Mother Superior all night, watching her. With all the chores I have to do as well, I barely get any sleep.' She caught herself, realising she must have sounded lazy, adding defensively: 'There aren't that many novices, so we are all exhausted . . . Tomorrow, it will be Patricia.'

Prior Steven nodded. 'The Lord sees your sacrifice,' he said in a gentle rebuke.

She nodded, blushing, opening the door. Inside, Mother Superior Elsbeth lay on her simple cot, her forehead drenched in perspiration. In her clutched fingers she fingered her only precious possession, a Franciscan crown rosary, purportedly owned by one of the close disciples of Saint Francis himself. She was mumbling the Hail Mary in low fervent tones. She did not seem aware of her visitors until Steven stepped closer, his hand gripping the MEDICINE jar. For a moment the Mother Superior was overcome by a cloudy vision; her soul seemed filled with a sense of sinister foreboding. The robed cowled creature in her cell loomed over her prone flesh, a dark evil shadow clutching an unknown item of terrible power. Who was this stranger? Her eyes slowly focused upon his features. His gentle honest concerned smile finally lifted the dark shadow. 'Prior Steven?' she asked, relieved. 'It is so charitable of you to come.' She laughed at her silly fears, smiling at the Prior with unabashed trust in her piercing dark eyes.

'I confess, Mother Superior, that my memory has suffered,' he sighed. 'I am not sure of the proper method of this medicine's administration.' He pondered the dilemma for a moment.

'My Ma rubs my back with ointment when my back is sore,' chimed in Mary.

Steven nodded. That certainly sounded . . . normal. He was a little jolted by the idea of ointment rubbed into Mary's perfect young skin – the image sent a warm shiver down his back.

'Maybe she can have some mixed with wine or milk,' added Mary, proud of being paid attention to. 'I remember when I was sick, I . . .'

Prior Steven saw her chatter was tiring Mother Elsbeth. 'You have done well, my child,' he said. 'I will take it from here.' But he could not find any problems with Mary's logic. 'Bring some wine.'

Mary returned in short order with a modest jug. 'Is this good, my Lord Prior?' she smiled sweetly.

'Yes – that should be fine.'

He hesitated over the jar of salve. How much was enough? Considering her fever, he figured a little extra could not hurt. He dribbled a healthy pinch of the resinous grease into the wine, watching the sweet-smelling goo dissolve in the jug. He thought of tasting it, but then thought better of it. She may need the whole jar's worth – some medicines did not work unless they were used in profusion. He wet a cloth and dabbed the Mother Superior's lips with the potion.

Mother Superior Elsbeth smiled. The potion tasted sweet, wonderful. She eagerly sucked down the wine. 'Tastes so sweet,' she muttered thickly.

Steven smiled, relieved. He poured a goblet's worth into her waiting lips, careful not to waste a single drop. Her lips seemed to gain strength with every swallow. The Mother Superior's eyes gained a measure of brightness that was not there before.

Elsbeth felt strange. The sweet taste rushed through her body, sharp wicked bursts of delicious pleasure. She has never felt the like before. This was not a sensation she had experienced before, ever. Mother Superior Elsbeth had never had an orgasm. She had never even kissed a man, much less a woman. Suddenly, in the prime of her life, she felt an excruciating need, an insistent moist longing in between her legs. She had no idea what to call this intense filthy craving. She gasped as she watched Steven's hand dip into the jar of salve, greasing his strong manly fingers, preparing to touch her flesh. She felt she would die if he touched her, die of pleasure.

'You look better,' he said, his voice proud, strong, wonderful. She gazed upon him with adoration.

'I feel better.'

He slowly, gently uncovered the bare minimum of skin on her shoulder, and softly rubbed the resinous salve into her skin. She lay there, unmoving, her womanhood screaming for attention. She felt as if there were a thousand fingers on her feverish skin, touching her softly, insistently, everywhere. She suddenly felt horrible guilt –

how dare she think such thoughts of the Prior? He was practically a saint! A single tear travelled down her cheek. Prior Steven noticed it immediately.

'I think you've had a long trying day.' He covered her back up. 'I will return tomorrow with more medicine,' he said, gently.

She said nothing – the idea of him doing this to her again nearly blanked her mind. She wanted to rub her legs against one another. She wanted to rub herself . . . to rub herself *there*.

'Leave, Patricia,' gasped the Mother Superior. 'It's bad enough the Prior has to see me like this.' She moaned softly. The tall solemn blonde beauty curtsied, her eyes full of gentle concern. 'Yes, Mother Superior.'

'Such a pretty child,' whispered the Mother Superior, her eyes following the retreating novice.

Steven nodded. 'She certainly cares for your welfare.'

He smiled gently. He dipped his hand in the jar, the resinous grease sticking to his fingers. As always, he uncovered a small patch of skin of the Mother Superior's shoulder. Her skin was warm – could her fever have returned? He softly rubbed the Mother Superior's skin with the salve, praying it would ease the pain of her shoulder, heal this saintly kind woman. The thick pasty resin tingled against his fingers, a strong lively sensation. The scent was overpowering, sweet – he felt a strange, somehow familiar, sickly stirring, but dismissed it. It was selfish to question the efficacy of medicine, out of some odd sense of superstitious foreboding. It was not abnormal, even for a man of late middle age, to feel the stirrings of lust when kneading the flesh of a woman. The attractive saintly nun looked at him gratefully. She smiled. 'It tingles so . . . so *nice*,' she said, her voice breaking a little in mid-sentence. As he rubbed more salve into her shoulder, her breathing got faster. He stopped. 'Are you all right, Mother Superior?' he asked, concerned.

'Yes,' she barked. 'Don't stop.' Her voice had a very

peculiar, pleading sound to it. 'Please, don't stop,' she added, her voice oddly weak, lacking its customary moral authority.

He rubbed vigorously, spreading the salve on her shoulder. She squirmed a little; her soft feverish skin pressed against his fingers. He felt the stirring intensify below his rope belt, an unwelcome temptation of the flesh, and he removed his hand again.

The Mother Superior leaned into his hands. 'Prior, please . . .' she begged. 'I can feel the medicine working.'

He resumed his labour with a sigh, chanting Hail Marys in his mind, concentrating on the words. His fingers kneaded her back, her shoulders, felt muscles knotted with tension. Her skin seemed to soak in the resinous salve. A soft whimpering moan escaped the Mother Superior's lips and she screamed softly, her entire body shuddering with a sudden release of tension. Her face was drenched in perspiration. 'That was wondrous,' she said softly, her eyes unfocused, dazed.

'Feel better?' he asked, strangely disturbed.

'Yes . . . yes, feel much, much better,' she answered in the same weak tone.

Steven felt a little disconcerted about the healing session. The Mother Superior certainly looked better – much better – but he did not think it was proper to touch her flesh with his hands, particularly now that she seemed past mortal danger. He admitted it to himself – he was not entirely above the temptation of the flesh. Better to let one of the novices see to the Mother Superior's welfare. He did not wish to surrender the entire jar of MEDICINE to any of the young women without proper instruction, of course. Women could not be uniformly trusted to dole out medicine in the appropriate dosage. He would provide the nurse of the Mother Superior with the drug, and let her administer it. He cornered Patricia after Mass and gave her detailed instructions.

'You are to put a tiny pinch of the medicine in sweet wine. Give her no more than a single goblet, mind you.' He measured out a small pinch of the precious medicine, demonstrating. Given its obvious strength, he thought it was prudent to cut down from the amount he used on Mother Elsbeth the last time.

'Yes, Prior,' said the novice, awed at the responsibility.

'Massage her shoulder, where she said it hurts, with a little bit more. Make sure you are not too rough with her skin.'

'Yes, Prior.'

He handed over the jar, overcoming a strange reluctance to part with it. He watched Patricia's retreating slender body, chiding himself for his weakness at the same time; nonetheless, he still could not look away.

For the next two days, he was left to his own devices; he had the run of the Convent. Most men who came here were not allowed to converse with the nuns. The Mother Superior thought men were lustful evil creatures, tools of temptation. He secretly shared her belief, except his thoughts mirrored hers with regard to women. The Mother Superior was regaining her strength rapidly – she ate heartily, taking large portions of venison and wine at dinnertime. He normally disdained such practices, but her condition excused a great deal. He caught her watching him avidly – he felt a little uncomfortable, but then realised many of the other nuns mimicked her behaviour. A man, even a monk, must be a novelty here. Still, Mother Elsbeth did not linger much with the other nuns – nearly immediately after dinner, she would excuse herself and retire to her cell. Patricia or one of the other novices would visit her, administering the miniscule glob of salve provided by Prior Steven.

The nuns attributed her recovery to his arrival, to the liberal dispensation of his miraculous salve. He did not argue – secretly, he thought the same. He dismissed his loathing of her recent taste for rich expensive foods and liquor. She needed such fare to aid her recovery.

She summoned him the next night. He was reciting the rosary, lying awake on his cot. The young pretty novice who admitted him upon his arrival – he searched his mind for the name – Livia – came running into his cell, her dark eyes glittering clouds of anguished concern.

'Prior Steven, Prior Steven!' She shook him.

'I am awake.' He sighed and put the rosary down.

'You must come at once. The Mother Superior is not well.'

He was fully alert immediately. 'What's wrong?'

'She says she feels horrible.' The pretty dark eyes of the novice were swimming in tears. 'She said she was dying! She said the only thing that could save her now was your miraculous salve.'

He felt terrible sadness. He hurried to the Mother Superior's side, following the young nun, his heart churning with sorrow. In his hand he carried the MEDICINE jar, the large pink letters flickering as they passed torch after torch after torch. He suddenly lurched to a puzzled halt, staring at the jar in his hand, his heart filled with foreboding. The slender pretty girl ahead of him looked back, her eyes frantic.

'There is no time, Prior!' she cried and took him by the hand, dragging him through the torch-lit shadowy corridors. They came upon a heavy dark oak door. The novice knocked, a peremptory token gesture, and entered the chamber without waiting for a response. Her hand was a warm vice on Steven's fingers.

Mother Superior Elsbeth was lying on a simple spartan cot. Her face was white, drenched in sweat. She was covered in a thick wool blanket, all the way up to her chin. Her breathing was shallow.

'Go. Go now, Livia.' Her voice was shrill. The novice hesitated for a moment. Steven nodded to her, troubled but steadfast. 'I will take it from here.'

A mere glance at Elsbeth's features was enough to convince Steven of the seriousness of her condition. He peered at the jar in his hand, still somehow disconcerted. Why was he so worried? Obviously, he was here to tend to Mother Elsbeth. There was no other rational explanation for his presence. On his way here with the salve, he fell off his horse and knocked himself out. The salve was obviously working. She asked for his help. It must be right – but it didn't *feel* right. He heard Mother Elsbeth's rapid breathing, her face excited, flushed. He smelled a peculiar odour – sweet, cloying, somehow familiar. The back of his head crawled with a cold eerie sensation. What was happening? His hand shook, nearly dropping the precious MEDICINE. She whimpered – her eyes were filled with a helpless unspoken plea. Her shoulders trembled. The thick wool slid off her neck, then her shoulders – she was naked, it seemed, at least up top. He looked away, embarrassed. He did not want to see her breasts – he felt a strange loathsome stirring below his rope belt, a familiar cloying sensation, a disturbing filthy caress. He resolutely determined to withstand any and all temptation that may come his way.

Mother Elsbeth was on fire. Her shoulder had became her second cunt, her helpless degraded pussy. She wanted her cunt stroked, petted, licked, touched. The need was excruciating. On a purely intellectual level, she understood the obscene fact that it was Prior Steven himself who had brought the disgusting grease, the foul substance that robbed her of her virtue. On a physical level, her clit was a trembling needy slut on a bender. She needed more salve, more touching, more touching, more touching. For the past two days, her fingers had barely left her sore drenched sex. At first, she prayed, fondling her Franciscan crown rosary and profession crucifix with Hail Marys and Our Fathers of progressively decreasing coherence. The prayer soon degenerated into an endless session of lewd filthy masturbation. She developed surprising skill in pleasuring herself, the rosary turned into a convenient bumpy sexual aid over and around her starving demanding clit. All she could think about was Prior Steven's hard immense cock plunging into her drenched hungry virgin sex. She summoned the novices and the younger nuns to her side, not daring to show her weakness before women who may identify her obvious craving, forcing the young women to pray for her health. She did not dare to tell them that the real problem was her intense desire for the monk's member. Elsbeth took comfort from their presence, until her need became all pervasive. She would send them away to allow her solitude for uninterrupted, hours-long sessions of masturbation.

Sometimes she couldn't stop herself from touching her clit even when the novices were in the cell. This was particularly true when Patricia or Mary came by with the pathetic gob of grease they tried to pass off as the proper dose of her precious MEDICINE. She started thinking about Mary's lips, her hand slowly manipulating her sopping wet femininity, carefully, keeping the motion as subtle as possible, all fingers, no hand motion underneath the thick wool. She climaxed constantly, disguising the obscene spectacle with faked moans of pain. The prettiest of the novices, Patricia, caused her a lot of trouble. All she could think about was kissing her soft lips, touching her, seeing that statuesque young body naked. Yesterday, she nearly licked her hand as the unsuspecting novice wiped her forehead of sweat. The poor young woman thought the Mother Superior was sweating in a fever. In a crying moment of desperation, she sent her away. Livia came to relieve her – she began to think about Livia in the nude, rubbing her young flesh against hers. Finally, she could not stand it anymore. She ordered Livia to bring the monk. Anything but this – she did not want to be the cause of a young woman's corruption. Giving herself to a man was infinitely preferable to the disgusting idea of fornicating with another nun.

Her voice was full of need. 'Please rub my shoulder,' she gasped, sitting up. The blanket slid to her waist. She was completely naked. Her breasts were still firm, the nipples long and hard.

Steven felt a wave of filthy desire – suddenly, a vision of long pink painted nails flickered in his consciousness. He shook his head.

'Please,' she moaned. Her hand ripped the blanket off her naked body. The ascetic lifestyle had kept her muscles well toned. She was ripe, firm, a vision of torrid temptation. 'I will die unless you rub some more salve into my shoulder,' she moaned, her voice subconsciously becoming a manipulative needy whine.

His fingers trembled. Something was terribly wrong. His head hurt. Steven touched his shaved skull, rubbing his head. He did not want to remember. His trembling arm fell to his side, still holding the jar. The lid slid off the earthenware container and the potent sweet scent enveloped the spartan cell.

Mother Elsbeth moaned.

Steven's member, dismissed and ignored for the past few days, suddenly twitched, growing more and more alert with each sweet breath of scented air. The image of a gorgeous blonde woman floated before him for a flicker of an instant, naked, luscious, her shaven cunt brazenly displayed before him. He shook his head to clear his mind. 'What . . .' he gasped. 'What do you want me to do?'

'Rub my shoulder,' she begged. Her sob was frantic when he hesitated. 'Please. Please rub my shoulder.'

He touched her shoulder, his fingertips stained with the resinous salve. She leaned into his touch, her voice a weak filthy moan. The Prior's cock twitched again, raging against his coarse robe. The sensation felt completely degrading, an intense sullied caress of pleasure on his shaft. He massaged the Mother Superior's shoulder, his fingers fondling her naked skin. Her virgin nipples became erect. 'Yes . . .' she muttered thickly. Her hand snaked up and captured his own, her honest working hands gripping his busy fingers with fanatical strength. 'Massage my shoulder . . .' she whispered. She slowly moved his fingers down, from her shoulder to her chest. 'Massage my breasts . . .' she told him in a frozen whisper, her voice less than a shadow of its former self. 'Please . . .' Her lips formed the unfamiliar word. 'Please touch my . . . touch my tits.' Her nipples were very erect, sensitive little columns in a church of lust, straining against Steven's hand.

Steven's erection was a raging quivering rod of iron in between his legs. The tingling of his fingers travelled up his arms, jolting his mind. He suddenly remembered a gorgeous wanton harlot inside a confessional, legs spread open, her pink pussy a gateway to eternal damnation. Pre-cum oozed from his member. His eyes were glued to the Mother Superior's bared flesh, his mind awhirl with images of Stephanie's pussy play, the torrid picture alternating with the openly offered tits of the Mother Superior. He moaned with the overwhelming force of the sudden revelation and rammed his hand into the jar, smearing more of the resinous salve onto his fingers. The tingle brought more images, the scenes of filthy corruption stiffening his drooling erect cock. He rubbed the nun's eager full breasts, her panting matching his own. 'You like?' he asked, unable to stop himself.

'Yes,' she answered, equally weak. 'Please play with my tits.'

He fondled her breasts, rubbing his crotch against her sickbed. 'Play with your pussy, Mother Elsbeth.' He was surprised to hear his own voice.

The Mother Superior eagerly circled her clit with her fingers at his command. Her helplessness stirred him. 'You are my little pet, aren't you?' he gloated.

'Yes.' She rubbed her pussy with obscene vigour. 'I am your little pet.'

'You want to become my helpless pussy-pet, is that right?' He added his fingers to her own in between her legs. Her cunt was a torrid hot hell-hole, practically dripping with Elsbeth's virgin juices.

'Yes, yes, yes,' she intoned. 'I want to become your helpless pussy-pet.' She spread her legs wide, her eyes glazed, staring at Steven's erection. 'Please fuck my virgin cunt, Prior Steven,' she begged. 'Please fuck me . . .' she repeated, sobbing.

Steven rubbed some of the resinous salve into Mother Elsbeth's quivering cunt. The twisted needy harlot on her back no longer resembled the Mother Superior of the Convent of Saint Eleanor. She was a pussy-pet, a whore with legs spread open, a cunt with no purpose other than to fornicate. The Prior mounted the Mother Superior. His dick slid into her, taking her innocence. He slid in and out of her wet pussy, her gasp of pain quickly replaced with squeals of mindless delight. She moaned with perverse pleasure as each thrust desecrated her body and office.

'Thank you for fucking my cunt, Prior Steven,' she gibbered. 'Thank you, thank you.'

She came on his cock, moaning, gyrating her hips. He came at the same time, shuddering.

The daze lifted from her mind, a red velvet curtain lifting to reveal a newly formed cesspool of corruption. She stared at her soul's mirror within her mind. Her tears were as sudden as her obscene climax. 'What have I done?' she whimpered, staring at Steven in helpless anguish.

He petted her head, expecting something like this. Quick as a snake, he rubbed some of the resinous salve in between her legs and lowered his face over her glistening fleshy knob, his tongue a practised fornicating whirlwind over her clit. Feebly, she tried to scurry away, but her flailing weakened, then stopped completely as his lips wrapped around her drug-laced pussy lips, gently sucking the wet aroused flesh of her femininity into his mouth. The salve on his tongue was a sweet taste of sin, a luridly lit resinous gateway to his memories. With razor-sharp clarity, he remembered every moment of his obscene corruption. The Prior tongued the nun's trembling drenched clit until she came, and came, and came again. Mother Elsbeth quivered, her tears forgotten in the explosions of raw red lust. Her dark bush reminded him of Heather.

He tugged the nun's moaning weakly lolling head over towards his obscenely erect member. She looked at it with undisguised lust, licking her lips with carnal appetite. He slid his manhood inside her virgin mouth, closing his eyes, remembering. Steven recalled Stephanie's shaved pink sex, his helpless surrender inside the confessional as she stood over him. The vision invoked the by now welcome familiar sensation of filthy caresses over his member. His eventual climax became an obscene fountain of seed inside Mother Elsbeth's eagerly suckling lips. The Mother Superior gagged. 'Swallow, Mother

Elsbeth,' he commanded, mockingly. He watched her eyes cloud with perverse pleasure as she swallowed, her addicted pussy rewarding each new act of humiliation with fresh waves of obscene pleasure.

Mother Elsbeth licked her lips. 'I am your bitch, Prior Steven,' she moaned. She had never felt so filthy, so alive. 'I am your whore.' She fondled her dripping pussy, her plain unadorned fingers a blur. 'I am your fornicating cunt, my Lord.' She raised her cum-stained mouth and kissed Steven's salve-drenched hand. She tasted the sweet addictive grease and wrapped her lips around his fingers, her hope of salvation a forgotten useless luxury in the face of her overwhelming need. She licked his hand clean, one finger at a time, her pussy so wet she nearly cried with unmet base need. She begged the agent of her corruption on her knees, subconsciously assuming the posture she used before the altar. 'Please finger me.'

Steven pushed one finger into her cunt, then another. She was moaning softly like a bitch on heat, bucking on his hand. He rubbed some salve into the area around her sex with his other hand, and his finger slipped, the resinous salve mixing with the thin film of perspiration and pussy juice. The drug-laced digit slipped into her anus. She squealed, a high-pitched pitiful moan of helpless fornication, shoving her ass all the way onto his finger.

She moaned. 'Yes, yes, finger me there.'

He chuckled, amused, and began to finger her anus, the drug-laced finger a corrosive file on the nun's remaining shreds of dignity.

She sobbed, pain mixed with pleasure as she shoved herself all the way onto his hand. It felt wonderful, this new degradation. She wondered what would feel even better.

'Please sodomise me, Lord,' she begged, her saintly face a mask of drooling lust. 'Please stick your cock in my ass.'

There was not a lot of MEDICINE left. He pondered the sadly depleted contents before him. Mother Elsbeth couldn't care less about her convent anymore – all she cared about was the welfare of her well-lubricated pussy. She kept sending for him and his MEDICINE, awaiting his arrival on all fours, her habit pulled up to expose her trembling eager bottom. In the privacy of her chambers he just called her his pet whore.

The senior nun, Sister Emma, no longer thought of Steven as an angel of mercy – she had the temerity to question Mother Elsbeth about the nature of their relationship.

'The Mother Superior spends a lot of time with Prior Steven.'

'I am still ill,' said the Mother Superior, with undisguised impatience. Her cunt was a quivering needy pit, constantly wet. She thought of Steven's cock in her ass and nearly screamed at the irritating wrinkled nag. Couldn't the old bitch see that she was busy?

'The Mother Superior looks . . . healthy . . .' the old woman sighed.

'Obviously, your interest in my affairs is attributable to your lack of productive employment,' said Elsbeth, icily. 'I suspect that can be cured. I want you to meditate on the sin of Sloth, Sister Emma – for a week, at least, on the peak of Mount Eleanor.' That ought to keep the irritating hag out of the way.

'But – Elsbeth –'

'*Mother Superior* Elsbeth, Sister Emma.'

'. . . Yes, Mother Superior. What about my duties here? I must oversee the novices . . .'

'Obviously you are no longer able to carry out the duties of your office. I will see to your replacement while you are away.'

Stunned, her wrinkled face sad, Emma bowed and left her chambers. The old woman passed Steven in the hallway, her eyes mirrors of frustration. 'Go back to your monastery, Prior!' barked the nun, her eyes filled with tears of anguish.

Elsbeth heard Emma's frustrated cry. She used the warning of Steven's approach to get on her hands and knees and raise her habit, exposing her bottom. She began to salivate.

Elsbeth was beginning to bore Steven. There were younger, prettier nuns, and her incessant whiny pleading for constant play began to get on his nerves. When he climaxed, his need to fornicate barely abated. He had his best orgasms when he pictured Stephanie, imagining scenes of licking, tasting, and worshipping her beautiful shaved pussy. He ordered the Mother Superior to shave her sex. It helped some, but it still wasn't the same. At his suggestion, Mother Superior Elsbeth raided the storage room of the convent – some women of questionable virtue had taken refuge here years ago. Upon joining the Order, they abandoned their powders and rouge, high-heeled shoes, lace fripperies and other implements, along with everything else of their former sin-filled lives. Mother Elsbeth dressed herself in the shameless garments, applying all the rouge and powders to please him. He watched the formerly prim ascetic woman degrade herself for him, her lips forming a daily ring of pink rouge around the base of his member. The stain reminded him of the time Stephanie sucked on his cock – he found himself obsessively thrusting his member inside the nun's wet mouth, his mind wrapped around Stephanie's arched feet, her long pink fingernails, her luscious tits.

He stifled a frustrated curse. This stupid slut was delaying him. He waited until he gained a moment of satisfaction in her mouth before he spoke. 'I need to get to the monastery.'

'Please don't leave . . . please don't leave your pet whore,' moaned the Mother Superior, cum dribbling down her cheek. 'I will do whatever you say.'

He looked at her with distaste. He explained as if to a child. 'To get you more salve, we must give Lady Peabody what she wants.' He slapped her quivering naked ass. 'You don't want to run out of salve, do you?' he asked mockingly.

'No,' she gasped. 'Pet needs more . . .'

'Tell your servants – tell your nuns – to saddle the best horse you have.'

'Can I come with you?' she asked eagerly.

He frowned. Her presence would afford him convenient access to pleasures of the flesh – but Anders was not a fool. He would see through her façade to the cock-crazed whore that she had become. The Sub-Prior had the key to the treasury box; he needed a plausible excuse for accessing it, not a middle-aged corrupted Bride of the Lord.

'You will stay here. I will bring you more salve when I get it.' The shadowy outline of a disgusting evil scheme touched his mind. It somehow felt familiar, as if it was not the first time he had thought of it. 'Oh yes, I will bring plenty, plenty of salve.' He grinned. 'Won't that be nice?' He raised her chin with his hand. Her eyes were empty, uncomprehending, yet dazed with base lust. She nodded, agreeing with whatever he said.

Sister Emma saddled his horse for him. Her habit was a torn stained mess. It had taken her many days to return from Mount Eleanor. Elsbeth did not permit her to obtain a new garment. When she was sent away, the other nuns were puzzled at first upon hearing of her harsh sentence. Their puzzlement quickly gave way to a muted shameful glee. Sister Emma was not a popular nun. She was the mistress of novices, a harsh unyielding fanatic, and her downfall was secretly applauded. With the Mother Superior so busy with Prior Steven and her illness, the nuns relaxed their rigorous routine. They ignored Sister Emma's angry sermons on sloth and gluttony, knowing full well that her words would find no reception with Mother Elsbeth or the new Mistress of Novices.

The nuns – except for Sister Emma – were pleased when Mother Elsbeth declared that it was not sinful to eat meat every day. The simple gruel and plain bread that was the customary fare at the Convent quietly gave way to hearty dishes of stew, rich pastries and wine. Some of the nuns refused the new rich fare, particularly the older ones, but the majority felt it was not against the word of God to enjoy life a little. Mother Elsbeth took any criticism of the new ways personally, and levied harsh punishments on those who expressed outrage. Sister Emma was given the most arduous jobs. She had just begun to muck out the stables when Steven rode up, his feet clad in his high boots, spurs bright in the morning sunshine. She stared at the Prior with undisguised hatred.

'You have become a tool of the devil,' she hissed. 'You have poisoned this well.' Her eyes were piercing vengeful daggers.

He laughed. 'I will return with more medicine. Now stand aside, hag.' He applied his spurs, the rearing horse nearly riding Emma down, and rode out into the sparkling morning.

Four

He made good time – within a mere hour or so he was at the copse of tall birches surrounding the Priory. The monks were singing a hymn – was it time for Mass? He barely remembered the time when he would attend Mass as a matter of course. He occasionally went at the Convent during his few weeks there, once nearly falling asleep after a night of particularly satisfying fornication with the Mother Superior. He was bored every time, irritated at the annoying interruption to his busy schedule of massaging, fingering, pleasuring the Mother Superior. He considered his next move. Riding a horse into the humble monastery like some kind of Earl would do nothing to help him gain his objective. He dismounted, leading the horse towards the stable. Just in the nick of time, he remembered to take off the boots. His feet were uncomfortable on the grass, having grown soft and pampered in the silk slippers he wore at the town house. He did not have a chance to toughen the softened soles here – he was barely ever on his feet, otherwise occupied in Mother Elsbeth's chamber of fornication.

Brother George was tending the animals. He greeted the Prior with euphoric joy. The young man had just taken his vows – his eyes were gleaming with holy fervour. He worshipped the Prior, a man of God he hoped to model his life after. He had been getting worried about the Prior's absence – there were rumours he had been taken ill. 'I am so pleased you have returned, Prior Steven,' he gushed.

'Whose animal is this?' he asked, bewildered, gazing at the mistreated horse.

'It belongs to the Convent,' answered Steven. 'See to it – I have urgent business with Sub-Prior Anders.' He decided the less he said the better. Long lies were like fat fish – they were caught with less fine nets. He hurried out of the stable, ignoring Brother George's obvious puzzlement. He crossed the main courtyard and entered his personal room, a spartan, tiny cell with a simple wooden crucifix on the wall. He frowned with distaste. This was no chamber for a Prior!

He sat on the cot and considered his next move. Could he remove the jewels without telling Anders? Obviously, that would be ideal. He would need the key from the Sub-Prior, of course. Why would Anders give him the key? The Prior could demand it, of course . . . but a monastery was not a kingdom. He had to watch his step – theoretically, the other monks could strip him of his office, if his offences were egregious enough. Certainly, his embezzlement . . . He sat bolt upright, frowning. By God, he had forgotten about the winter coats! How was he going to explain this to the Brothers? He recalled his drooling doglike fornication with Heather, the stacked pile of silver clinking on top of her ass each time he thrust inside her. His member stiffened and he began to fondle himself, but he was too distraught to make a decent job of it. He stopped shortly and gathered his wits about him. He needed a good excuse for losing the money. A plan floated through his mind, a dark glittering gem of a scheme. He seized upon it.

He summoned Anders and embraced him. 'I am glad to see you again, Brother,' he said, gravely.

Anders smiled. 'I am also glad to see you, Prior. We were worried about you.' The Prior did not look well – he looked haggard, in fact. If it wasn't for the weight he seemed to have gained during his absence, Anders would have thought Steven had been on a long fast. The Prior had the same look worn by those brothers who have gone on long fasts, or a foreign pilgrimage – a preoccupied feverish gaze, as if they were not entirely with you when they engaged in conversation. 'We even prayed for your return – it seems our efforts were rewarded.'

'Yes, yes, Brother.' Prior Steven looked disconcerted. He turned away, burying his face in his hands. He lowered his hands and turned around. There were tears on his cheek. 'I must seek the harshest penance possible, Sub-Prior,' cried Steven. 'I failed this monastery, I failed our orphans.'

Anders had never seen Steven cry. He was shocked. 'What do you mean, Prior?' he asked, distressed.

'I must start with the story of my journey to town,' began Steven. 'I passed by a poor man's corpse with a slit throat and an empty purse by the side of the road.'

Anders gasped.

'I pressed on, determined to complete my mission. Upon my arrival at the Bishop's palace, I looked around for an honest merchant with the wherewithal to supply our needs – alas, there was not one who did not try to cheat me.' He buried his face in his hands again. 'I decided to return with the money.' Steven's face was swimming in tears. 'I even borrowed a fast horse from the Bishop to make the return journey faster, and safer.' He sighed. 'I just wanted to make the purchase in Nottingham or London, to avoid the robbers on the road.'

'What happened?' asked Anders, dreading the answer.

'I found myself lying on my back in the forest, my head in terrible pain.' He lowered his tonsured head so Anders could see the remnant of the injury, a small scar on his head. 'The brigands took the Bishop's horse, the silver . . . All the silver!'

'Those blackhearts shall burn in eternal hellfire!' cried Anders. 'I am just glad you are alive, my Lord Prior.'

'I crawled to our convent, the Convent of Saint Eleanor. Mother Elsbeth, despite her recent illness, was kind enough to nurse me back to health.'

'She is a good woman, a living saint.'

'Yes. Yes she is,' said Steven woodenly, his lips two tightly pressed lines. He continued after a moment of silence. 'My own life is meaningless, Brother. We must think of what must be done to see to the orphans welfare. Winter is coming.'

'Yes. Winter is coming,' agreed Anders.

Steven sighed. 'If only there was a way to make up for the loss . . .'

Anders thought hard. 'What about the Peabody estate?' he asked. 'Surely you have not forgotten about the late Lord's charity, my Lord Prior?'

'Of course!' cried Steven, relieved. 'You are certainly a man of sharp intelligence, Brother Anders. But . . . those jewels were meant to expand the orphanage.'

'My Lord Prior, not much point to expanding the orphanage if the orphans have frozen to death in the harsh winter,' said Anders. He felt a quiet sense of triumph – the old man would just collapse without him to think of good solutions, good ideas. 'Why stop with the jewels?' he smiled, pleased at his ingenuity.

'What do you mean?' asked Steven, sharply.

'My Lord Prior . . .' began Brother Anders. Steven could see he had thought about this before, and rehearsed his speech. 'The Peabody estate also has several accounts receivable for shipments of wool to Flanders. Any one of those account letters can act as collateral for a sizable loan from a moneylender.'

Steven was not of a financial frame of mind. His brain struggled with the concept of a loan. He was thinking about what Anders said. All that money . . . The idea of all that gold, ready for use at his beck and call, stirred him. Women would be attracted to all that wealth, to the trappings of power. He thought of Heather's wet excitement as she greedily collected his silver.

He smiled. 'Yes . . . you are right, of course.'

His tears had dried up completely, Anders saw. The Prior was obviously drained emotionally, ravaged by the demands of his journey. No wonder – being robbed, knocked out, it must have really got to him. Anders considered his physical condition. Prior Steven was no longer a young man – he looked terrible, despite the care he said he had received at the Convent. Perhaps, if Steven was ready for retirement . . . If he could be convinced of Anders's ability, would his fellow monks acclaim him with the mantle of leadership? Anders knew he would make a good Prior. The idea excited him.

'Brother Anders . . .' pondered the Prior aloud. 'Any property may be used as collateral in such manner?'

'Yes, of course, my Lord Prior.'

Steven thought furiously. 'You are obviously a man of more worldly ability than I ever have been.'

Anders beamed at the compliment, nodding his head in humble acceptance.

'I have no doubt *you* would get a good price for the jewels in town.'

Anders nodded again, pleased at Steven's recognition of his abilities.

'Sub-Prior, I would be pleased if you came with me to assist with these matters. I trust we can both leave the monastery for a brief period.'

'I would be delighted, Prior Steven,' smiled Anders.

'Well . . . let us gather the jewels and those "accounts receivable" about our persons and head off to town.'

Anders nodded. He fished out the large iron key of the treasury box from under his robe and led the Prior to the Church. The treasury was in the chapel, within a locked windowless chamber. Without the key, it would have required siege equipment to break in.

Steven marched inside. There were gold goblets, sacred relics of precious metal, a jewel-encrusted cup, a small chest and a walnut box with papers inside. He immediately grabbed the small chest containing the jewels. Without turning around, he spoke. 'Sub-Prior, it will be safer if we split the valuables about our persons. If we meet robbers, at least one of us should try to escape. Keep those papers – those account receivables – with you – I will hold on to the jewels.'

Anders could find no fault with Steven's reasoning. 'Yes, my Lord Prior.' The Sub-Prior picked up the walnut box. After a moment's pause, he added: 'Perhaps we should hire some men-at-arms. Those jewels are very valuable.' He felt he had to explain further. 'Although nobody knows about these account receivables outside of Flanders, I would be more comfortable if we had an escort.'

Steven blinked. 'Nobody knows about them?'

'Well, my Lord Prior, everyone knows they exist – just not how many there are, or what they are worth.'

Steven swallowed, hard. The reward for bringing such riches to the gorgeous temptresses at the town house turned his member into a stiff goad beneath his monastic robe. 'I see,' he said, terse. 'Make sure you are a conscientious custodian of those papers, Brother Anders.'

Steven politely waited for the Sub-Prior to leave the chamber. He did not want the other monk to see his erection, the gift of a secret filthy vision of squealing naked luscious maidens. He slid a gold cup dedicated to Saint George beneath his robe, next to the thick slice of onion he had used to tear his eyes. Steven smiled broadly at the waiting Anders outside.

Patricia was going crazy. For the past few days, she had been fighting with Mary and the other novices for the privilege of taking care of the Mother Superior. Since Prior Steven left, her condition had deteriorated. It was very pleasant to massage Mother Elsbeth's shoulder, spreading the wonderful sweet-smelling tingling salve on her hands, rubbing the gentle stuff into the Mother Superior's soft warm skin. There was very little of the gooey resin left – she secretly wanted to rub her own skin with it, but refused the temptation. She thought that greedy little bitch Mary was dipping into the jar for her own disgusting purposes – whatever those might be. She dismissed the filthy idea. What would Mary do with the salve?

She shook her head to chase away the incessant thoughts of the pretty, gossipy girl. She certainly had pretty lips, thought Patricia. She stared at a torch on the wall and willed the fire to cleanse the sinful shadows of her mind. Patricia was careful with knocking on the Mother Superior's door. Sister Susan did not knock once, and Elsbeth was apoplectic with rage – the nun was sent to

Mount Eleanor as penance, to maintain a useless fire, 'a beacon of God's warm presence' for an entire week.

'Come!' yelled the Mother Superior. As always, Elsbeth was covered up to her chin underneath her blanket. Her arms and hands were covered as well. Her eyes were dazed, yet hungry. She smiled at Patricia, an eager yearning gesture.

'I brought your medicine, Mother Superior.'

'Yes, yes,' whimpered Elsbeth. She sat up instantly, her skin glistening white in the candlelight.

Patricia noticed her nipples were erect, jutting out, as if she had just come from a cold bath. She smeared the tiny pinch of resin over her fingers, enjoying the sensation, drawing it out for as long as she dared. Elsbeth grabbed her arm, her fingertips hot daggers on her arm. The fleeting thought flickered across Patricia's mind that the Mother Superior was growing longer nails. 'Please . . .' gasped Elsbeth.

With something akin to regret, Patricia rubbed her hands over the Mother Superior's naked shoulder. Elsbeth closed her eyes – her trembling subsided a little.

'My . . . my shoulder is doing better,' moaned Mother Elsbeth.

Patricia smiled. That was good – perhaps the Mother Superior did not need any more of the precious MEDICINE.

'My . . . my bosom hurts,' she said softly, a feeble whisper. 'Here.' She grabbed Patricia's salve-stained hand and pressed it against her chest. Her skin was hot, her nipple a stiff warm poker against her fingers. The tingle in her hand seemed like a red flame – the sudden fire travelled up her arm, through her suddenly erect, full nipples, down her belly, finally finding a home in between her legs.

'Mother Superior . . . Mother Superior wants me to rub the medicine on her bosom?' asked the beautiful slender novice, her eyes dazed with the fiery sensations coursing through her womanhood.

'Yes!' cried Elsbeth. 'Please rub my . . . rub it.' She clasped her fingers around Patricia's hand and forcefully rubbed the girl's fingers against her naked heaving bosom. 'Yes . . . like that. Like that.'

Patricia rubbed the Mother Superior's tits with her hands. She vaguely realised the salve on her hand had been used up already, but she couldn't seem to stop fondling the nun's shapely breasts. The nipples were so erect, so nice in between her fingers. Her skin was soft, warm, inviting. She was fondling Elsbeth's quivering tits, abandoning all pretence of simply applying medication.

'Yes . . .' moaned Elsbeth. 'Suck on my nipples, Patricia.'

Patricia's clit was a raging inferno – she had never touched a woman like that before, but the Mother Superior's command tore the inhibitions from her addled lust-crazed mind. She lowered her lips over Elsbeth's breast as the Mother Superior's hand slipped beneath her habit. Elsbeth reached her clit at the same time that the novice's lips locked around the Mother Superior's aching nipple. Her breasts were soaked with the resinous salve – she found her lips locking around Elsbeth's nipples, sucking in the sweet moisture. The Mother Superior stroked the young woman's soft blonde bush with her fingers, her motions mimicking each more and more frantic nibble on her breasts. Finally, Patricia climaxed in a great shuddering wave, an avalanche of addictive filthy pleasure coursing through every pore of her virgin body. The novice collapsed on Elsbeth's cot, a weak heap of gorgeous downy young flesh in a nun's habit. Physically, she was completely exhausted, a passive observer of her fate – mentally, she was still obscenely aroused, incapable of contemplating anything other than the needs of her womanhood. The Mother Superior began to stroke the novice's body with her hands, greedily stripping her sacred garment. She tenderly fondled the naked aroused girl, her passivity only broken by occasional shrill moaning squeals. Finally, she lowered her face over the young woman's trembling glistening pussy, greedy tongue descending on her clit.

'Patricia! Patricia!' Mary's happy vivacious voice was tinged with irritation. 'Where are you, girl?' She burst into Patricia's tiny cell. Now that the Mother Superior –

against all tradition – had removed Patricia from the common room where all the novices slept, Mary realised she missed the stiff solemnly pretty young woman. What made her absence particularly galling was its reason: Patricia's elevation into the Mother Superior's permanent nurse. Mary would have laughed at her feelings a few weeks ago – who wanted to nursemaid the strict ascetic self-flagellating Mother Superior?

She sighed and glanced at the supine sleeping body of the novice on her cot. She looked so exhausted, so pretty . . . She blushed when she realised she had just thought of another woman as pretty. Well, she was! She looked around Patricia's chamber, unable to stop herself. It was spartan and simple, as all such cells were. Her eyes strayed over the tiny bedstand – an all-too-familiar earthenware jar stood next to a dust-covered bible. Mary's eyes grew large. She had been sent to collect Patricia by the Mother Superior – she told her she felt ill, she needed her medicine. She was grumpy, demanding why Patricia was not by her bedside. All too often, the novice spent the night with the Mother Superior, praying for her welfare by her cot. Patricia's eyes, lined with fatigue at each meal, definitely supported this story. Despite her relative lack of responsibilities, Mary was not far from Patricia when it came to fatigue. She kept falling asleep during Mass, barely able to do her most basic of chores. She could not sleep at night – her dreams were full of strange silky touches, the most vague of intimate caresses. She secretly missed taking care of the Mother Superior. She kept suppressing pangs of envy whenever she met Patricia in the hallways. Mary felt sorry for her – now that she had to be with Mother Elsbeth all the time, it was definitely taking its toll on her. The tall blonde girl seemed to enjoy strutting her new office before Mary – whenever she ran into her she would stare at her, as if she was some kind of a spectacle.

She only managed to avoid penance because of the continued absence of Sister Emma. The strict Mistress of Novices kept getting on the bad side of the Mother Superior – this week, the old woman had been sent to gather firewood in the forest. Many of the older nuns complained, only to find themselves keeping company with Sister Emma. The younger nuns and the novices secretly gave sighs of relief. The dining hall filled with laughter and the clinking of forks, as new delicacies were brought in from town. Mary did not think any of the new dishes tasted any good. The sweetest of pastries tasted like ashes in her mouth. She could tell the other novices who took care of the Mother Superior felt the same. If only she could just get Patricia's job . . . It's not like she was any worse at rubbing the Mother Superior's soft pretty skin.

She found herself moving closer to the bedstand. Mary's fingers trembled as she picked up the jar. She carefully uncorked the container and peered within. What she saw took her breath away. There was barely any of the resinous salve inside – it was practically empty! She could not suppress an anguished loud sob.

'Mary!' Patricia's voice was full of outrage.

Mary was so startled, she nearly fainted – she juggled the precious jar and dropped it, the earthenware container shattering into a hundred pieces on the stone floor. For a moment, nothing happened.

'Mary!' It was the loudest whisper in the world.

Suddenly, both of them were on their hands and knees, desperately scrambling around the clay remains for the last tiny gob of resin.

'I am sorry, I am sorry . . .' sobbed Mary. 'I will – I will –'

'What will you do, Mary?' snapped Patricia. 'Drop it again?'

Mary was crying incoherently. 'She sent me to fetch you,' she sobbed. 'She told me to bring you and the medicine.'

'The medicine is nearly gone,' sighed Patricia. She stared at Mary. The brunette looked away, blushing. Patricia's eyes seemed lost in a different world, focusing on Mary's soft lush red lips. 'It's fine . . .' She hugged the vivacious young girl, murmuring soft phrases of assurance in her ears. 'Don't worry . . .' Patricia rested her head on Mary's shoulder, her eyes still scanning the ground – suddenly, she saw the gob of resin, smeared on a shard of glazed pottery. Still hugging Mary, she leaned down, scooping up the tiny piece. A sudden flash of inspiration seized her. She held up the salve on the tip of her finger, displaying her find, a peculiar smile playing on her lips. The wonderful gorgeous tingle resonated through her hand, her arm, her entire body, centring in between her legs. She held out the salve to Mary. 'Go on,' she urged her in a breathless whisper.

'What – what do you mean?' asked Mary in the same way.

'She doesn't have to know it wasn't gone yesterday . . .' said Patricia, slowly moving her finger towards Mary's beautiful sensuous mouth.

Mary smelled that wonderful intense sweet scent. 'It smells so good,' she sighed. She felt her lips part as Patricia's long pretty finger approached her mouth. Mary's breathing grew shallow, becoming a basic panting as Patricia's grease-stained finger invaded her mouth.

Mary felt nothing but sweetness; an explosion of intense compelling pleasure pouring through her taste buds into her very heart. Her lips tingled. She closed her eyes. Suddenly, there was a soft pleasant sensation on her mouth, the warmth of skin, pleasant caresses against her flushed full lips. She opened her eyes – Patricia was showering her lips with tiny kisses, her breath a cascading echo of the wondrous sweetness in her mouth. The blonde girl's huge emerald green eyes seemed to stare into her soul. She felt an odd, intensely erotic tingle in between her legs – her knees buckled and she gasped, leaning against Patricia. Each time her lips touched her mouth, sweet explosions of intense pleasure flooded her being.

'Thank you. Thank you,' she gasped in between kisses. She couldn't seem to stop herself. 'Don't stop. Never stop.'

Patricia's soft little kisses slowly became an in-depth exploration of Mary's gorgeous full mouth. Her tongue slid in between her lips, seeking to unite with Mary's. The buxom pretty brunette moaned softly, her entire being transformed into Patricia's shivering melting accomplice.

She could smell every strand of Patricia's beautiful blonde hair, hear every breath escaping her lips.

'I love you,' whispered Mary, gazing at Patricia with unabashed adoration.

'Of course you do,' smiled Patricia, softly stroking Mary's silky dark hair.

Steven did not bother with any of the other monks. He had known most of them his entire adult life, indeed, some of them he considered his best friends – before his trip to town. Now, they were nothing but irritating delays on the way to Stephanie's coterie of whores. He tried to think of his imminent reward as little as possible – his erection was always nearly instantaneous, obvious to even the most distracted observer. He justified the extreme haste of their departure with a concern for the orphans, as well as the fear of an early winter storm. He left the convent's horse in the stable. They would travel by coach, with two men-at-arms riding escort. Steven's plan did not require a fictional roadside robbery. They might as well get to town safely. He did make sure, of course, that the men-at-arms were hired with the knowledge that they would be dismissed shortly after their arrival in town. There was simply no need for them – indeed, their presence might jeopardise the plans he had for the Sub-Prior. They set out at dawn.

Steven grinned. 'Brother Anders, it is a wonderful day today.' He rubbed his hands together, ostensibly against the chill – in reality, he was barely able to contain himself. He was on his way with the Peabody jewels, princess Stephanie would reward him, perhaps she would rub her pretty stiletto heels against his cock and let him . . . He realised he was drooling. 'What did you say, Brother Anders?'

'I hope we shall make good time.'

'God willing.'

'God willing.'

There was a pause in the conversation. Anders started it up again. 'Your journey – your injury – must have been truly exhausting, Prior.'

Steven glanced at the Sub-Prior – Anders was usually not a man for useless chatter.

'Yes . . . It was a most difficult and distressing journey.'

'A man of advancing years – however diligent in prayer – might grow weary of so many responsibilities.'

Steven nodded slowly, just realising where Anders was hoping to steer this whole awkward exchange. He considered this new angle. 'Yes . . . I do occasionally feel the weight of my office. It is a most heavy burden.' He pretended to close his eyes, as if fatigue overcame him. Anders carefully covered him under a wool blanket, pulling it up to his chin – but his eyes were weighing the Prior with unabashed ambition.

They pitched camp every night at sundown. Steven secretly would have preferred to push on to town, going without sleep, but he could not openly justify such a risk. The men-at-arms built a fire, set up a tent, and one of them slept while the other kept watch. They both looked bored, and slightly put out by their obligation to guard – of all priestly types – monks. Steven was most careful about not opening the small chest with the jewels in their presence. He did not share his concerns with Anders, who spent a great deal of time studying the papers in the walnut box.

The men-at-arms were typical of their breed. They quarrelled, drank dreadful watered wine, ate salted pork and belched constantly. Stopping too often for breaks, the men ate hearty chunks of roasted pork. The monks ate bread and drank water. Steven glanced at the men-at-arms' jug of wine with carefully disguised yearning. He had grown used to rich food and good wine, and the lack of both made him short-tempered. The men were not pleased by the quality of their drink – their cursing in the presence of men of God irritated Steven, and enraged Anders. 'Such men to safeguard us from brigands,' frowned the Sub-Prior. 'Scum of this earth.' He would have spat but for his robe and office.

One of the men, Henry, turned bright red – he must have heard Anders.

'Men of action may not act like men of God – but when they protect men of God, they are just as holy,' intoned Steven. Henry looked mollified, but his eyes remained sullen. He stopped talking to the Sub-Prior entirely. The few occasions when he was forced to interact with Anders, his eyes were full of malevolent, piggish anger.

Steven smiled.

They reached a familiar-looking glade at nightfall. Steven looked at it with the expression of a man who knows he has been to a place but can't really recall why or when. He frowned, then slapped his tonsured head with his hand. 'This is where I was robbed. We are not far from the convent.' He pointed to his right. 'That way, not far at all. We will lodge there, at the convent.'

Henry grinned, taking a bite out of a fat yellow onion. He laughed coarsely. 'Virgins, by God!'

His companion grinned back. 'I don't suppose they see too many real men out here.'

Five

Prior Steven ordered a nun to see to the needs of their animals. The decrepit haggard old woman looked crushed, emanating a strange sort of sadness. She led the animals inside and unsaddled them. Anders saw others occupied in similarly difficult work – another older woman was mucking out the stables, yet another was splitting wood. From the size of the enormous pile, she had been at it for some time – maybe a few weeks. None of them looked eager to talk. Anders did catch the eye of one of them, an old mean-looking woman in a torn filthy habit. She was carrying bundles of firewood, apparently just returning from the forest. If a look could kill, Anders thought he would have died an instant death. What was going on here?

'They are serving penance. They are all under a vow of silence,' said a voice from the doorway.

Anders has met Mother Superior Elsbeth once already, at the time of her investiture. He did not think she was a perfect choice to head the convent. Too harsh, even then she had a reputation as a fanatic. It seemed his concerns were borne out. He examined her pallid unhealthy-looking skin, the circles under her eyes, her unstable angry posture, and reconsidered his harsh opinion. Perhaps her illness could excuse her lack of patience with the sinners. Behind her, a few younger women jostled to get a look at the visitors. One of them was taller than the others, a stunning beautiful blonde maiden. She occasionally reached out a hand to steady the Mother Superior, her fingers massaging Elsbeth's shoulder with practised ease. She caught his eyes and held them for a moment – the most striking green eyes he had ever seen – before demurely looking away. Even so, Elsbeth noticed.

'Prior Steven, I hope you are not bringing men of sinful appetite into this house of God?'

Steven suddenly began to cough. He seemed unable to stop. 'Why would you say such a thing, Mother Superior?' he asked finally, his eyes rich with the tears of his coughing fit.

'Your monk practically devoured Sister Patricia with his shameless eyes.'

'Is that so, Brother Anders?' asked Steven, gently.

Anders blushed and lowered his eyes. This was no way to impress the Prior with his ability for higher office. He felt intense relief when he heard Steven's chuckle.

'Do not worry, Mother Superior. Brother Anders has taken the same vows I have. He just feels the weight of his years – the lack thereof, rather.'

The Mother Superior frowned, but looked too preoccupied with something else. 'Prior, let us talk in private. I have much that I must discuss with you, right away, in my cell.'

Steven nodded and followed Elsbeth inside. Her attendants clustered around them. The tall girl left their company at the next corridor – Anders could not suppress a pang of longing.

Steven faced him. 'Sub-Prior – I have business with the Mother Superior. Don't wait for me at vespers.'

'Of course, Prior Steven.' Sometimes the business of God had to take a back seat to the business of governing. He secretly thought he would make a good Prior because of his pragmatism – his lack of fanaticism.

Anders found his eyes straying to the novice table. He could tell they were novices because they wore no rings. The only nun who had taken her vows was the slim tall beauty with the blonde hair. She sat primly at the head of the table. On her right, a buxom friendly-looking novice sat with pretty, silky dark hair. She barely ever took her eyes off of her beautiful dinner companion. Suddenly, the blonde girl looked up and calmly met the Sub-Prior's fascinated gaze. It was like lightning hitting him. Her eyes were like verdant promises, her lips, ruby gates of paradise. Those eyes were like deep green emeralds, framed by the face of the Madonna. Her gaze was steady as a rock as she looked into his eyes. Eyes like a deep green lake. He felt the stir of desire. After a few moments, the heat from those eyes suffused his face; it turned the colour of crimson and he lowered his gaze at once, staring into his bowl of succulent venison, ashamed and confused. The food was amazing; these nuns ate better than some of the local gentry.

He had an ominous feeling that he was more than merely tempted to jump into that lake with no thought of the consequences. Relieved, he was glad Prior Steven was not here to witness the spectacle – what would he think of him! By divine grace, instead of eating, the Prior volunteered to personally tend to the sickly Mother Elsbeth.

He noticed a shadow before him. It was cast by the buxom dreamy-eyed brunette from the novice table. She was standing in front of him, smiling. Her lips were luscious, full, somehow mischievous, even – or particularly because of – her holy garments. Anders began to get an inkling why laymen were not allowed in a convent. If a monk of office, a Sub-Prior, could be so tempted by the beauty of a Bride of the Lord, what would have happened to the men-at-arms?

'Sub-Prior Anders,' chimed the young woman, curtsying. Her bosom jiggled with the movement under her black and white habit.

'Yes?'

'Patricia, the new Mistress of Novices, begs your advice and good counsel.' She motioned towards the table with the astonishingly beautiful, tall young woman at its head.

Anders swallowed the rest of his water. His mouth still felt as parched as the desert. 'Tell . . . Tell the Mistress of

Novices I will be delighted to help with anything . . . my humble skills . . . knowledge . . . at her disposal . . . they are.' He rambled to a strained conclusion. He found it difficult to concentrate. Across the dining hall, Patricia caught his eye. She solemnly faced him, nodded in agreement as if she had heard his assent, and broke into a slow dazzling smile. His knees would have buckled if he had been standing. She got up from her seat, graceful in every single economical motion, and walked towards him. Her walk was more of a glide – no, she was a winged angel, she was flying, he corrected himself. It felt like the sun was coming over. He lowered his eyes again, blushing furiously. He heard her soft gliding footsteps. She was standing next to him. She came so close, he thought he could smell her, the scent of a thousand spring flowers on a sunny mountainside.

He heard a sound – was it a chuckle of amusement? – from the direction of the novices' table, but he could not seem to concentrate. She put a hand on his shoulder. He nearly fainted – her fingers were warm, light, fragrant. 'Prior Steven told me you were a man of exceptional ability,' she said softly. Her voice was crystalline honey.

'The Prior is too . . . kind,' he managed to utter.

'Prior Steven told me you had papers with you . . . Papers for something called account receivables,' said Patricia.

'Yes, that is true,' frowned Anders. Why would the Prior tell this woman – however ravishing and wonderful she was – about the papers?

'Mother Elsbeth asked me to learn of such things. Will you please teach me?' she asked softly.

'Yes,' he found himself saying. 'Of course I will.'

'I am just a silly naïve girl.' Her smile was so dazzling, her eyes so beautiful, he could not seem to follow the conversation. 'It may take some time. You don't have to leave with the Prior, do you?'

'I do . . .' he said, disconcerted.

'Won't you stay for a few more weeks, at least? I am sure Prior Steven will let you go if you ask him.' She slowly sat down onto the bench next to him and rested her chin on Anders's trembling shoulder, her long incredible eyelashes filtering the green light of her eyes as she gazed up at him from less than a foot away. 'Please . . .' she sobbed, slowly unveiling her devastating green eyes through the rising curtain of her eyelashes. 'I will be eternally grateful.'

'I – I really can't . . .' managed Anders, heartbroken. Her proximity made it impossible to think. His manhood was wide awake and standing at eager attention, a nearly forgotten, suddenly rediscovered relic of ancient power.

'Oh no . . .' whimpered Patricia. 'Who will I learn from? Prior Steven said you were the very best at these difficult things. I am too ignorant of these papers of men – Mother Elsbeth will make me do penance . . .'

He smiled at her with fondness. 'There, there . . .' He petted her perfect warm cheek, the touch driving him wild. 'Not all of us can be beautiful and clever at the same time. There, there.' He petted her cheek again.

'No . . .' She smiled. 'You will help me . . . Won't you?' she smiled playfully, her green eyes pulling him in.

Duty pulled him from within his heart. Deep inside, he was a man of principles. 'I will return as soon as our mission is complete.' He meant it. Of course, he also realised this was impossible – he would be sitting beside the object of his desire day after day, dying inside as their vows to God kept them from one another's arms. Eventually, his resolve would erode and he would lose his way to Heaven. He could never see Patricia again. His mouth tasted like ashes. He wished he had never come along with Prior Steven.

Patricia led him to his cell. She abruptly stopped and faced him in the corridor. Her sudden halt forced a jarring closeness. Her lips were so close to his own, he thought his heart would stop. 'Here you are,' she smiled. 'I wanted to make sure you were given adequate accommodations. This is my own cell. I will be sharing Mary's cot tonight.'

Somehow, the idea of the lovely Patricia sharing a cot with the nearly equally lovely Mary did nothing to quiet the troubled waters of Anders's private ocean. The idea . . . the idea only made him *bothered.*

Anders had a rough night. He could not sleep. He kept staring at the ceiling, Patricia's clear green lake-like eyes a torrent of raging waters through his memory. He thought of the sensation of her head on his shoulder, the smell of her soft fragrant hair, the crystal sweetness of that amazing dulcet voice. He turned on his side, unable to sleep. It didn't help. The spartan bedding was saturated with her flower-fresh scent. He gathered the blanket in his hands and buried his face in the rough homespun wool, breathing in her smell. He suddenly discarded the blanket and hit the stone wall with all his strength, leaving his knuckles bloody. Duty called. There was no room for lust – or love.

Finally, a fitful slumber claimed him. He was not sure what awakened him. Was it a sound? He sat up.

He heard it again. A cry of pain? He wasn't sure. He hastily put on his robe. He peered out into the corridor. It was empty. He heard it again – this time, he was sure it came from Mary's cell. Definitely the sound of a sharp whimpering cry. He hurried over to the door and slammed it open. 'Are you all right?' he asked, concerned.

He saw Patricia standing in the centre of the cell, lit by the light of a single flickering wick in an oil lamp on the tiny table by the cot. Two nun's hats were lying on the coarse wool bedding. Her wild gorgeous golden hair formed an exciting sinful contrast to the sacred black and white of her habit. She was so beautiful, so astonishingly desirable that for a moment his mind could not quite process the rest of the scene.

He vaguely realised she was holding a riding crop in her hand. Below her, on her hands and knees, lay Mary's sobbing form. She was fully clothed in her sacred garment, but she held the hem of her habit in both hands, raising the fabric, exposing her round naked white bottom. The downy skin was lined with angry red welts. The gorgeous Mistress of Novices raised the riding crop and with a single practised swish added another thin line onto Mary's exposed bottom, the sharp sound of leather on skin nearly muffled by Mary's throaty muffled cry of pain.

Patricia glanced at him. 'I am administering penance.'

Anders still could not move, or say anything. There was something intensely, erotically compelling about the contrast between Patricia's factual statement and the obscenely arousing reality of the whipping. The view seemed a living thing, diving through his eyes straight into his stiffening member.

'Tell Sub-Prior Anders why I am punishing you, novice.'

Mary whimpered, shaking her head vigorously. 'Please . . .'

Patricia raised the riding crop high in the air and struck her bottom again, her height affording her quite a bit of leverage. Anders winced.

A high-pitched squeal of pain escaped the pretty brunette's lips.

'Tell Sub-Prior Anders why I am whipping your bottom, novice.'

Patricia smoothly placed the riding crop between Mary's thighs, sliding the stiff leather out in a single efficient stroke.

Mary moaned, a helpless drawn-out sound. She began to speak. 'The mistress caught me touching – touching myself.'

'Shameless harlot!' barked Patricia and struck again. 'And where did you touch yourself, novice?'

'There . . . *there*.'

'Where is that?' smirked Patricia. 'Certainly not in the Holy Land, now is it?' She slid the riding crop back in between the young brunette's legs. 'Does this jar your memory, novice?'

Mary gasped, convulsing through her pretty body as the riding crop invaded her secret place. She seemed to lean into the whip, straining. '. . . Yes, Mistress.' Her voice was barely audible.

'I don't think Sub-Prior Anders heard you. In fact, I don't think I heard you either.' Patricia slid the riding crop out from the shadows in between Mary's trembling thighs.

She raised the riding crop high and struck the air, the stiff leather making a sharp hissing sound.

Mary cried out in fear. 'Please, Mistress . . .'

'Show Sub-Prior Anders your filthy disgusting sin.'

'Please, Mistress . . .' Mary moaned. 'I am ashamed.'

'You should be ashamed. Go on, spread your legs wide. Show the Sub-Prior how you desecrated your sacred calling.'

Anders's eyes were glued to Mary's beautiful welt-covered rear as she spread her legs wider. Her body slumped forward as her right hand snaked in between her legs. He could see a rhythmic motion of her body as she began to moan.

'Raise your bottom up a little higher, harlot,' ordered Patricia. 'Let the Sub-Prior get a good look of your needy cunt.'

Mary raised her bottom even higher, her head now resting against the stone floor. Anders could now see her fingers, a circling blur of shameless wanton masturbation against the auburn hair of her womanhood. He had never felt so aroused. His cock was a twitching iron-hard rod of lust.

'How dare you masturbate in the presence of the Sub-Prior?' screamed Patricia, enraged. She struck again, and again, and again, the welts appearing on Mary's gorgeous peachy ass with monotonous regular precision. The shameless moans of the buxom novice only seemed to grow in strength with each strike, the pretty brunette completely lost in a haze of shameless pleasure and pain.

'You shameless hussy!' Patricia turned to the frozen statue of the monk by the door. 'My job is so hard, Sub-Prior.'

'Yes,' he said lamely, unable to say anything else. 'Yes. So hard.'

'You must help me. My hand has grown weary. God demands your service in the discipline of a sinning wayward child.' Patricia handed the Sub-Prior the riding crop. He held out his hand without thinking, immediately regretting it. He began to lower his arms, but the gorgeous disciplinarian clasped his hand in hers, and the refusal on his lips died with the touch of her fingers. 'You hold it like *this*,' she said.

'Did you sleep well, Brother Anders?'

'Uh . . .'

'I'm sorry, I did not hear you. Did you sleep well?'

'. . . Yes, I did, thank you Prior.' Anders heard himself say, the dark circles under his eyes a fitting complement to the churning state of his soul.

'I couldn't sleep at all. Such ruckus! Some novice was being punished for some trivial sin – I heard her cries of pain all night. Didn't you hear anything?'

'. . . Ah. No.'

'Hmm. Really? I thought she was loud enough to wake the dead. Moans of pain! Screams! Squealing like she was being flayed alive!' Steven's smile was positively predatory.

Anders did not notice – he was too busy staring at his bowl of porridge, his tonsured head the colour of the setting sun. He desperately tried to think of some appropriate comment. 'Mother Elsbeth is certainly a strict disciplinarian.'

Anders hit Prior Steven a few more times in the back, but whatever he was choking on seemed to go away on its own.

Patricia walked into the dining hall. She looked over at Anders. Those emerald-green eyes met his, calmly, confidently, and she smiled at him, that dazzling drawn-out spectacle that made him weak in the knees. Desire rose within him like a tidal wave.

'Prior.' His voice was so low, he could not possibly be heard. Anders began to pray that maybe Steven did not hear him. Duty called – there was no room for lust. Please, God, let Prior Steven not hear me. Deliver us from evil, save me from temptation . . . His inner voice trailed off as he realised that Prior Steven, indeed, failed to hear him.

'Prior!' he said loudly, shaking his shoulder with both hands. 'Would it be all right if I stayed an extra week or two? Patri – Sister Patricia, the Mistress of Novices, asked me for some lessons on finance,' he blurted out.

‘Anders, what about the orphans?’ asked Steven.

Anders wanted to hit the sanctimonious old man – wasn’t it he who got himself robbed and got Anders into this den of gorgeous young off-limits temptation? He felt himself growing erect just thinking about it.

‘I . . .’

‘You are not tempted by the lure of the flesh, are you my son?’ asked Steven.

‘No, of course not!’ cried Anders vehemently.

‘These are nuns, daughters of God. When they are tempted into sin, they are severely, severely punished. You wouldn’t want one of these young women to suffer so?’

Anders was nearly in tears. ‘No,’ he mumbled. He stared straight ahead, lost in a private world. He promised Patricia to help with Mary’s penance for as long as he stayed at the convent. He was eagerly looking forward to it. In fact, he could not stop thinking about it. That is all he could think of, for that matter. He heard Steven’s voice. How long had he been talking?

‘In that case, you have my blessing to remain for a while. Of course, I will have to take the papers along with the jewels.’

‘Of course.’ It made no sense to Anders, but he was too frazzled to dispute the Prior.

‘I trust your stay here will be a credit to the monastery.’

‘Yes, Prior,’ said Anders, weakly.

After breakfast, Steven hurried to Elsbeth’s cell. He simply locked the door and lifted her habit. She wore lurid pink lace panties under her sacred garments. He fucked her like an animal, the Mother Superior squealing like a bitch on heat. Steven’s fantasies were now all-consuming. Now that he was rich, Stephanie would allow him to pay constant homage to her beautiful shaved pink slit. He closed his eyes thinking about her luscious ripe tits, her stiletto heels resting against his worthless face. He withdrew as he climaxed, his seed drenching the flimsy pink lace.

He read through the account receivables in the coach. His eyes grew wide as he realised the sheer extent of his wealth

– he could not spend all of it, of course, just nearly all of it. He would leave a token sum with the monastery, the value of one or two of these letters. He was so aroused by his imminent rewards he nearly touched himself inside the coach. They finally reached the road by dinnertime. Instead of stopping to eat, he promised the men-at-arms a gold piece each if they made town by nightfall. The men-at-arms rode like devils possessed, Henry whipping the gentle gelding pulling the coach, the other riding ahead. They were making excellent time, despite the occasional delay brought about by other, slower travellers on the road. Steven stared at yet another family dragging sacks of turnips south and cursed lividly. 'It's market day,' he told Henry. The thug nodded. 'I don't care how many we have to ride down, we must make it to town by nightfall.'

Henry nodded. He was used to masters without patience. The monk was simply unusual in that he wore a coarse brown robe – but he was no different from an Earl, it seemed. The next family they came upon barely had the time to save themselves. Their last harvest before winter – apples, or turnips? They were past the wailing mob too quickly to tell – was smashed below the hooves of the horses.

Steven leaned back on the bench, holding on for dear life as the coach practically flew over the bumpy road. It was too dark to see anything from inside the coach, but Steven still managed to figure out when they reached the town gates. He smelled the characteristic cesspool scent of the canal exiting the walls. The disgusting smell was ever present in town, less so in the rich quarter, more so in the poor. The smell invoked the memories of countless hours of filthy fornication at the town house. He could not seem to stop fondling his erection. He overheard Henry identify him to the gate guard.

'Prior Steven. He is here on urgent business.'

They rolled into town, coming to a shuddering stop a scant fifty feet inside the walls.

'Prior – Prior, we are here, we made it before nightfall.'

Steven considered his next move. What he really wanted to do was sell the papers at a moneychanger, deliver the jewels to Stephanie, and spend the rest of his life fornicating with the pretty widow and her coterie of whores. He was also hungry – maybe fornicating and eating at the same time. Moneychangers were always open – even at night. Perhaps particularly at night, he thought. 'Take me to a moneychanger. Or a rich merchant,' he ordered. 'The richest one.'

It was a warm night for late autumn. It being market day, there were a lot of people on the streets. Henry asked another man-at-arms escorting a rich-looking merchant for directions.

The merchant was curious – he asked them who was in the coach.

'A baron with no patience for fools,' sneered Henry. Steven liked that – him, a baron! Well, why not? He was as rich as a baron! He decided to give Henry a bonus, enough for a good whore or two. He should have given them orders anyway to safeguard his identity. Only a fool advertised a trip for money, of course. Following the directions supplied by the nervous merchant, they turned uphill, passing the Cathedral, finally coming to a shuddering stop before a hulking white stone house.

Henry banged the large cast-iron knocker against the stout oak door. 'Who is it?' asked a tentative cautious voice, nearly immediately.

Henry glanced at the Prior and announced him. 'My master is here to conduct business. Open up!'

The door slowly creaked open. A short careful-looking man with a bushy yet well trimmed salt and pepper beard stood outlined by the glow of candlelight. He held a mean-looking bludgeon in one hand. His eyes dismissed the men-at-arms at once. 'I will wake up the master if need be,' he said calmly, addressing himself only to Steven.

Steven ground his teeth together. Yet another fool he had to deal with before he could make his way to the town house! 'Tell your master I have letters from Flanders, instruments of commerce. They are worth a great deal of gold – I wish to discuss their sale. I have need of the money now.'

He took one of the letters from the walnut box and showed it to the doorman. He pulled it back as the lackey tried to put his hand upon it. 'You question my honesty?' he asked, growing hot with anger. 'Do you not see my monastic robes?'

'I see them . . .' The man thought for a moment, then decided not to say what was on his mind. 'Very well – I will wake up the master.'

'Wait for me here,' Steven ordered the men-at-arms. He saw one of the windows come alive with the flickering light of an oil lamp. Soon enough the servant opened the door again.

'Follow me.'

Steven followed him inside. The house was opulent, full of expensive antiques. There were a number of Turkish rugs, expensive tapestries from the continent, silk wall hangings . . . He nearly cried out in surprise as he stared at a particularly lovely silk carpet – it was Hereke silk, and the last time he had seen it, he was rubbing himself against it in a drunken gluttonous daze.

'You have a good eye,' said a deep melodious voice from the red glow of a massive ancient hearth. 'That carpet may be the most valuable antique of my collection.' The master merchant was a man in his late fifties, perhaps, with alert sharp blue eyes, sun-streaked bronze skin and a graceful bearing. He looked more like an Earl than some kind of money-grubbing merchant. 'I am John, I trade in wool, goods of precious metal, weapons – everything,' he said simply.

Steven nearly questioned the man about how he had obtained the carpet, but thought better of it. He had urgent needs that had to be met. Without another word, he opened the walnut box and handed over the contents, saving only two slim sheaves of parchment on the bottom.

'I wish to sell these,' he said quickly.

The merchant examined the documents by the light of the fire. He looked up after a few minutes. 'I may be interested.'

The merchant sent for food and wine. Steven ate and drank heartily while the merchant wrote figures on a piece of parchment by the firelight. He asked for more wine. When the man finished his fiddling, he named a figure.

Steven frowned. 'That's less than half the value I anticipated.'

'You need the money now. I can give you that much now – or a little more later.'

'It is for a good cause.'

'I am sure it is,' said the merchant, his tone carefully neutral. 'Like I said, if you wait until spring, I can add another hundred in gold at least. These letters will keep.'

Steven's gaze wandered over to the Hereke rug. He thought he could see the tiny stain on the beautiful silk – his cock stirred with the memory of that day.

'Very well. Give me the gold now.' His voice was thick with frustrated lust and wine.

The merchant bowed and left to get his strongbox. Steven's erection steadily stiffened in the meantime. He drank more wine to calm himself. The man finally returned carrying a heavy crimson chest. Steven hurried over, his hand caressing the painted wood. 'Let's see!' he drooled.

The merchant flipped the chest open. It was filled with gold, shiny round coins, beautiful glowing money. Steven grinned. He pushed his hands deep into the pile of clinking metal. Each coin was a little round hole for his cock to slide into, shiny pussy on his fingers. His erection was a massive goad under his monastic robe. He gathered a fistful of coins and looked for a container.

'Allow me to help you with that.' The merchant rang a bell and the bearded servant from downstairs appeared. 'Michael, bring my spare belt and purse for Lord . . .'

'Lord Steven,' sneered the Prior, his head reeling with wine and the imminent promise of fornication.

'Lord Steven.'

Michael left to return shortly with an elaborate belt lined with soft white fur. It had a silver buckle in the shape of a coin. A rich red brocade purse hung upon it, empty.

Steven fastened the belt around his gut and shoved the

money in his new purse. He kept four gold coins in his palm.

'I will have Michael escort you.'

'I have men-at-arms,' replied Steven carelessly.

'Sometimes all men are tempted by greed.'

Steven nodded – this was true. Maybe he should dismiss the men before they saw him with the money.

'Where are you staying?'

'I have a town house.'

'Ah!'

Steven remembered something. 'I have to stop by Garode's first. I have an order to pick up.'

'Of course.'

With some reluctance, Steven took off his splendid new belt and went outside, leaving it with Michael. The servant stood in the doorway, watching impassively as he gave each man-at-arms two gold coins. The men's faces were masks of avarice. 'You are dismissed. Enjoy yourselves,' said the Prior.

Henry whistled happily. 'Thank you, Lord Steven.'

His companion mimicked him. 'Thank you, Sir.'

They mounted their horses and rode off, heading in the general direction of the whores' quarter. Steven returned to the house. Michael handed him his new belt and purse and he put it on.

John's men loaded the box onto the coach. Michael took the driver's seat. Garode's was only a few minutes by coach. When they got there, Steven motioned to Michael to stay with the coach. A doorman stood on the street by the elaborate sign: GARODE'S: MASTER TAILOR AND FURRIER. When the doorman saw the coach stop, he smoothly bowed to the monk, not missing the heavy purse and the ermine belt. 'You are welcome at Master Garode's, my Lord,' he said, opening the door.

The first item of interest he noticed was a very pretty, tiny maiden in her late teens. Her hair was a cascade of red ringlets all the way down to her shapely perfect little bottom. She wore a pretty dress of white Belgian lace and high-heeled dancing shoes. Her corset was laced so tight, and her waist was so tiny, he thought he could wrap his fingers around her with a single hand. Compared to her delicate frame, her breasts looked positively huge. She was talking to a portly richly dressed man in a velvet tunic and a gold chain. She stomped her tiny feet. 'I was promised a new dress by Daddy.' Her voice was a petulant whine. 'He said I could have one even prettier than this one.'

'I am so sorry, Miss. Your father said to me, very specifically, that he would not pay for any more dresses.' The merchant's voice was soothing, yet sorrowful. 'I would be the first to petition him to change his mind, Miss. I am sorry.'

She stomped her foot again, her voice rising into a hysterical shriek. 'I want to go to the ball next week and I have to have a new dress, everyone has a new dress except for me, it's not fair, it's not fair!' She hurled herself into a pile of silks awaiting Garode's needle and sat there, pouting.

Steven couldn't take his eyes off the girl. Her tits were heaving as she sobbed, petulant.

'Can I help you, my Lord?'

Steven frowned and turned to face the tailor. 'I am here to pick up an order.'

'Ah!' Garode smiled. 'Certainly! Who ordered, what, when, for what occasion?' His face assumed that cloying ingratiating expression he used for paying customers.

'Lady Stephanie Peabody ordered a mink coat from you a few weeks ago. I am here to pick it up.'

Garode's smile broadened until it seemed to fill his entire face. 'I did not think she could . . . I mean, after all that happened . . . Well, this is good news. Very good news! A lady of excellent taste!' he cried. 'I will assemble her entire order.'

Before Steven could ask what he meant by 'entire', the merchant bustled off. The doorman bowed to Steven and brought him a tray of cheeses and a goblet of wine. He drained the cup and handed it back to the fellow for more. The wretched man looked surprised but then his face smoothed out and he disappeared in the direction of the wine cellar. Steven looked around. He was alone in the shop except for the pretty little redhead. She was looking at a gorgeous white lace dress in the corner, prominently displayed on a wooden dummy. He saw her stand next to the dress, sighing, her breasts heaving with longing. He walked over. This close, he smelled her perfume, the heavy scent of jasmine flooding his senses.

'You would look very pretty in that dress,' he said conversationally.

'I know.' She sighed. 'Daddy is so stupid sometimes.' She stomped her foot again. The motion made her tits quiver. 'I would do anything for a new dress. Why can't Master Garode understand?'

'Anything?' he asked, his cock twitching beneath his robe. He unlaced his nearly bursting, heavy purse. Her eyes grew as wide as saucers as he showed her the shimmering pile of gold coins. 'Ooh . . .' She breathed in deeply, eyeing the contents with nothing less than avarice. 'I could buy a new dress . . . Daddy would never know.' She eyed him playfully. 'What would you have me do?'

He whispered in her ear. She giggled and clapped her mouth with her tiny hands. 'If I let you do that you will buy me any dress . . .?'

'Yes.'

Garode's servant arrived with a dusty jug of wine. Steven handed it to the girl after a moment's hesitation. 'We will be outside, getting some fresh air,' Steven told the servant.

She eyed the wine with a wicked gleam in her eye. 'Daddy doesn't let me drink at all! He says I get tipsy from the tiniest cup.' She raised the jug and sucked on the contents, her face contorting as she took great gulps. 'That was tasty.' She wiped her mouth with her hand.

He took her to the coach. Michael said nothing – he opened the door for her and she slipped inside. She giggled drunkenly. 'You want to feel my titties?' She put his hands on her full white tits. Her breasts were firm, white, hot to the touch. 'And you want to see my pretty panties?' She put up her high-heeled dancing shoes on the monk's shoulders. He could see her panties, plain white satin hugging her perfect tiny bottom.

She tittered drunkenly. 'You are so much better than Daddy. He wouldn't buy me a new dress, but you will. You are a much better Daddy.' She giggled and put her hand on his robe, right over his throbbing member. 'Eeeew.' But she did not move her hand away.

'Can I lick your clit?' he said, his voice trembling.

She blushed but giggled coyly. She moved her hand up and down over his straining member. 'Two pretty dresses are sooo much better than one . . .'

'Two dresses,' he gasped, agreeing.

She squealed with delight. She removed her hand from over his erection and pushed her panties down, her shoes still on either side of his tonsured head. He leaned forward, his eyes locked on her fresh red-trimmed pussy. It was perfect, beautiful, more gorgeous than he could have imagined. The gorgeous redheaded harlot moaned softly as his tongue disappeared in between her legs.

'I am a virgin,' she declared with triumphant glee as he sucked her pussy lips into his mouth, his tongue circling her clit. 'That feels so good. Yes, yes . . .' She panted hard. 'Lick me, lick me, eat my pretty red cunnie.' She ground her young red-haired pussy in his face, her white satin panties pulled tight over her wide-open legs. He rested his chin on the white satin while he tongued her clit.

Her pussy tasted like fresh cream and jasmine. He was nearly delirious with lust – he wanted to fuck her so bad it hurt. 'I want to put my cock in you.'

She laughed and playfully slapped his tonsured head. 'Naughty little monk. No cunnie for you.'

'Will you at least put my cock in your mouth?' he asked, weak with desire.

'Three dresses . . . and a new hat. And you can't fuck my cunnie.' She giggled, a sleazy vapid sound. 'I have to guard my virtue.'

He eagerly signalled his assent. She opened her mouth wide and used her pretty hands to guide his cock into her fresh warm mouth, her lips enclosing his erection with surprising skill. She milked his balls with her tiny hands, her lips soft, warm, her tongue a firm rasping file of wetness on his member. He came nearly immediately, thrashing against her pretty face. She swallowed every drop, milking his prick until it was nearly painful. 'I didn't want you to stain my dress by accident,' she explained, her tongue licking her red lips clean.

The pretty redhead gasped when he opened the red chest. The moonlight glinted off the huge mound of gold. 'Ooooh . . . I love my new Daddy.' She propped herself on Steven's knee and caressed him behind the ear. He grabbed two fistfuls of rich yellow gold, showing her the bounty she had earned. She was cooing with excitement, her face suffused with naked greed. They got out of the coach. Michael had the collar of his coat up – they could not see his face. He did not turn to look at them as they walked back to the shop, the little redhead prancing before him on her high-heeled dancing shoes.

'Three pretty lace dresses for such a little thing.' She giggled again and kissed him lightly on the cheek. 'If I need you, where can I find you, Daddy?' she asked, her voice assuming the tone of a petulant, demanding child.

'At the Peabody town house,' answered Steven. As far as he was concerned, she was worth every penny. He had not had an orgasm like that since he came in Amber while licking Stephanie's stiletto heels. Thoughts of the beautiful manipulative gold-digger stirred him again.

Inside the shop, Garode was directing three of his men. They were putting boxes of all shapes and sizes in an impressive pile on the floor. 'Lady Peabody's mink coat,' said Garode, pointing to the largest box. 'Lady Peabody's . . . nightclothes. Specially ordered from Brussels, as she requested.' He pointed to a pile of shoeboxes. 'And those, of course.'

'And three lace dresses and a hat,' piped up the exquisite, tiny little redhead.

Six

Michael drove him to the town house. It was very late by now, but he was sure Stephanie would be delighted to see him anyhow. The coach was full of boxes from Garode's. In his hand he carried the oak chest with the Peabody jewels. His lust was as if it was never sated. When he closed his eyes, he could see Stephanie's gorgeous shaved slit as she would open her legs wide and allow him to worship her sex. He knocked on the door, squirming with lust. He closed his eyes, imagining her gratitude. She would ride his cock while Amber and Heather took turns sitting on his face. She would . . .

The door opened. His eyes snapped open. It wasn't Stephanie. His mind tried to match the girl with one of the whores he left at the town house. It wasn't Amber, it wasn't Stacey, it wasn't Heather. The girl's conservative plain shift did not match with any of the sleazy pictures painted by his filthy expectations. She raised the candle in her right hand to get a better look at the Prior.

'Prior Steven?' Her voice was one of immense relief. 'Thank the Lord, Prior Steven!' She sobbed and hugged him. He was speechless. Who was this stupid slut? Where was Stephanie? What had happened to his Mistresses?

'Don't you remember me, Prior Steven?' The girl smiled, a gentle hopeful gesture that seemed to turn her face from pretty to beautiful. 'I am Laura, Lord Peabody's daughter.'

He nodded dimly. His erection seemed to have deserted him.

'I am so glad you are here, Prior. You would not believe what I've been through over the past two weeks. I wish I could offer you a place to stay,' she sighed.

'What happened here?' he asked weakly.

'My father's town house . . . that harlot turned it into a house of ill repute! There were whores fornicating on my mother's bed . . .' Laura broke down, sobbing. 'Painted harlots were fornicating under my mother's crucifix . . .' She leaned against Steven, her body wracked by pain. '. . . until that evil slut sold it for silver! I could not believe Master Tisdale when he . . .'

'Why are you here?' he asked, trying to sound gentle and understanding. Where was Stephanie?

'Where do you want all these boxes, my Lord?' Steven gaped at Michael.

'I am just a humble monk,' he managed through gritted teeth. 'Do not call me a Lord. This is a Lady, though. This is Lord Peabody's daughter, Lady Laura.'

Michael bowed. 'Your Ladyship.'

'Forget the boxes.' He tried to convey as much authority as he could into as innocent a remark as possible.

'Yes, my L . . . Yes, I will.'

'Go home, Michael. I will be all right. I can stable the coach here.'

Laura glanced at the horse. 'The horse should be all right – but you will never consent to staying overnight in a place such as this. It reeks of spiritual corruption.'

'My child . . . I am a man of God. I am immune to such taint.' His voice brooked no argument.

'There is no cot – the harlot threw them all away and replaced them with feather beds. You will have to sleep on the floor. The beds reek of perfume, the stink of endless fornication.'

Steven practically swooned. 'I will sleep on the floor, then.'

'Why are you wearing a belt and a coin-purse, Father?' asked Laura, somewhat accusingly.

'I was . . . buying winter coats for the orphanage. The belt and purse were a gift from the . . . merchant. The boxes in the coach . . .' He trailed off.

Her expression softened. 'Of course! How could I have forgotten? You stayed true even after Father met her. You were always the only one who truly loved me like a father should.' She threw herself on the irritated monk and hugged him tight, burying her face against his chest. She laughed softly. 'Did you preach in a flower bed, Prior Steven? You smell pretty, like a field of flowers.'

'So what happened to Lady Peab – Steph – to Miss Hayes?' he asked lamely.

'After I finished mourning my poor departed father I tried to find the Lord Prior, but I was told he had gone to Salisbury. I still had my poor departed aunt's keys to the family Town House and I decided to follow.

'When I saw Father's sword at a pawnshop here in town I knew she was responsible. I did not know she was here at the town house. Master Tisdale sent word.' She pointed at the town house across the street. 'He said my stepmother was here, keeping unacceptable company. I rushed over and saw a painted evil whore open the door for a servant delivering boxes. I went to the sheriff, of course.'

'You got Ste – You got Miss Hayes arrested?'

She frowned. 'He came. He went inside and did not leave for hours. When he came out he told me to mind my own business or else. He stank of wine and perfume! Of course, I didn't leave it at that. I went straight to the Bishop.'

Steven sat up, ramrod-straight. 'Warener is back from Rome?'

'Yes, he just returned a week ago. I couldn't find you. I was told you rode off on the Bishop's best horse and still hadn't returned. I sent word to the monastery but they said you were not there either. I did not know what to do.'

'What did Bishop Warener say?'

'He said he was worried about you.'

'I mean, what did he say about . . . Miss Hayes?'

'Oh, he ordered some of his men to throw the whores out,' she said with infinite satisfaction.

'What?' Steven's voice was a wooden whisper.

'They came by one morning and threw them all out. It was wonderful! I was here to watch the whole spectacle! I wanted them to tar and feather her, but the Bishop is too lenient about these things. He just had the common whores tossed in the Whores' Quarter. He ordered Stephanie held in the palace, to repent and seek penance before her trial.'

Steven's mouth was open. He stared at Laura as if he had seen a ghost. He wanted to hold his head and moan.

'Are you well, Prior Steven?' she asked with concern.

'What – what will she be tried for?'

'She stole from you, of course. Weren't you listening to what I said, Prior Steven? She has been stealing Father's things – all the things he left to the Priory and to me – and selling them on the street to keep herself and her whores in luxury.'

Princess was in trouble because he was too late with the money and the jewels. He took too long banging away at Elsbeth's needy cunt. She will be so angry with him!

'When is her trial?'

'Three days hence. The Bishop is assembling the court now. He told me in private that it was a formality, she will be found guilty and stripped of Father's title. They will torture her until she admits to every single theft. Maybe they will even cut off her arm for stealing from the Church.' Laura's voice was dripping with satisfaction. She frowned. 'Of course, not that I would ever believe her, if she repents, the court just might order her whipped in the town square.'

'No . . .' gasped Steven. If Stephanie talks about her pussy-crazed pet monk, he was done for.

'I agree, my Lord Prior,' said Laura, misunderstanding his horror. 'She has sinned too much against both God and men. She should burn at the stake.'

He nodded absently, agreeing with her. He needed to think. He needed to think hard on what had to be done. 'I am weary of my long journey,' he said, pretending to yawn.

He drove the coach into the shed by the side of the town house. Steven carried the boxes in, one at a time, refusing to let 'Lady Peabody' soil her fingers with such a mundane task. He piled the boxes in the late Lord's private bedchamber. The room had a huge elaborate French four-poster bed with red silk curtains dominating it in the centre. He nearly began to play with himself as he was looking at it – Stephanie occasionally allowed him to watch her play with her pretty friends upon it. Sometimes she would allow him to manipulate himself as he watched. He slid the chest of gold and the jewels under the bed.

Laura knocked on the door, carrying a simple wool blanket. She smiled at him and laid it down on the floor. 'So you won't catch a cold tonight.'

'Thank you, Lady Peabody.' He smirked to himself – Lady indeed! He had all her father's money, she was nothing but a common servant now.

At dawn, he stretched out over the luxurious red satin sheets and got up, yawning. The reality of the situation slammed into him like a cold avalanche. He hurriedly dressed himself, his hands fumbling with that godforsaken triple knot. He stopped himself from putting on his belt and his purse. Shivering in the late autumn air, he hurried over to the Bishop's palace. He tried to put a humble expression on his face and pull in his bloated gut. He tightened his rope belt. He tried to calm himself as he waited in the antechamber of the Bishop's private office, practising his story in his head.

Bishop Warener was an energetic no-nonsense kind of man in his late forties. He had not found his true calling until relatively recently. He was a Knight Templar who actually fought in the Holy Land, a strong right hand of Prince Henry and a man of absolute, true piety and honour. He received his appointment to head the Diocese when he took a cut to his left leg, leaving him unable to ride a warhorse in battle. Despite his secular background, he became a spiritual caring Bishop, a true shepherd of his flock. His sermons were famous throughout the county as divinely inspired. From what Steven heard, the stiff-backed fool had no vices at all.

'Prior Steven.' Warener's voice was deep, resonant, powerful. 'You took my horse. Come into my office.'

Steven entered the well appointed, but still tastefully decorated chamber. A wicked two-handed sword leaned against a corner. Over the hearth, Warener's old Templar shield reflected the red flames of the roaring fire. It was reputed that the Bishop always carried his sword with him on all his trips, even when he went on pilgrimage. Two heavy impressive illustrated bibles sat on a wall shelf.

Steven bowed stiffly. 'I apologise, my Lord Bishop,' he said calmly. 'I heard grave news of Mother Superior Elsbeth's illness and rushed off at once to see to her care. I am skilled at healing. Thanks to my intercession and God's grace, she is fully recovered. The horse, unfortunately . . . It suffered a small cut on a leg and Brother George is tending it at the monastery.' Steven had no idea if the horse had even survived the brutal spurred ride from Salisbury to Redfork. He reminded himself to contact Brother George to inquire about the animal. If worse came to worst, he would pay the Bishop the price of the horse. Suddenly, he realised he was thinking about the wrong horse – the horse from the convent, not the Bishop's horse. The Bishop's horse disappeared when he was knocked out in the forest. He opened his mouth but closed it again – anything he could say right now would just sound like a pack of lies.

The Bishop's sharp grey eyes locked with his own. He studied the Prior for a long moment, his sharp gaze betraying some concern. 'Prior Steven, I have been hearing some strange rumours.'

'Yes, my Lord Bishop?' Steven fidgeted nervously, his bare feet cold on the stone floor. He was not used to walking around without boots anymore – or walking much at all, at that. The Bishop had not asked him to sit.

'You left this palace well before you took my horse on your mission of healing.'

Steven strained but failed to hear any sarcasm in Warener's voice.

'I heard an angelic voice in my dream, directing me to go outside and pray.'

Warener looked sceptical. 'Pray for an entire week?'

‘I was possessed by the Holy Spirit, my Lord Bishop. As if I was no longer me in my own body!’ Thinking about it, Steven realised his second sentence was true in a way.

‘Well, no matter what or why, it is all water under the bridge,’ the Bishop sighed. ‘I assume you did not let that harlot widow into the town house?’

‘Harlot widow?’

‘Stephanie Hayes, Peabody’s . . . *wife*.’ Warener practically spat the word.

‘Of course not; the town house belongs to the Priory.’

‘I am happy to have been of service to the Priory.’ Warener crossed his fingers before him. ‘Stephanie Peabody is awaiting trial. After her arrest, I had her kept in a simple clean room within these walls. She tried to tempt me – me! – with an offer of fornication. A Bishop! She offered me her sin-drenched flesh. She is a willing tool of the devil.’

Steven picked up a bible from the wall shelf and opened the Good Book randomly to shield his sudden erection from view. He glanced at the passage.

‘A harlot of hell.’ His voice trembled. ‘I am proud of your . . . strength of virtue, my Lord Bishop.’

‘Yes. She is an attractive woman for a spawn of Satan. When I was but a knight, I had my choice of women – I did not go much for blondes. There was this one girl, this tiny slip of an Irish lass with long pretty red hair . . . But that was a long time ago.’ The Bishop shook his head to clear the cobwebs. ‘I considered putting her in the dungeon – but I want her to live through the trial, at least. I now have her gagged and chained to the wall.’

‘That sounds very harsh, my Lord.’

‘Harsh? She would have cost me my soul, man!’ Warener’s voice was rich with contempt. ‘As if some conniving harlot could tempt one of the Knights Templar! I cannot charge her with the crime, of course. She never actually asked me to touch her. Just intimated – just intimated . . . Women are crafty, cunning creatures, full of a loathsome cleverness.’

A servant entered with a tray with a simple wooden goblet on it.

'Boiled water. Wine is a tool of the devil.' He waited silently while the servant drank from the goblet and passed it over to him. He drank the rest with relish.

'Yes, my Lord Bishop.'

'You don't sound convinced. Well, I still kept her out of the worst parts of the dungeon. I have one of the serving women wash and feed her – I don't want her raped, either, despite her lack of virtue.'

Steven felt somewhat better.

'Anyway, Brother Bougric is coming from the continent.'

Steven paled at the mention of the inquisitor's name. The man could make rocks confess.

'She is holding something back. I know – I can tell. I can always tell when someone is not telling the truth.' Warener's eyes were sharp grey swords. 'I want to know what else there is to this sordid filthy story, that is why I sent for him.'

Steven swallowed hard.

Warener eyed the Prior with unbridled curiosity. 'I was told she last confessed . . . to you.'

'Yes.'

'She will confess all anyway when Bougric puts his hands on her. You might as well tell me what she said.'

'My Lord Bishop!'

Warener sighed. 'Robert told me you would refuse.'

'We have a sacred trust, my Lord Bishop.' He did not have to make his voice sound outraged. Decades of ingrained habit made his body shake with anger.

'All right, all right, I just thought I would ask . . .'

Steven forced his face to relax. 'I understand, my Lord.'

'You are the one who most suffered by this creature's thievery. Why, she nearly cost your Priory the orphanage. Without the Peabody gold you would have no way to keep it going through the winter.'

'All so true, my Lord.'

'This is why I have no trouble granting this wretched creature her wish. She wishes to confess before Brother Bougric arrives. I can trust you, as you were the most aggrieved victim of her crimes.'

'I will . . . of course . . . have no trouble . . . I mean, certainly, I am at your service, my Lord Bishop.'

'I do not want you to think I am sitting somewhere by the confessional, trying to listen in.' He raised a hand to ward off Steven's vehement refutation to the contrary. 'I know you are a man of honour, Prior. I asked around about you. We are alike in many ways.' He grinned at Steven, the smile of a man who has seen everything. 'I will give you the keys to the chapel – you can lock it before you begin her confession.'

His filthy wave of arousal upon hearing the word 'confession' did not completely blank his mind. Understanding dawned on Steven. 'My Lord Bishop never wanted me to break the sacred trust – just wanted to make sure I would not do so myself.'

'You are not a stupid man, Prior.'

'May I . . . May I study the scriptures now? I wish to prepare myself.' Steven held the large book over his crotch, his face sweating in the firelight.

'Of course. And send someone for my horse!'

Steven bowed and took his leave, shielding his arousal with the Good Book.

He was jarred awake by the sound of the latch on his door being tried. 'Prior Steven!'

He recognised Laura's voice.

'Prior Steven, are you awake?'

He stumbled out of the great silk bed and kicked the untouched sheets on the floor with his bare feet. He looked at the result with a critical eye – yes, it looked slept in. Without any more hesitation, he unlatched the door, putting on a concerned expression. 'Yes? It's the middle of the night –'

'Prior Steven, you have a visitor.' He could not fail to notice the tone of accusation in Laura's voice.

'Who is it?'

'I have never met the young woman, Prior. I am sure you have a good reason to meet her in the middle of the night, lace dress and dancing shoes and all.'

‘Uh . . .’ He covered his nightclothes with a thin linen robe and hurried downstairs without another word. Who could it be? His vague suspicions were confirmed when he opened the door. The tiny exquisite redhead stood in front of the house, her red lacquered fingernails busily stripping a peach, carving the downy skin with her crimson-tipped talons. She wore a white lace dress, the corset pulled so tight her breasts nearly popped out of the delicate, nearly transparent material. She wore silver dancing shoes with very high heels.

When she saw Steven, she smiled happily. ‘Daddy Steven!’

His cock responded to her shrill vapid contralto with immediate rapt attention.

‘Yes . . .’ he managed. As he stared at the sexy little vision before him, he heard the window open overhead. Laura was listening to every word! He saw the redhead’s pretty blue eyes suddenly gleam with calculated mischief.

‘I am sooo glad to have found you so quickly . . .’ she purred. ‘You remember me, don’t you?’

‘Yes, yes, of course . . . you are – you are –’

She smiled sweetly. ‘Evelyn . . . My name is Evelyn.’

‘Uh . . . my child . . . I am glad as well. You must be cold in this dress . . .’ he continued after just a moment’s pause. ‘Just having been admitted to the orphanage, still without your new winter coat . . .’ He silently mouthed the word ‘please’ while pointing straight up in the direction of the window, shielding his finger from view from above with his body.

She gaped at him for a long, long moment. ‘Orphanage?’ she giggled. ‘Wha –’ Her voice cut off as he simply mouthed the word.

She mouthed it back, silently. ‘*Dress*?’

He nodded. Aloud, he spoke. ‘Why don’t I come by tomorrow at your place of lodgings and drop off your new coat?’

She grinned and stepped closer. ‘You are soooo kind, Da –’

‘Prior!’ he hissed in a low tone.

'Prior Steven! You are wonderful!' she cooed, stepping closer and hugging the nervous monk. Her tits pushed against the thin linen of the robe he had thrown on. 'Can I have my new coat now? It's sooo cold tonight . . .' Her eyes were huge, pleading. 'Being an orphan and all . . . I really have nobody . . .' she sobbed. 'Please . . .?' She actually managed to produce a tear – Steven was impressed. He was also becoming very aroused. The little harlot's hands were busily manipulating his erection through the thin linen of his nightclothes. Laura could not see it, of course, with his body blocking the view.

Evelyn was stroking his manhood, her fingers toying with him as she talked. 'Can we go and get the coat now pweeease . . .' Her hand moved on to fondle his balls. 'Please, Prior Steven . . . I will be soooo grateful . . .'

'Which box is it? I will bring it down.' Laura's voice was like a bucket of ice water on Steven's head.

Evelyn giggled. 'You are sooo kind!' She rolled her eyes.

Steven nodded, groaning.

'Don't trouble yourself, Lady –'

'Lady Peabody,' filled in Steven. 'I will find it, Laura. Go back to sleep.'

He heard her sniff loudly – the sound someone makes when they are irate over being left out and are unwilling to let it go. The windowpanes shut overhead. He slowly let out a sigh of relief. The gorgeous redhead was smiling sweetly at him, calculating rapt greed shining in her pretty blue eyes.

'It's difficult to explain . . . I would be grateful if you . . .'

'Say no more, Prior Steven,' she giggled. 'Why don't I pick out my new coat from the pile of boxes myself?'

He wanted to say no – but she suddenly pulled his head forward, into her bosom. His lips brushed against her perfect white skin, the hot flesh of her tits like white fire against his lips. The scent of jasmine was like a cloud around her.

'Come in, please,' he mumbled.

Once they were inside the room where Steven kept the boxes, Evelyn tore through them like a whirlwind. Steven nervously closed the door. 'You know we can't – we can't play, now.' He swallowed hard as Evelyn held up a pair of red dancing shoes, twins to the ones Stephanie wore.

'Are you sure we can't play?' she cooed innocently. 'My tiny little feet would look so pretty in these . . .' she sighed.

'Yes. Laura Peabody – she is an innocent.'

'So . . . If she wasn't such a goody-two-shoes . . . I could come and play . . . I could have all this for my very own?'

'Well, some of it, at least,' he said quietly, his eyes glued to her pretty, tiny feet.

She sat on the edge of the huge four-poster bed, daintily going about the chore of putting on the red harlot's shoes. She raised and dangled one slender stiletto-clad foot. The shoe slid up and down on her tiny foot. 'It's too big!' she sobbed, real tears streaming down her face. 'You will buy me one that's the right size, won't you, Daddy Steven? Orphans should have pretty shoes too . . .' She smiled wickedly, touching her upper lip with the tip of her wet, red tongue.

'I – very well.'

'So, these orphans, do they wear pretty dresses?'

'No . . . For the most part, they wear wool or homespun.'

'Eeeew. You want me to be one of those?'

'You – you don't have to wear wool or homespun. We could say you are the daughter of a rich merchant whose ship sank . . . and his estate is paying for your keep at the orphanage, in the manner to which you are accustomed.' He warmed to the lie. 'You did not want to enter the convent . . . and as a Lady of good breeding, you are –'

'This one is sooo pretty!' cooed Evelyn, holding up a sleazy silk corset. 'Will you at least let me have this one?' She cruelly began to strip, displaying her full tits and perfect tiny bottom. She was not wearing any panties. Her red bush seemed to blaze like a bonfire, consuming the remaining shreds of his dignity.

He took a deep breath. 'We can't –'

She giggled. 'Can't what, Daddy Steven?' she asked innocently. She put on the corset. 'I can't tighten the laces,' she whined petulantly. 'Will you help with the laces, Daddy?' Her voice was a manipulative filthy caress on his soul.

He found himself pulling the laces tight, tugging on them with his hands.

'Tighter . . .' she pleaded, her voice a whining insistent caress, feather light on his cock.

He pulled tighter until she was satisfied. Her tits looked huge, on full display over the revealing corset, her tiny waist accenting her sinuous curves. She sat back down on the bed and dangled her feet. 'I can't put my shoes on laced up like this . . .' she pouted. She raised one leg and prodded him on the side with her tiny perfect foot. 'Put my shoes on, Prior Steven.'

His erection was so hard, it was difficult to kneel down before the red-haired seductress. He carefully brought the shoes to her feet, putting his hand on her ankle to permit the manoeuvre.

She giggled with the welcome sensation of this rich powerful cleric kneeling before her, carrying out her every whim. She arched her pretty foot, watching the Prior of Redfork's drooling gaze on her shoes. 'Where is the coat of the prettiest orphan in the world, Prior Steven?' she asked mockingly.

Steven's eyes travelled up from her high-heeled shoes towards her sex, devouring her slender perfectly proportioned legs. They were tightly pressed together, depriving his lecherous eyes the view they so desperately desired. The scent of jasmine and cream seemed to tease his very soul. 'There is – there is a coat,' he heard himself say.

'I should have it . . . shouldn't I?' she slowly parted her legs. Her beautiful red-crowned pussy seemed to mock him, freezing him like a statue, his erection a hammer crumbling away his resistance. She continued to pull her legs wider until she was in a full split. Her high-heeled dancing shoes were on either side of the four-poster bed. She put a tantalising, red-tipped finger over her clit and began to tease herself. 'Bring me my pretty coat, Daddy . . .' She took her moistened finger out from in between her legs and put it in her pouting petulant mouth. She began sucking on it, her eyes huge, wide and blue in her angelic red-crowned face.

He shoved a few boxes aside until he found the large one, the one with the fur. He brought it over to Evelyn. She giggled happily as he handed over her prize.

His knees buckled in front of the bed. He found himself on all fours before the little redheaded slut, her beautiful pussy a scant inch from his drooling lust-crazed lips.

'Ooh . . . this one is in such a nice box . . .'

He tentatively extended the tip of his tongue, nearly cumming as her flavour pervaded his being. He began to lick her pussy, his tongue a subservient helpless slave of his overwhelming need. He heard the sounds of her hands making quick work of the packaging as his tongue circled her clit. He pulled her pussy lips into his mouth as he pleasured her, sucking in her scent, her flavour. Vaguely, he heard her coos of delight as Stephanie's gorgeous mink tumbled out of the box, the warm soft fur cascading over his kneeling body, covering the obscene display of his mindless pussy worship.

'Good little monk . . .' She giggled. He felt her hands stroking the soft fur over him. 'Good boy . . .'

She cruelly pushed his head away. He groaned with unmet need but stood up as well. She was a vision of temptation. She wore nothing but the luxurious fur coat, her high-heeled dancing shoes and the tight sleazy corset. She did not bother to close the coat, the lewd display of her body a calculated cruel goad of lust. The fur was too long – she nearly stumbled in her stiletto heels as she strutted about. She stomped her pretty foot. 'All these things are too big for pretty little Evelyn,' she pouted. 'Where is *my* coat?' she demanded, her voice shrill, uncompromising.

'I – I will buy you another one. I can't let you be seen leaving with this one on anyway,' he sighed. 'Laura might be watching.'

She frowned. 'Laura Laura Laura! I thought you liked me . . .' She rubbed herself against the monk. 'Don't you like me . . .?'

She smoothly dropped to her knees before the Prior, baring his massive, more than ready erection with the skilled motions of someone who has done this a hundred times. She wrapped her pretty lips around the head of his cock, staring at him with her huge blue eyes at the same time. She sucked him in, slowly, her warm mouth enveloping his erect member completely.

He whimpered softly, clamping his hand on his own mouth. She seemed to take perverse delight in pleasuring him. Her mouth manipulated his erection with consummate skill. That little pink tongue traversed up and down his shaft until it found a special spot just below the head of his cock. He felt the imminent climax in his balls. His hands weakly latched on to her glorious red hair and he began to fuck her mouth with eager abandon. The warm moist cave of her mouth demanded immediate tribute. He came in her mouth, keeping himself from a scream of release with every ounce of his lust-eroded will.

He hurriedly put on his robe and checked the hallway, then the foyer. The crack underneath Laura's door was dark. He quietly opened the front door and gazed up at her window from the street. The panes were shut. He quickly walked back up to the bedroom containing the boxes and the impatient and bored redhead.

'Come on,' he whispered. 'She is asleep.'

She nodded and walked out. In her hands, she carried a pile of expensive Brussels lace. She did not bother to take off the corset.

He did not press her – he secretly felt she had earned it.

At the front door, she faced him and planted a kiss on his cheek. 'I will come by tomorrow . . .' she giggled. 'I want to make a new friend.' She looked up at the shuttered window and smiled.

Seven

Stephanie's voice was an angry petulant hiss, exasperation mixed with a kind of broken disbelief. 'I am here to confess.'

His erection was so massive, so all pervasive, he could not open his mouth to respond. He saw her vague outline through the cross-lined lattice partition. She made a hasty sign of the cross.

'Bless me, Father, for I have sinned.' She sounded resentful. 'Say something, damn you. I really will confess, whoever you are . . . I don't want to die on the rack unshriven.'

'Princess,' he managed finally, his voice no more than a lust-crazed adoring whisper. 'It is I.'

A disbelieving silence was finally broken from the other side. '. . . Steven?'

'Yes.' He frantically pulled up his robe and freed his throbbing cock, stroking the engorged member. 'Yes. It's me, Friar – Friar Slut.' His voice broke as he spoke his name at the town house, a mockery of his calling.

She giggled, her voice gaining sudden strength. 'I see you have not changed, Friar Slut.'

He got on his knees before the partition and obscenely fondled himself before the cross-shaped hole. 'Yes, princess.'

'I assume from your . . . stance . . . that we can talk safely. This accursed wench Laura is ruining everything. I tried to have her sent to the convent when I married that drooling idiot, but that stupid bitch Elsbeth refused to keep her there against her will.'

'Yes, Princess.'

'Stop playing with your cock for a minute and pay attention, Friar Slut.'

Frustrated, he groaned but obeyed.

'Where have you been?'

'I fell on the way to Redfork and hit my head on a tree. I couldn't remember anything. I found my way to the convent where I stayed with Elsbeth.'

'That sanctimonious bitch.'

'Uh . . . not anymore. She was injured . . . I used – I used a certain jar of medicine.'

Stephanie's laughter was like a cruel, serrated edge of crystal on crystal. 'Perfect.'

'The salve in the medicine made me remember. I – I still couldn't leave for quite some time – Mother Elsbeth became one needy slut.'

'Maybe there is a way . . .' Stephanie's calculating throaty whisper trailed off as she thought. 'In the wine cellar at the town house there is a barrel of winter apples in the northeastern corner, in a hidden alcove. I showed Heather where it was. I want you to get the clay pot in the bottom of the barrel.'

'Clay pot? Princess, you will be tortured!'

'Shut up, Friar Slut. Get the clay pot to Sylvia. Little masturbating monk remembers Big Tits Sylvia, doesn't he?'

'. . . Yes. Yes . . .' he panted.

'Stop it, Friar Slut. She knows what to do . . . But she can't get into the town house. You will have to do it.'

'Yes, princess.'

'Is there anything else you wish to tell me?'

'Yes, princess. I have a lot of gold . . . I picked up your order from Garode's . . . and I have the Peabody jewels in a chest too.'

Stephanie giggled, a satisfied triumphant smirk of a sound. 'You are a good little puppy. Puppy can stick his cock through the cross now.'

* * *

'With great surprise I must report that the shameless harlot really seems to have repented.'

'I don't believe her. You should not either.'

'I have greater reason to disbelieve her than anyone. She is truly contrite.'

'What makes you think she is telling the truth?'

'She cries as she recounts her numerous crimes. She tears her hair with her hands. She prays to the Lord and demands penance, more severe even than the ones I have thus far levied upon her.'

'She really made this picture of the blessed Virgin herself?' Bishop Warener held up the crude, but somehow compelling charcoal sketch.

'I watched her do the drawing. She seemed completely overcome with rapture.' Steven did not have to pretend satisfaction. Stephanie made sure he had every reason to look forward to her confessions.

'Hmm . . . hmm . . .' Bishop Warener drummed on the surface of his desk. 'I am still unconvinced. But as you say, you are indeed the most qualified judge of her character. No one has suffered as much as you at her hands.'

'. . . Uh. No. No one.'

'What do you suggest we do with her? If she really repented . . . I can't give her to Brother Bougric. Nevertheless, she must still pay for all the thefts and her attempt at seducing a man of God. Perhaps a public stoning –'

'That is the same as an execution, my Lord Bishop. Perhaps I can offer a better solution . . .'

'Go on.'

'She could enter the convent.'

'A woman like her? That is preposterous!'

'There have been precedents. Some of Mother Elsbeth's best have come from . . . let's just say questionable backgrounds. Sometimes the most beautiful rose grows from a field of dung.'

'I am not sure I want someone like that near anything holy. Maybe a consecrated gallows, huh?'

Steven chuckled along with the irritating fool.

* * *

He walked back to the town house. He had to get Laura out of there. Strictly speaking, Laura had title to the town house – he only held rights to the town house if it was used as an orphanage. Still, he had to figure out a good reason to evict her. Using the truth occurred to him for a funny moment, leading to an oddly compelling fantasy.

'Laura – leave.'

'Why?'

'I need the town house to fornicate in peace.'

'Is that all?'

'Not entirely. I need to get the drug in the cellar so your father's widow can turn Bishop Warener into a drooling fornicator.'

'Very well. Let me take off my garments and pleasure you before I leave.'

He shook his head, grinning. That was not going to work. Why would Laura have to leave? She was an orphan now – she had no family. That idiot girl thought of him as her father, now, Steven realised. He could ask her to perform small missions for the monastery, perhaps . . . He was still unsure of a course of action by the time he arrived at the town house. He knocked on the front door. There was no answer. He fished out the key and opened the door himself, thinking of how some servants could definitely come in handy.

He found Laura in the kitchens. He was surprised to find her kneading dough. Next to her tall flour-covered shape stood a tiny, redheaded girl in a conservative grey linen dress. Steven nearly gagged as he recognised those devastating curves and that cruel vapid smile.

'Hello, Prior Steven!' piped up the tiny redhead.

'Hello . . . Evelyn.' He smiled weakly.

'Prior, Evelyn told me you wanted her to stay with us for a couple of days, at least until you could arrange for a coach to take her to the orphanage.'

'Uh . . . yes.'

'Of course, if you are turning the town house into an extension of the orphanage, I don't see why she can't just stay here.' Laura stared at Prior Steven. 'I realise you do not wish to live with women, Prior – but she is just a child! Could you not make an exception?'

He glanced at the little redhead. She was wearing the most innocent smile. What was she doing here?

'I just want to earn my keep, Prior Steven! Lady Peabody will teach me how to –' she made a tentative motion with her useless lacquered fingernails towards the dough and the kitchen table '– do that!'

'You really want to learn how to bake?' asked Laura, smiling.

'Yes! I am so lonely without my Daddy . . . we can be best friends!' She turned around and hugged the startled girl. 'It will be wonderful!'

'Do you at least have a mother, my dear?' sighed Laura, closing her eyes in empathy. She only knew too well how horrible it was!

I must remain a dutiful daughter and speak nothing ill of my mum,' said Evelyn. 'She wishes to see me married as soon as possible . . . or enter a convent. I was my father's best friend and . . . uh . . . strongest support during his sickness,' she improvised, '. . . and without him, my mum feels that unless I marry as soon as possible, my best chance for a proper upbringing lies with Prior Steven's orphanage. She is a dutiful mother, she is . . .'

Tears streamed down Laura's face. 'You poor creature. I know what it is like to lose a father . . .' She hugged Evelyn back, their bodies merging into one. Her eyes were pleading with Steven over Evelyn's shaking shoulder. She mouthed a silent 'please'.

The Prior sighed. 'Very well. You can stay, for now, Evelyn.'

'Thank you, both of you!' Evelyn curtsied to Laura first, then to him. Laura could not see her expression as she faced the Prior – it was a mask of gleeful greedy cunning.

'Oh, Laura. It is so hard to knead this dough,' she sobbed, raising her hands from the awkward mess on the kitchen table.

Laura sighed. 'You do it like this.' She began to redo the entire pie. The girl was completely useless, she thought. All she could talk about was dresses, and shoes, and lace and dancing. Why, the girl would be miserable at the orphanage.

'You are so wonderful!' squealed Evelyn. 'Can I just watch for a little while?'

'My shoulders hurt,' mumbled Laura. Of course they hurt, she thought – she was doing all the work.

'Oh, don't worry, I know something that can help you with that.' Evelyn giggled and dragged over a small footstool. She took off her dancing shoes and clambered on top, barefoot. 'Just relax, Lady Peabody.'

Her fingers began to knead Laura's shoulders. The tall girl was surprised to find that Evelyn's fingers had unusual strength. The pain receded and was replaced by a pleasurable warm sensation.

Laura smiled. 'That feels wonderful!'

'I am glad you like it. I've been told I am a very good masseuse.' She slipped her fingers below Laura's shift.

Evelyn's fingers felt so light, so warm on her bare skin, Laura could really learn to like this.

She leaned back a little and smiled directly at the tiny redhead. The cloud of jasmine surrounding Evelyn mixed with the pleasant sensations of her fingers. Laura has never felt this relaxed in her entire life.

'Relax, Lady Peabody . . .'

'Oh, just call me Laura.'

'Thank you, Laura. Of course, this is not nearly as nice as when I give a full massage.'

Laura closed her eyes. She stopped kneading the dough. It was just too easy to do nothing, to listen to Evelyn's tinkling little voice, to give in to her expert warm fingers. She leaned against her hand. Those fingers bared a little more of her skin, slipping the shift lower, until the linen slipped all the way over her breasts. They were still covered, but just barely so, and her nipples started to rub up against the fabric with each kneading motion of Evelyn's hand. Her nipples stiffened; it felt so good, she let a soft moan escape her lips.

Ever so slowly, Evelyn's hand kneaded its way lower and lower over Laura's bare back. The already unlaced shift slid lower and lower on her back with each skilful movement. Only her nipples, utterly erect, kept the shift on her chest; the fabric snagged on her breasts.

Laura's breathing grew ragged. 'Maybe – maybe we should stop,' she whispered quietly.

'You are right,' giggled Evelyn. 'This is just silly, I should give you a full massage.' She deftly slid Laura's shift off completely, freeing her aching breasts.

Laura gasped. 'What – what are you doing?' She covered her chest with her arms.

Evelyn shrugged. 'Giving you a full massage, of course. Lie down on the table.'

'But . . . I am naked!'

'No, silly. You are not naked yet. To give you a full massage, of course, you should be naked. But this once I will just give you an upper body massage. Is that all right?'

'What about all this dough? We have to finish the pie!'

'Relax, Laura. We will finish the pie afterward.'

Laura glanced at the complete mess on the table. It's not like they wouldn't have to start all over again anyway. And the massage felt so nice.

'Oh, all right . . . How do you want me to lie down?'

'On your stomach, please.'

Laura felt so silly – she clambered on top of the table, sweeping the floury mess into a bucket. It was still cold and a thin layer of flour remained. She let out a soft screech as her breasts pushed against the cold wood. Her nipples were still so hard . . .

Evelyn's hands were back on her shoulders. She rubbed her muscles, slowly at first, then with increasing speed and vigour. 'I can't do it like this . . . I have to get on top of you.'

It felt so good, Laura forgot to protest when she felt the tiny girl's weight on top of her bottom. Evelyn kneeled there and leaned forward, massaging her back. Her long lustrous red hair fell forward. The strands softly fell onto her skin, a thousand falling jasmine flower petals. Laura moaned softly. 'Your hair . . . It is so beautiful . . .'

'Thank you . . .' Evelyn giggled and lowered her hair until the tips of the strands just barely touched Laura's skin on her shoulders. She slowly, teasingly moved her head over Laura's body, stimulating her back with her hair. Laura felt a thousand tiny fires over her skin. She emitted a peculiar whimper as Evelyn's hands moved steadily lower on her back, massaging her muscles around her spine. She felt an unusual warm wetness between her legs.

Evelyn reached her waist. 'Do you want me to continue, Laura?'

'Yes, please. It feels so good . . .'

Laura shuddered in delighted surprise as she felt Evelyn's fingers slip beneath her shift on her bottom. Her secret shameful parts felt strangely alive, warm, moist. She thought she was sopping wet in between her legs. 'It feels – it feels so good,' she moaned as the redhead began to caress her ass.

Evelyn giggled. 'You keep saying that.' She pulled off Laura's shift completely and examined her drenched panties with a critical eye. She crawled on top of the softly moaning girl and traced her hair from top to bottom, this time, all the way from her head to her feet. Evelyn slid her hands beneath her undergarments and pulled off the shameful drenched panties.

Laura just lay there. She told herself she wanted to get up. 'This is wrong,' she mouthed weakly, without actually making any sound. Her pussy was a thoroughly soaked, demanding mistress in between her virgin legs. She was writhing in ecstasy as she felt the soft warm flesh of Evelyn's tits press against her back.

The redhead disrobed herself and crawled on top of the solemn tall daughter of Lord Peabody, a white-skinned, red-taloned predator gloating over her freshly trapped prey. Evelyn slid a hand over Laura's clit and began to stimulate it with a single finger. 'It feels so good, this full body massage, doesn't it?' she giggled.

All Laura could do was moan.

Evelyn carefully maintained the girl's continuous debasement as she slipped off the table. She leaned close until her hair was like a nest of red snakes covering the moaning writhing girl's face. She leaned in and kissed her. Her tongue slid inside Laura's shocked lips.

Thoughts of resistance crumbled with each skilful touch of Evelyn's lips, coupled with the obscene manipulation of her sex. Laura's struggles gave way to ecstasy. She lost herself in the kiss, her prim moral upbringing crumbling into shards of red-hazed oblivion as she came on Evelyn's hand.

Laura wept for hours before she went to Prior Steven.

'Prior . . . I must confess!' Her face was drowning in tears.

'Uh . . . Of course, of course. Come to the . . . den.'

'Not – not the chapel?'

Steven blushed with sudden shame. Laura Peabody, of all people, would not want to fornicate with him in her late father's den. 'Of course . . . the chapel. I am frazzled this late. Affairs of the monastery consume much of my time.'

He followed Laura to the chapel.

'There is no confessional in this small chapel, Lady Peabody,' he said, gently. 'But such a place is not necessary to levy penance and grant absolution. Tell me what troubles you, my child.'

'Prior Steven!' Laura began to bawl. Heavy tears stained her shift as she began to speak. 'I . . . Evelyn . . . Evelyn and I did a terrible thing!'

'Calm down, child, and tell me exactly what happened.'

'She – she gave me a massage, and one thing led to another . . . and we – we – I think we fornicated!' She threw herself before the Prior and buried her face into the fine linen of his new robe. 'Please . . . tell me Prior Steven, is Heaven forever lost to me now?' Prior Steven looked at her with a strange tight-lipped expression. He gently pushed her head away from his robe.

'No. Not if you serve penance and gain absolution. Tell me exactly what you have done.'

The Prior sat in the chair and rested the family bible over his lap as he listened to Laura's account of her seduction. She did not leave anything out – she wanted to serve penance, to earn absolution. Desperation lent power to her description. Prior Steven nodded occasionally. He seemed very attentive.

Her confession stumbled out of her in an incoherent jumble. 'And then . . . I felt this amazing wave of pleasure coursing through my . . . Through me . . . As Evelyn . . . Well, as she . . . She put her hand over my . . . she played with me . . . I felt so weak, it felt so good . . . and then I broke down in tears and ran away to my room, and then to the chapel. She laughed at me! She has been trying to talk to me but I know she is an agent of the devil . . . I lust for her touch, still, Prior Steven, please help me!'

'Of course . . . Of course . . . You have done the right thing coming to me. This sort of thing is not unknown between young women, my child.'

'It isn't? But I thought –'

'I have personally seen Mother Elsbeth discipline several girls in her care for similar infractions. It is of no great concern.'

'But –'

'It is still a sin to act in such manner, of course.'

Laura lowered her eyes in shame. 'Of course, I know that Prior Steven.'

'The key here, of course, is for you to – to stand steadfast in the face of temptation.'

'What do you mean?' Laura became confused. 'You want her to leave, I assume . . .'

'That would remove her from your sight, of course . . . but it would not prove your strength of character. Nay – you must prove the strength of your character in spite of her presence.'

'I – I see.' She could not expunge a note of dismay from her voice.

'I will speak to her as well. For the next few nights, you will share a cot with her. Neither of you is to touch the other. You are to pray during every waking moment – except when you are cleaning or doing chores. The rosary.'

'Yes, Prior Steven.'

'Your character – and hers as well – will emerge from this challenge tested and cleansed of taint.'

Laura nodded dutifully. 'As you command.'

'It is for Lady Laura Peabody,' the page repeated. He was grinning widely, enjoying the view. Evelyn was wearing a flimsy white shift, her breasts nearly exposed to his appreciative eyes.

She pouted. 'Are you sure it's not for me?'

The boy tapped his fingers on the satchel with the leather tubes of parchment in it. 'This message is for Lady Laura Peabody. Tell your mistress to –'

'I am not some filthy little serving wench, boy!' Evelyn shrieked. 'I will tell Laura to come down for her bloody message.'

The boy nodded silently. Evelyn could feel his eyes on her bottom as she walked up the stairs. She hammered on her bedroom door with her fist. 'Laura! Laura!' The stupid girl was not there. Where could she be? After a moment's reflection, the redhead directed her steps towards the family chapel. Her hunch was correct – Lord Peabody's daughter was in the Peabody family chapel, on her knees, praying. Her fingers were obsessively moving from bead to bead on the rosary, her lips repeating the Hail Mary, over and over. She was staring at a passage within the immense heavy black form of the Peabody family bible, her lips never ceasing the incessant Hail Marys.

When Evelyn stormed into the chapel, she stopped her prayer for a moment, keeping her fingers on the rosary. Laura instinctively glanced at Evelyn. She immediately blushed and averted her gaze, returning it to the words in the book before her. She addressed the redhead without looking up from the bible. Her voice was wracked by conflicting emotions. 'Yes? What can I do for you, Miss Wentworth?'

Evelyn rolled her eyes. 'You have a messenger at the door, a page by the look of him.'

'Really?' She never had visitors! Her evil wicked transgression forgotten in the excitement of the moment, she ran downstairs. The novelty of the visitor transformed her solemn countenance into a vision of breathless exuberance. She looked truly radiant as she faced the page; her face glowed with excitement. Laura's long healthy chestnut hair reflected the morning sun. The messenger could not help but smile back. Such contrast between this girl and the shrill redheaded bitch who answered the door!

'Lady Laura Peabody?'

'Yes . . . I am Laura Peabody,' she inwardly sighed. She never thought the title could feel so hollow without the trappings of the wealth that she had taken for granted for most of her life. She knew she would have most of her father's estate back when she turned nineteen, but until then she had resigned herself to a life of monastic asceticism. Prior Steven's unexpected fondness for rich food and expensive robes was a surprise, yet no largesse dribbled down to her plate from his. He did not buy her dresses or books. She caught herself envying Evelyn's numerous new dresses, her shoes, her jewellery, the pearls accenting her pretty red hair . . . It was obvious the redhead's father took pains to leave her a sizeable sum to see to her needs, and, no doubt, for a dowry.

'I am charged with delivering the messages of Prince Henry.' The young man withdrew a leather tube from his satchel. 'This one is for you, my Lady.'

'Thank you,' she smiled at the page. She took secret satisfaction from the young man's sudden flush of colour, the way his eyes traversed over her face, her body. Yet another sin to confess to Prior Steven! Maybe she should enter the convent, keep herself from temptation . . . She never really liked the strict rules of Mother Elsbeth, but perhaps it was best for her to be a member of such a community, to keep her soul from succumbing to lustful impulses. Softly, she closed the door and leaned against it, holding the tube tightly in both hands. She suspected the message was an invitation.

'Well? What is it?' Evelyn's shrill contralto cleaved into her excitement.

'I – I don't know.'

‘Read it, silly.’ The redhead walked closer. She seemed to move in a cloud of jasmine petals.

Laura breathed in the scent without wanting to. She opened the tube and extracted the parchment. ‘It is an invitation.’ She shrugged and lowered the parchment.

‘Well, read it! Where is it inviting you to?’

‘I am not going wherever it is. I am only a Lady in name. I have no money of my own, I have no castle, I have no dowry, I have nothing!’ Laura’s voice was tinged with bitterness.

‘Relax . . . You still have your title. Read the invitation! Please . . .’ Evelyn’s bitchy voice acquired a smooth lilting tone. ‘Please . . . Laura . . . Be nice . . . Read the invitation.’

Laura sighed and unrolled the parchment fully. She cleared her voice. ‘It is addressed to me . . . Lady Laura Peabody, et cetera . . . Here it is: Prince Henry requests the pleasure of your company at the coming of age ball of his sister, the Princess Annabelle, this coming Saturday night.’

‘That’s wonderful!’ Evelyn’s voice was soaked in envy. ‘I can’t believe you are not going!’

‘I don’t know how to act at a ball . . . Anyway, I have nothing to wear, and nothing to say if someone asks about my estate. The men will want to know about my situation . . . And I have no situation.’

‘I wish I could go . . .’

Laura shrugged. ‘Go, then. Where is your invitation?’

Evelyn glowered at her. ‘I don’t have one, Laura. I don’t have your title.’

Laura blushed. ‘I am sorry, Evelyn. I – I forgot. If I went I could take you as my companion.’ She sighed. ‘I am not going, of course. I am sorry, Evelyn.’

‘No trouble . . .’ The redhead smiled. ‘I wanted to tell you that I am sorry about what happened . . . I got carried away. Sometimes I just want to physically touch someone . . . Since my father died, it has been so hard . . .’ She began to sob.

Laura looked at her with concern. ‘I know. I know exactly what it feels like. It will be all right.’ She hugged Evelyn, her arms tentatively embracing her. The redhead buried her face in Laura's shoulder, sobbing. Her breasts softly pushed against her own. 'I am so glad you are contrite about what happened, Evelyn.' Laura could not hide the relief she felt. 'I confessed to Prior Steven what happened.'

'You did what? I mean . . . why?' Evelyn's voice went from shrill rage to a calculating, even tone in a heartbeat.

'Don't you fear going to hell, Evelyn? We – we sinned back in the kitchen.'

'Well . . . What did Prior Steven say? Was it a sin?'

'He said it was not at all unusual . . . He said this has happened before at the convent.'

'Really?'

'Yes . . . He said – he said he was going to talk to you about it as well. Didn't he talk to you last night?'

'Uhm . . . Yes, of course he did.' Evelyn's nightly session of fellatio with the Prior earned her a new bracelet, paid straight out of the Peabody loot – not much was discussed besides the transaction. 'Which part exactly do you mean?'

'The part about us sleeping together . . . To test each other's resolve against temptation.' Laura's eyes were downcast, yet resolute. 'I do not wish to burn in Hell, Evelyn!'

The redhead rolled her eyes and petted the tall girl's dark locks. 'Nobody wants to burn in Hell, Laura . . . It's fine . . . It will never ever happen again.' The old goat! No doubt he wanted her to do his dirty work for him, and turn the annoying pauper into his whore. Well, he can just wait until the judgment day for that. She had better things to do than rub up against some penniless slut when she could milk the old goat himself. Something Laura said suddenly loomed large in her mind. 'What did you say about the ball?'

'What do you mean?'

'You said you could take a lady companion?'

'Of course. That is just how it is done. Usually it is an older matron, a chaperone, but in my case nobody would begrudge if I brought a friend. It is unfortunate that we cannot go. I am sure you would have enjoyed it.' Laura smiled a bitter little smile.

'Please let us go . . .' Evelyn whined.

'No! We still must serve our penance. Balls are not for those who are doing penance.'

'No . . . I suppose you are right. I will go and see Prior Steven right now for my penance.'

'Oh, Evelyn! Thank you!' She hugged the little redhead with unabashed joy. She was worried Evelyn would fail to see the error of her ways. How wrong she was! She smiled at her. 'I hope he will not be overly strict with you.'

'I hope not,' said Evelyn, chuckling to herself.

She hurried downstairs to see the Prior. She knocked on the door of the den.

'Yes?'

'Open up.' She did not bother to add an honorific.

Evelyn sauntered inside, picking up the monk's pet goblet. It was hammered gold, depicting Saint George slaying the serpent. She had introduced him to the choicest French wines – he only drank the best Bordeaux and Madeira now. 'What game are you playing?'

'What do you mean?' He looked guilty, she decided.

'I mean, what is this stuff about Laura sleeping with me and doing penance?'

'I thought she would never consent to it . . . I figured she would leave, go to the convent or something.'

'Or I would turn her into your little playmate?'

Steven grinned. 'You have an evil mind, Evelyn.'

'Well . . . It looks like she is going through with it. And you are to severely punish me here, in your office . . . something that requires a lot of . . . moaning . . .' She giggled.

He stepped closer. She could hear him panting, excited. 'What do you mean?' he sounded hopeful.

'Not *that*. I don't want to kneel and pray all day with Laura, but I want her to feel sorry for me.' She looked around. 'Is there a whip somewhere around here?'

'There is a tawse in the stable . . .'

'Get it. I will wait here.'

She uncovered her tight white bottom and lay on her stomach in the middle of the bearskin rug by the hearth.

Her unblemished smooth flesh was lit by the red light of the flames. Steven arrived in a moment – he must have run to return so quickly. In his hand was a tough leather tawse, used on the occasional mule that was stabled at the town house. Steven's eyes were riveted to her naked bottom.

'Spank me.' She rolled her eyes as he eagerly stepped closer. 'Lock the door first, fool.'

He nodded and locked the door. He raised the tawse.

'Hit me.'

He hit her, softly. She yelped but it turned into a giggle. 'I need you to make a mark, silly. Hit me harder.'

He tentatively raised the tawse and hit her, this time with force, the sound of leather swishing through the air nothing compared to the stinging slapping sound it made against her skin. She screamed, her high-pitched contralto shattering the silence of the town house.

He smiled nervously. 'Do you want me to stop?'

'No . . .' she gasped. 'That was perfect. Hit me again.' She wiggled her bottom.

He struck her bottom, again, and then again. He saw she was writhing like a snake in heat. A soft whimper escaped her lips. 'More . . .' she gasped. Softly, almost imperceptibly, she added: 'Please . . .'

He spanked her bottom until it was lined with smooth red strokes. She was moaning with each stinging slap, wriggling her ass, raising it high in the air.

'I am a naughty little bitch, Prior Steven,' she panted.

'Yes you are. You are a little slut.' He rained a steady shower of stinging blows on her perfect smooth skin. He saw her hand snake between her legs – she began to pleasure herself as her 'penance' continued.

She suddenly shuddered and collapsed in on herself, purring contentedly. He grabbed a fistful of red hair and raised her head, pushing his erect member in between her unresisting lips.

'I am so sorry, Evelyn,' Laura sobbed. 'I cannot believe Prior Steven is . . . torturing you. I thought he would make you say prayers like he made me . . .'

‘He is cruel but fair,’ said Evelyn.

‘But . . . Look at you! Your bottom is lined with welts!’

Evelyn sighed. ‘I am paying the price for my lustful nature. The blows hurt, but not nearly as much as the touch of hellfire.’

‘Can I – can I do anything to make it feel better? I feel awful . . . I feel like I should have told you to stop.’

‘It’s all right . . . maybe – maybe you could put some snow on it? I saw a few flakes coming down outside.’

Laura walked to the window. Sure enough, a thin blanket of snow was covering the filth of the street outside. ‘I will bring you some as soon as there is enough for a clean handful.’

Evelyn hugged the tall girl. ‘You are like a sister to me.’

Laura stifled a tear. She was so lucky to have a friend like Evelyn! In a little while she judged enough snow had fallen for her purpose. She went outside and collected cool refreshing snow in a bucket. It took some time to find enough to fill it to the brim. She was shivering. Avoiding the den, she made her way upstairs. In her absence, Evelyn had disrobed and fallen asleep on her stomach. She looked beautiful, calm, stunning with her glorious red hair. Her exquisite white body was exposed, the smooth white expanse of skin on her bottom marred by angry red welts. Laura felt anger – how could Prior Steven do this? She sighed as she put down the bucket. She would have to wake Evelyn up . . . Or she could just do *this* . . .

A mischievous spirit seemed to spring out of thin air and land right on Laura’s shoulder. It whispered its sly counsel in her ear. She never had any fun! It was always the Evelyns of the world who got to play with others . . . It was her turn!

Laura picked up two handfuls of white snow and smeared the ice-cold crystals all over Evelyn’s tight bottom.

The redhead shrieked at the top of her lungs, shocked awake in such a rude manner. ‘What – what?!’

Sparkly eyed, Laura laughed, her fingers dripping with melting snow.

'You bitch!' Evelyn slapped her, hard. Her long painted fingernails left raked vivid marks down her cheek.

Without thinking, Laura slapped her back. 'Bitch?!'

In a moment, both of them were clawing and pulling each other's hair. Laura shrieked as her shift tore in Evelyn's vengeful hands. Both young women were rolling around on the cot, hands flailing. Laura finally managed to put her hands around Evelyn's wrists, pinning the tiny redhead underneath her. She snarled and tried to bite her hand, but she could not bend her head enough. She was trapped, and too tiny to dislodge the tall girl on top of her.

Laura became extremely aware of Evelyn's breathing. Her breasts rose and fell in rhythm. Her lips were slightly parted, angry, red, inviting. The scent of jasmine seemed to soak into her from the little body beneath her. She felt Evelyn struggle and instinctively lowered her arms to give her leverage, to keep her pinned on the cot. Her lips were a mere foot away from the redhead's beautiful face. She felt the angry quivering tension suddenly leave Evelyn's body.

'So now that you have me . . . what will you do with me?' The redhead slowly raised her head from the cot. To Laura, it seemed like she was falling forward into Evelyn's inviting lips. She could not seem to look away, to escape. Those lips seemed to fill her being. Suddenly, they were not visible anymore – they were touching her lips, probing, nibbling, caressing, moving from her lips to the nape of her neck. The touch of those pretty pouty lips was hot, exciting, the spark of a roaring fire spreading through her body, centred on her sex.

Laura lost all strength in her fingers – she dimly felt Evelyn's hands escape her grip. All she could feel was the redhead's tongue in her mouth, the sensation of their merged lips, the rubbing of their bodies against one another. She whimpered and pressed herself tightly against Evelyn.

The redhead giggled. 'Now that's better, isn't it?'

Laura had just finished scrubbing the floor in Evelyn's room when the little redhead waltzed in.

'It's time for the ball!' Evelyn was brimming with excitement. 'We are going dancing!' She twirled around in her new dress and her new dancing shoes. She showed off the glittering amber and gold bracelet on her wrist. 'Isn't it beautiful?'

'Yes . . . it is.' Laura looked at her with desire. Evelyn was looking gorgeous, as always. Her deceased father must have left her a fortune to spend this kind of money on dresses and jewellery.

'Mmmm . . .' Evelyn stroked Laura's hair with her fingers. She leaned closer and pulled the tall girl's face low until their lips met. They kissed for a long time, their tongues intertwined.

'Why are you not getting ready for the ball?'

'I don't have a dress,' she sighed. 'When I was still Lord Peabody's daughter I had a whole wardrobe full of them. Now I don't even have one!' she sobbed.

'Don't worry . . . Prior Steven will get you one.'

'Oh no, I could never ask him to spend the money on a dress when he needs every penny just to keep the orphans warm. What's so funny?'

'Nothing . . . You are right. I still think it's the least he could do . . . It's not like he counts his money anyway. He has this fat purse stuffed full of gold coins in the den. All you have to do is take some . . . enough for a dress . . . He will never ever know.' She nibbled on Laura's ear. The tall girl slumped against the door. Of late, her sex seemed the centre of her being.

'Even if he finds out, he is a man like all men. Just show him a little skin . . . touch him here . . .' Evelyn caressed Laura in between her legs. 'Use your mouth if he doesn't succumb, at first. He will buy you whatever you want.'

'No! That would be – that would be wrong!'

'Don't you want to come to the ball?' Evelyn cruelly stroked her here and there. She stopped when Laura's panting made it obvious she was losing control. 'Come on . . .' She led her downstairs, to the den. 'I saw him hide the key under the floorboards . . .'

She watched Laura extract the small key, her fingers trembling with the enormity of her crime. 'Go on . . .'

whispered Evelyn. 'It's so easy . . . think of the fun we can have . . . just the two of us for the whole night . . . we can hold each other, naked, and drink champagne.'

Laura closed her eyes. The vision was so tempting, it felt so real . . . She opened her eyes and pushed the key into the lock, opening the door in the same motion. Everything was as Evelyn described it. She saw the purse on the elaborate fur-lined belt – it was, indeed, heavy with coin. She took it off the wall and unlaced it. She filled her hands with gold and put the belt and the purse back on the wall.

'Here it is!' she reported to Evelyn. She showed the redhead the gold in her hands, her face flushed with a mixture of guilt and delicious excitement.

'Let's count it!'

The girls ran upstairs and locked themselves in Evelyn's room. Evelyn counted the coins, one at a time, on her bed. 'One shy of a score of them.'

'That's good, isn't it?'

'Not bad – but not enough for a dress.'

'Not enough? I thought it was a fortune!'

'It's enough for shoes . . .'

'That's all we can do? So . . . we can't go to the ball?' Laura could not hide her disappointment.'Why don't we go to Garode's and see what we can do with what we have?' smiled Evelyn.

'Oh . . . very well.' Laura felt a little relief. Maybe they could just pick slightly less expensive dresses and still go.

'How do I look?' Evelyn twirled around, displaying the golden dancing shoes on her feet. The heels were very high.

'I thought we were looking for dresses.' Laura could not hide the tension from her voice. Those shoes were expensive!

'Don't be such a worry wart.'

'I'm not a worry wart. I just want a dress so I can go to the ball. You already have a new dress and new shoes, anyway.'

Evelyn smiled and caressed Laura's cheek. The redhead's fingers were burning firebrands on her skin. Her breath caught in her throat.

'So how do I look?' She arched her foot, displaying the stiletto heel.

Laura swallowed. 'Very pretty . . .'

Evelyn hugged Laura. She smiled and stared directly into the girl's eyes. 'I really love these shoes, Laura . . .' she began to sob. 'I really, really love them.'

'But –'

Evelyn's eyes began to tear up. 'Pleeeease . . .' She stepped closer to Laura, pressing her body against hers. She rested her head on her shoulder, hard cold blue eyes drilling into soft warm brown. 'With them on I am almost as tall as you are.'

It felt wonderful to have Evelyn's head on her shoulder. She smelled intoxicating. 'Oh . . . very well. It's not like we have enough for dresses anyway.'

'I know . . . perfect. We will take the shoes.'

Garode bowed, beaming. As he counted the gold from Laura's purse, he spoke, as if he had not even heard Laura's admission of their lack of funds. 'Will you be requiring dresses for the ball? We have new creations just arrived from the continent.'

'Do you have to go for an entire week?'

'Aaah, my little Prior, missing me already?' Evelyn giggled.

'Yes,' he answered tightly. 'I don't want to be here all alone with that holier-than-thou idiot.'

'Don't worry . . . I am taking Miss Insatiable with me.'

'What are you talking about?'

'I told my father that Lady Peabody and I have become best friends. He was thrilled that I was friends with a woman of character, finally.' Evelyn's vapid giggle rose in pitch. 'He said we can chaperone each other at the ball.' She slowly crawled over Steven's lap. Smoothly, she raised the hem of her skirt to expose her perfect round white bottom. Like a tiny red-haired serpent, she began to grind herself against his rapidly hardening member. 'We need dresses, Daddy Steven . . .'

'No . . . I want to fuck you.' he gasped.

'No cunnie for you. Not unless you are a rich prince who wants to marry me.'

'I am willing to buy you a dress . . . you know that,' he groaned as she manipulated him. Her buttocks seemed to grasp his member through the thin fabric of his night-clothes. 'But I have to have something in return . . .' The sleazy little seductress pulled his hands to cup her large firm breasts. Her nipples poked into the flesh of his hands.

He found it difficult to concentrate. 'Anyway, Laura Peabody will never accept an expensive dress from me. She thinks I am using all the money for charity.' Something just occurred to him. 'Why are you calling her Miss Insatiable?'

'Mmmm . . . Because she is, Daddy Steven. She is willing to do whatever it takes to get that dress . . . She really wants to go to the ball!' Evelyn giggled. 'I am soooo bad . . .'

'Yes . . . Yes you are.'

The door to the study opened. Laura gasped as she beheld the sordid scene. 'Prior Steven!'

Laura's eyes were glued onto Evelyn's exposed writhing body. She wore her plain linen shift. The thin worn fabric did nothing to hide her arousal. Her nipples hardened as the scene burned itself into her soul. 'What – what are you doing?' Her lips were trembling as she looked at Evelyn. Betrayal! She would have given anything to have Evelyn on top of her like that . . .

'I am just doing this so Prior Steven will buy you a dress for the ball . . .' pouted the redhead. She leaned back, her glorious hair enveloping Steven's head. The scent of jasmine wafted around Evelyn like a cloud of rolling seduction.

'No!' cried Laura. 'I – I can't let you – I can't let you lose your virtue over my dress.'

Evelyn giggled. 'If only there was a way for me to save my virtue . . . but Prior Steven has to be satisfied or neither of us can go to the ball.'

Laura found herself walking towards the sordid display. When she was close enough, Evelyn's red fingernails snaked out to latch onto her arm, pulling her closer. Her lips were so close, so beautiful ... She smelled so wonderful. Laura's eyes drank in Evelyn's, lingered on her beautiful hair, on her perfect skin. She could not seem to stop moving forward – Evelyn's lips grew larger and larger until she saw nothing else. With a soft whimper of helpless need, she leaned forward and merged her lips with those of the beautiful vision on Prior Steven's lap. Or was it Evelyn who kissed her? She could not seem to think. Her trusted best friend's manicured hand slipped beneath her shift. By the time she surfaced from the kiss, Evelyn's skilful fingers found just the right spot of her sex, beginning her debased thorough manipulation.

'Evelyn ...' she moaned softly.

'Laura ...' Evelyn's finger slipped inside her whimpering victim. She purred softly, seductively in Laura's ear. 'If you let Prior Steven stick his cock in you ... he will buy us all the dresses we want ...'

'No ...' gasped Laura. She wanted to push Evelyn away ... She wanted to ... What did she want ...? Evelyn's finger on her clit made her want to get on her back and spread her legs wide.

'I will make sure it will feel good ...' cooed Evelyn, continually fingering the quiet studious daughter of the late Lord. 'Virginity is such a little thing ...'

Like a sinuous serpent, she slid from Steven's lap and kneeled before Lady Peabody, raising her shift above the crimson locks of her hair. Her head disappeared underneath.

Laura felt her warm wet tongue replace the fingers over her clit. She cried out, a strangled whimpering expression of mindless lust, and crumpled onto the floor. Her knees opened wide, surrendering her sex completely to the debased ministrations of her seductress.

Evelyn's exquisite tiny body and red-lined, round little bottom was a tempting bobbing vision in front of Steven. Lust pervaded every fibre of the Prior's being as the beautiful temptress exercised her skills on her latest victim.

Her tongue brought Laura to the very edge of a mind-blowing orgasm. All Laura could do was moan as

Evelyn's skilful mouth latched on her pussy lips and her tongue circled the fleshy knob of her clit. Laura gasped. An overwhelming need seemed to rise within her, a heretofore unknown volcano of gibbering, demanding passion. 'I have to taste you,' she begged.

Evelyn resumed fingering her, freeing her painted lips for speech. She smirked. Her shrill vapid voice was mocking. 'Want to lick my cunnie?'

'Yes. Please let me lick your cunnie, Evelyn! Please!'

Evelyn giggled triumphantly, slowly lowering her gorgeous welt-lined bottom over Laura's mindless lust-crazed face. She began to grind her sex against the girl's mouth. The redhead pushed her legs tightly against both sides of Laura's head, robbing the helpless writhing Peabody heiress of her hearing. Pushing her tits together with her red-taloned fingers, she faced Steven and smiled. 'Dresses and more shoes, Daddy Steven. You can fuck her cunnie while you suck on my tits.'

Laura was licking Evelyn's clit with an insatiable perverse appetite. Her sopping wet pussy welcomed the touch of rigid warm flesh. A momentary sensation of pain was overcome by a shuddering wave of lustful pleasure.

The demanding little harlot was selfishly using Laura's lips for her wanton gratification. She pressed her clit over the lips of Lady Peabody and gasped with pleasure, her vapid shrill voice oozing with satisfaction.

Steven's cock slid in and out of Laura's eager drenched sex. The monk fondled the greedy little redhead's full breasts as his manhood explored Laura Peabody's tight virgin depths. He used a steady methodical motion, constant strokes, brazen and continuous, while his eyes roved over Evelyn's naked body.

Laura felt a momentary pang of sorrow over her sullied virtue – but the sensations emanating from in between her legs made further contrition impossible. The act of shameless fornication with Evelyn made her sex so wet and her desire so overwhelming that she did not feel the least bit of pain from the loss of her virginity. She wanted to taste Evelyn for the rest of her life. Laura licked her pussy lips, sucked on them, worshipped every part of the beautiful redhead's sex. She felt Evelyn begin to shudder as waves of intense pleasure wracked her body.

'Lick my cunnie, lick me, Laura, lick my pussy you sullied little slut . . .' screamed Evelyn, grinding herself unto Laura's lips with even greater selfishness.

Steven pounded away at Lady Peabody, fondling Evelyn's jiggling full tits. He leaned forward and sucked on her nipples. There was no way his tortured cock could take any more of this torrid stimulation. With an inarticulate moan, he pulled out of the orphan who has been placed under his care and ejaculated all over the writhing tangle of naked flesh beneath him.

'I will take the Brussels lace. And the new dresses, of course. And the shoes.' Evelyn was happy. 'Have I forgotten anything?'

'What about my dress? And . . . I want those earrings.'

'And the earrings.' Evelyn caressed Laura's cheek. 'You earned it, sweetie.'

Garode bowed deeply. 'I will have my servants take the young Lady's measurements. I already have yours, Lady Wentworth.'

'Very good. Oh . . . Laura, I hope you don't mind that my dress is a bit more dear than yours . . .'

'It's no trouble.' Laura's voice was a bit strained. The tiny redhead's daring black dress was dear enough to buy a wardrobe full of silk.

Evelyn leaned up and planted a big kiss on her cheek. Her rouge left a heart-shaped red stain on the taller girl's skin. 'You are so nice!'

The merchant delicately turned away as Laura leaned in, eyes dazed with desire.

'Not here, silly,' giggled Evelyn, languidly pushing away the besotted heiress. 'When we get home . . .'

Eight

It had been two days since Evelyn and Laura went off to their ball and Steven was going crazy with unmet need. He went upstairs into Laura's room. For the most part, Evelyn used the space to store the countless dresses, shoes and lingerie she milked out of the addicted monk. Laura's simple shift was a crumpled forgotten relic from a forgotten age, tossed in a jumbled heap on the floor. He threw aside a corset and picked up a pair of lace panties, pressing the frilly fabric against his face, breathing in Evelyn's perfumed scent. The lingering scent of sex and jasmine evoked memories of countless nights and his member responded. He began to touch himself, thinking of his last night with them. Evelyn told him she wanted it to be as memorable as possible.

'Don't worry, I could not possibly forget you.'

She giggled. 'It's not that you will forget me . . . When you get really horny, just play with yourself. There is no reason to bring anyone else into the house. We keep you satisfied, don't we?'

'Well, yes.' He was not entirely truthful; he did not want to say that more and more his thoughts had turned back toward Stephanie Peabody. The gorgeous blonde widow was an ever-present distraction on his mind, an irresistible, insistent tug on his member even while he availed himself of Laura's charms and Evelyn's expert ministrations. 'Of course.'

'Very good, Daddy Steven. I will be back in a week. Don't do anything I would do.'

He laughed. 'I don't think I am that limber.'

He smiled as he remembered the exchange. Evelyn stripped Laura of her clothes in the foyer, leaving the girl completely naked except for her high-heeled shoes. Laura leaned against a bare patch on the wall, her hand weakly supporting her body as the little redhead manipulated her sex with her mouth and fingers. Remembering, Steven's hand was a blur on his cock. His eyes strayed over that same patch on the wall – it was where Lord Peabody's priceless tapestry hung, the one that was sold off by Stephanie and her coterie of whores during their stay here, to support their parasitic life of luxury. Thoughts of the evil widow pervaded his thoughts like a deadly corrosive fluid, dissolving the sordid scene of the delicious threesome in his mind. He frowned as his frustration mounted. He continued to play with himself, but the focus of his thoughts drifted from Laura to Evelyn to . . . to Stephanie. He could not seem to climax. Every time he thought he was there, *she* would emerge from the most shameful recesses of his mind and mock him, leaving him more and more agitated. Completely frustrated, he finally stopped and clothed himself. He did not bother with the monk's robes and the triple-knotted belt anymore. He donned a fine fur-trimmed cloak and riding boots, keeping the hood low to cover his face. He picked up a heavy walking stick from the carved ebony container by the door. The large cane was ornately worked with silver. He went out into the icy rain, carefully locking the heavy door of the town house behind him. Steven shivered in the early winter cold, pulling his heavy cloak closer about him. His feet seemed to know exactly where to go. Before he knew it, he had left the rich section of town and found himself in the shady decrepit buildings adjoining the Whores' Quarter.

He saw the slim figure of a young woman, small, firm-breasted, with impudent sparkling dark eyes. 'You, wench! I seek a whore . . .'

She slapped him, hard. He was too stunned to respond in a meaningful way. 'You dare call me a whore? You filthy pig! Whoremonger!' She was enraged. 'How dare you! You should be ashamed of yourself! Go to church and confess your perverted ways!'

Steven's shameful guilt was transformed into a nearly living wave of obscene lust when he heard the young woman's command to attend confession. He realised the confessional has been forever tainted for him. Stephanie had turned it from a holy place into an antechamber of delicious fornication, from a way to gain absolution into a place of perverse corruption. He shoved the outraged young woman aside and continued on. Children ran up to him, tugging on his finery.

'Kind Lord, alms for the poor . . .'

'Lord, my mum lies sick outside of town – she will die unless I bring her food . . .'

'Kind sir, our family lost the harvest . . .'

'Anything you want, sir . . . anything at all for a silver penny.' This last voice belonged to a young child, no more than twelve at most. Her voice sounded familiar – as if he had heard it before. He was never interested in children, of course, but perhaps he could use the child to find Heather.

He shook the questing hands off with distaste, raising his cane high in the air. 'Away with you, whelps, or I will beat you bloody!' He turned to the little girl who offered herself to him. 'You – stay a moment.'

She nodded, her face completely expressionless. 'Yes, Lord.'

'I do not wish to purchase your flesh. I may have a proposition for you, however.'

She looked relieved and hopeful. 'I have a miraculous picture of the Virgin that was drawn by my blind brother . . . Perhaps the Lord would be kind enough to buy it.'

He glanced at the offered picture. It was indeed a powerful vision of the Virgin. On a whim, he reached into his pouch and tossed the child a silver penny. 'There.' He rolled up the picture and put it in his mantle. 'Now, child, I am not here to buy pictures or talk to silly little girls. I seek a woman.'

Understanding dawned on the young girl's face. 'I can bring you any number of women, my Lord. A copper . . .'

He pulled out two silver pennies. 'You can have both of these if you take me to a woman named Heather.' He described the sultry brunette who took his silver and his virginity.

She sighed. 'I may be able to find her – but I don't know her, it may take time. I can bring you a lot of women who look a lot like her . . .' she trailed off, hopeful.

He shook his head. 'No. What about . . . Amber or Stacey?' He described the tempting pair of young women with painstaking detail. The girl suddenly looked intensely pleased. 'I know Amber, of course. I will take you to her.'

He followed the child, excited. 'How come you beg on the streets, so young? Have you no family, no support?'

'No, Lord. My parents died of the plague this summer. I hope to weather the winter here in Salisbury. The Prior of Redfork sent me to the orphanage, but Mother Elsbeth sent me away. She said the orphanage was full.'

So this was why she looked familiar! 'When was this?'

'Just before she left on pilgrimage. Three or four weeks ago, if I remember it right. The Mother Superior said there may be an orphanage founded here in town, but I have heard nothing, and I have to eat.'

Steven nodded. He did not know what to say. He was overcome with shame. He fished in his purse for a gold mark and pressed it in her palm. 'Go and buy yourself a winter coat and some decent food.'

'Thank you, Lord!' Tears streamed down her face. 'You are a truly kind man, my Lord. God shall bless you!' She pointed directly ahead, at the smoky entryway to a pub. 'There she is, she is always in there after market day, conducting – conducting business.'

He glanced at the doorway. It was covered with a filthy tanned hide to keep the warmth in. Smoke and flickering firelight lent a hellish halo to the edges of the doorway. He glanced at the beaming orphan next to him. She beamed back at him, her young innocent smile a sacred white sword of pure cleansing within his soul. He turned around. The street behind him was empty, swept clean of refuse by the deluge of rain. Fresh cold clean droplets of water hit his face, tiny hammers of guilt and the hope of renewal.

'Amber! Come out! You have a visitor, a Lord!'

He gaped at the girl, making frantic motions to shut her up. 'No . . .' he mumbled.

She smiled at him. 'I said I would bring you to her. Well, here she is! Can I still have the two pennies?' She held out her dirty tiny hand.

He became aware that the hide had been pulled aside and a figure emerged into the cold. He raised his eyes slowly, dreading the insidious pull of the all-pervading lust that was sure to rise if he was subjected to temptation. The vague outline in the doorway cast a shadow on the street, the delectable curves of the whore's body casting a spell of filthy cravings.

Amber wore a long blue robe of fine wool. When she saw this splendidly clad new client, she smiled, a lazy inviting gesture of pleasures promised. She very slowly opened the folds of her robe, displaying her luscious naked body beneath. Her nipples were stiff in the cold of the early winter chill. She did not seem to have suffered much since her eviction from the town house. Her body was lush, perfect, slender. Steven could not seem to look away. He felt the little girl tug at his sleeves and he absently released the two pennies into her palm. She curtsied, the awkward feeble copy of the gesture she must have seen from some Lady in church or at market, and scurried off with a nod to Amber.

She smiled at him appraisingly. Her voice was a honeyed purr. 'My Lord . . . I am so glad you have sought me out. I can make you feel most comfortable . . .'

His breath was a foggy cloud coming out of his lips. He desired her body, but he was fighting the filthy, obscene impulse with every last remaining unsullied fibre of his being. He shook with physical need and spiritual conflict. Slowly, he turned around, wrenching his gaze from the delicious flesh before him. He faced the clean cold street behind the gorgeous redheaded whore and took a step, then another.

'My Lord! Where are you going? You just found me . . .' He heard Amber's high-heeled shoes crunch on the frozen mud as she moved to intercept him.

He launched into a desperate, shambling run. His body, once a finely toned instrument of monastic life, complained against the unusual demand. He had grown fat and indolent over endless weeks of luxury and fornication. Wheezing in the cold air, his face grew red with exertion.

A frozen lump of mud, no doubt a sending of Satan, tripped him. He checked his fall with his hands, but the damage was done. Steven heard the sounds of her approach as he struggled onto his back, trying to catch his breath before getting up. Amber stood right above his prone body. She let the folds of her robe part again, displaying her naked body beneath. She smoothly dropped to her knees before Steven's magnificent robe, her eyes locked on his bulging money purse. Her fingers instinctively sought out his member through the layers of his finery.

'Your cock is so hard, my Lord . . . I can't let you get away so easily when I am so obviously needed . . .' She smirked with triumph as his erection grew even harder in response to her torrid manipulation.

'Go away,' he whispered.

'Did you say something, my Lord?' cooed Amber. She freed his aching cock, lowering her painted lips around his member, taking his flesh inside her mouth. A sneer of recognition flitted across her pretty face, but she did not stop his debasement, not even for a moment of crooning victory. She expertly sucked his cock until his struggles faded in a red haze of hellbound pleasure. His mind stopped its hopeless resistance; he let himself sink low into the filth and mud of the street, allowing this pretty succubus free reign over his soul through the mindless drooling sceptre of his manhood. Once she was sure of his surrender, she took his cock out of her mouth.

'Friar Slut!' Her voice was a smirking demanding command, not a simple statement of recognition. He felt himself nod against his will. She stroked his bulging money purse with her hand. 'Stacey and Heather will be so happy to see you again, Friar Slut . . . So happy . . .' She giggled cruelly as she put her red-nailed fingers around his erect member. She forced him upright, leading the lust-crazed

Prior around by the leash of his member. 'This way, Friar Slut. It would not do to have you run off now.' Her ass swayed rhythmically, seductively as she walked on her high-heeled dancing shoes before him. Her fingers were an unbreakable vice around his cock and his will.

He followed her, numb. His entire being seemed centred around his member. She slid her hand up and down his shaft every few steps or so, keeping him properly erect, compliant and obedient. 'Good boy . . .' she sneered.

They passed by a matronly old woman delivering milk in clay pots. She chuckled derisively as she beheld the pathetic scene. This rich merchant was being led by the cock by a haughty painted whore! Steven barely saw the old woman – his life was his throbbing oozing cock and the touch of Amber's fingers around it. He was being walked on his meat-leash.

She led him down a seedy alley towards a smoky entryway. He squeezed in behind her. Inside, he saw a large room with a huge crudely fashioned bed. There was a hearth and a large chest. The chest was open – he could make out the characteristic texture and shape of lingerie within. Heather and Stacey were lying in bed, holding each other as they slept.

'Girls! Look who crawled in from the street, bearing a fat bag of silver!' She contemptuously tugged on his cock. He groaned as he fell forward onto his knees.

Heather stirred, then Stacey. Their eyes opened and focused on the corrupted monk kneeling on the floor. The brunette gasped with delight. 'Friar Slut! You look very . . . very . . .' She was looking for a word. Stacey finished the sentence for her, her eyes locked on his heavy money purse. 'Rich.'

'Yes. Rich.'

Amber pouted. 'He tried to run away after he found me.'

Stacey playfully twirled her blonde locks with one hand as she casually reclined on the bed, her long slender legs sliding against Heather's skin. 'Princess will not be pleased about that.'

Heather nodded. 'No. Princess will definitely not be

pleased about a lot of things. I hear you found a new playmate.'

Steven thought furiously. How much did they know? 'She. she is gone – I came to find you . . . to rescue Princess.'

'Why else would he have come back?' asked Stacey.

'He is horny,' giggled Amber. She playfully squeezed his balls with her fingers. He moaned with desire, moving into the filthy caress with abandon. 'You are a disgusting little piggy, Friar Slut.'

'Tell me why you looked for us, Prior Pussylicker.'

He thought of resisting for the flicker of an instant, but Amber's insistent mocking debasement of his member made resistance impossible.

'Princess . . . Princess asked me to find you, mistress Heather.' He closed his eyes, thinking of Stephanie's pink fingernails caressing his shaft.

The sultry brunette raised an eyebrow. 'Is that so? She is held in a cell within the Bishop's castle, I hear.'

'Yes. She told me you knew where there was a secret alcove within the town house, a place where you keep a barrel of apples. Inside the barrel . . .'

'Enough. I know of what you mean. I meant to go back when the opportunity presented itself, to save the jar, but the risk was too great. With that busybody little slut Laura Peabody always there, and the neighbours knowing our faces after our eviction, it was impossible to go back. Now . . . There must be a way. I am sick of this filthy little hut and these smelly men with their few scraped up silvers.' Heather prodded Steven's money purse with her high-heeled shoes. The gold within jingled with a characteristic rich full sound. Heather smiled. 'Ooh . . . now that's nice.'

The women looked at each other. Their faces were portraits of naked greed. Stacey captured Steven's eyes – she leaned over Heather's exposed womanhood and began to lick the brunette, slowly, never letting go of the Prior's trapped gaze. Heather moaned softly and parted her legs completely, permitting Stacey's tongue full reign over her sex. Amber stripped the monk of his finery, stroking his cock with one hand all at the same time. She finished by picking up the heavy money bag and emptying the torrent of gold upon the naked bodies of the other two young women. She slid in between the brunette and the blonde and tugged on the Prior's member, pulling the monk into the tangled mess of gold-covered heaving flesh by the contemptuous pull of his meat-leash.

'You want habits, my Lord? The same kind that nuns wear?' Garode stared at the Prior. He hated asking questions of his clients, particularly when the client spent enough gold at his shop to pay for a castle.

'Habits, yes.' Steven considered. 'But they need only be habits on the outside. Line them with silk and velvet. I want them soft, comfortable. And – and make them easy to take off.'

Garode bowed, his face carefully expressionless. He was not paid to have an opinion of his masters' tastes. 'Will the ladies come by for the fitting?'

'No. Send a man to the Peabody town house tonight – I will take him to the . . . ladies. I am sure they will not miss out on a fitting. And . . . keep this between us.'

'Of course, my Lord. When is Lady Wentworth coming back, if I may inquire?'

Steven sighed. 'I don't know . . . A few more days, I suspect.'

Garode nodded diplomatically. 'She is a young woman of exceptional taste.'

'Yes, she is,' he smiled sourly, recalling Garode's identical comment about Stephanie, seemingly years ago. 'Exceptional taste' in Garode's book meant the lady cost a fortune for the man paying her bills. The tailor had not said another word about Evelyn's father after he paid for those first three dresses and the hat. Steven wondered for a fleeting moment how the exquisite greedy little redhead explained away the torrent of clothes, shoes and jewellery she milked out of his thoroughly addicted, happy member.

The ball was at the castle of Prince Henry, celebrating the coming of age of his sister, the Princess Annabelle. Prince

Henry was the most eligible bachelor in the entire realm. He was not a direct heir to the throne, but he was close enough to make life at court a certainty for any woman of eligible birth who happened to catch his eye. As a result, all the maidens of the realm did their best to secure the friendship of his little sister. As the daughter of a minor noble, Evelyn did not rate an invitation – but Laura did by virtue of her title as Lady Peabody. She was pleased to be able to allow Evelyn to attend the social event of the decade. Evelyn's mother, a shrill demanding shrew of a woman named Molly, chaperoned the two women. At one time she had been a great beauty – the resemblance to her daughter was obvious. Her lips seemed set in a perpetual scowl, her eyes were blue and filled with a cold calculating gleam. She was pleased about her daughter mixing with the most powerful members of the nobility, but it obviously grated on her to be forced to accept Laura's company as the price of admission. The angry middle-aged woman did her best to ignore the tall girl. She sniffed pointedly every time Laura opened her mouth.

'Remember, Evelyn, to show as much of your bosom as you can while you are in his presence. Wear the pearl necklace you got the other day. It really shows off your skin.'

'Yes, mother.'

'There will be other rich men here. The Duke of Gloucester has a son . . . His name is Thomas. I hear he likes to drink. Keep his cup filled, if you have the chance. Do that for Prince Henry too, while we are at it. The Duke himself should be there as well.'

'He is married, mother.'

'His wife is not here, I hear. She is attending her father's sickbed in Normandy.'

'Yes, mother.'

'Annabelle likes books. Talk to her about books.'

'I don't know anything of books, mother. You said they were a waste of time.'

'I know many books!' Laura's smile disappeared at Molly's scowl.

'You just show some skin, sweetheart. Remember to giggle prettily when they tell you something.'

'Yes, mother.'

'Kindly . . . Try to keep out of the way, Lady Peabody.' Molly practically spat her title through clenched teeth. She glanced at Laura's dress, adorning a dummy in the corner of the room. 'Her dress is rather revealing, is it not?'

Laura was mortified – her dress was an epitome of fashion virtue compared to Evelyn's sleazy French silk creation.

'Don't worry, mum. I am the prettiest girl there is, don't you think?' She twirled to display her charms.

Laura sighed with barely disguised longing. She walked out of the room and stood in the anteroom, looking at the sparse decorations of the wool merchant's respectable stone house. In the solar, the conversation continued.

'Yes, yes, you are pleasant to look upon . . . You never know about men, though. Some men like brunettes, some like blondes . . . Not everyone has good taste like your father or Sir Warener.'

'You never told me why you did not marry him instead. You said he was so good looking.'

'He was a knight. Knights have no money at all, not unless they come from a good family. Warener did not come from money. Now stand still while I tighten that corset.'

Evelyn stood stock still while her mother carried out her painful labour.

'There. Now those tits of yours look proper.'

Evelyn looked down at her bosom – her chest was pushed up by the corset nearly to the point of spilling out. She could see where the alabaster of her skin turned pink at the nipples. 'Are you sure, mum?' she mumbled uneasily.

'Mum knows best, sweetheart.'

'Yes, mother.'

'Your father had a lot of money back then. I remember my trip to Paris . . . It was wonderful. I thought those days would never end . . .' Molly sighed. Her lips twitched with distaste. 'If you do not want to end up like I did, married to a poor loser, you do as I say and show some skin.'

'Yes, mother.'

'And keep that tall know-it-all away from the men. Some men like women who know their letters. Make sure the rich ones keep staring at your tits instead.'

'Yes, mother.'

'Good, then. Keep her in line, show some skin, keep Henry's cup filled with wine . . . and we will be at court in no time.' Mother and daughter looked at each other and smiled.

'You want me to wear what, Friar Sl–, I mean, Prior . . . Uh . . .' Stacey giggled. James was taking her measurements with a bit of string. Garode's apprentice did his job with complete professional detachment – he seemed utterly unmindful of the delightful flesh all around him. The other two women watched him work with interest.

They heard heavy footsteps approach the door, followed by strenuous knocking. Amber walked to the door and cracked it open. She spoke in a courteous, but firm tone. Steven could not make out any of the words, but he thought he had heard a deep voice express frustration, perhaps disappointment. The caller left. They had turned away several clients already, flush with Steven's gold. A huge tray of expensive sweetmeats and a jug of potent dark wine stood untouched on the table. The women were too pleased to eat.

Heather picked up a length of shimmering white damask. 'That is nice fabric for a habit's lining.' She caressed her own cheek with the cool material. 'So smooth and silky . . .' She glanced at Steven, softly purring in his ear. 'I won't even have to wear any undergarments . . .'

Amber overheard. She giggled. 'None of us will . . . we will be naked before God!'

'I can't wait to be back at the town house.' Heather hugged Steven, her hands caressing his arms from behind. She pressed her breasts against his back. 'We will reward you properly once we are inside . . .' she whispered in his ear.

He groaned with unmet unyielding need. His arousal was constant. Every time he caught a glance of Amber he was reminded of the time she rode him while he licked Stephanie's shoes. When Heather touched him, he remembered her tongue buried in Stephanie's sex, and the taste of her lips on his own thereafter. He had to take them back to the town house to get his reward, the sooner the better, so he could think. Their faces were well known by the neighbours – dressing them up as nuns labouring at the new orphanage was the only way to get them back inside. He turned to James.

'I need these as soon as possible. Tomorrow.'

James nodded. 'It will not be excellent work, my Lord.'

'It need not be excellent work for now. There will be time to fix them up later. I just want them useable tomorrow.'

'As you wish, my Lord.'

When James left with the measurements, he addressed the women. 'Now be careful – when we head out, don't talk to any of the neighbours. Master Tisdale was probably the one who started the rumours about the town house in the first place. He owns the town house on the other side of the street, so if we meet him, try to act . . . holy.'

Stacey wiggled her fingers, displaying the long useless nails, painted red. 'What about these?'

'Keep your hands inside the habits. If he says anything, say nothing. I will say you are under a vow of silence.'

Heather nodded with approval. 'That's a great idea. Good boy! We will keep our mouths shut around Master Tisdale.'

Amber giggled. 'What about Mistress Tisdale?'

Heather's full pretty lips twisted into a cold evil sneer. 'You are so right, Amber. Perhaps Master Tisdale needs to be taught a lesson.'

James bowed deeply as he delivered the garments. They were wrapped in clean linen. 'Free of charge, my Lord.'

'Excellent.' He tipped the man a silver penny. The package was sizable – three habits, lined in silk, and shoes to match. He had nearly left when he remembered something. Hurriedly, he raided the chapel, taking some rosaries and some small crucifixes. Without the sacraments, the disguises could not possibly work. He hesitated before he picked up the first rosary. Sacrilege! his old self screamed through the lust-riddled holes of his soul. Filthy passion rose within him, overriding the momentary attack of conscience.

He hurried to the Whores' Quarter. A pretty woman with sparkling brown eyes approached him, smiling broadly. She was sauntering across the street towards him when another whore, a red-lipped harlot with lustrous dark hair, pulled her back, whispering urgently and pointing in his direction. After several repetitions of this same scene, he concluded (correctly) that Heather and her gang had put a marker on him – he was not to be touched by anyone other than themselves.

He knocked on the door. He heard the characteristic sounds of high-heeled shoes on the floorboards.

He heard Heather's voice. 'Who is it?'

'Friar . . . Prior Steven.'

'Prior! Do come in!' She unbarred the door to allow him entry.

The women were careful to maintain a seductive pleasing appearance for his visits. They never looked anything but desirable in his presence. Always, they were clad in lingerie and high-heeled shoes, and adorned themselves with rouge and powders. This time was no exception. He looked at them with lust. With some regret, he spoke. 'I fear you must take off the lace and the high-heeled shoes. And wash the powder from your faces.'

Heather nodded. 'You heard him!'

The women scrubbed their faces and changed into the habits. Stacey giggled. 'I love the feel of silk against my titties.'

Heather frowned. 'Don't look too pleased or happy. And don't walk like you were looking for trouble, Amber. You look like you want to fuck the Bishop, not become a Bride of the Lord.'

Amber grinned. 'You know me too well, Heather.'

'So, you are all . . .' Steven glanced at their ringless

hands and sucked in his lips. '. . . novices at Elsbeth's convent. Just arrived from . . . London.'

'Why London?' asked Amber.

'London is big. Nobody wonders why they don't know you if you are from London.'

'True enough. Who leads?'

'I will lead. Walk behind me. Keep the rosaries in your hands. If someone talks to you, keep your eyes averted, at the rosary. Can you all pray?'

Amber blushed. 'Not really . . . just a couple of words.'

'Mumble something.'

Amber tugged at his robe. 'What about that idea about the vow of silence?'

'I forgot about that . . . that would be just a touch too unusual, I think. Let's keep it as normal looking as possible. When we get to the town house and we encounter Master Tisdale or someone else who can be trouble, then pretend you are under a vow of silence. Is that acceptable?'

Heather nodded. 'I think we all agree.'

He led them outside. A sultry young whore – Gail, he remembered from a conversation he had with Amber yesterday – gawked at them as they emerged from the doorway. Suddenly, she collapsed onto the muddy ground, holding her sides. Her shrieking gales of laughter echoed throughout the street.

Heather bristled. 'This is not good at all. She is going to ruin everything!'

Steven sighed and walked over to the guffawing young woman. He unlaced his purse and slipped a gold coin in his palm. He showed her the soft yellow gold. The silence was sudden and instantaneous. Steven's whisper was terse and to the point. 'You have seen nothing.'

Her gaze did not waver from the gold. She nodded.

He tossed the coin in the mud and resumed the long walk back to the town house, the women following closely behind him.

'Sisters, sisters! Please bless my son . . . His hand is broken!' A bedraggled woman was holding out a bawling miserable baby to Heather. Steven quickly stood in front of the women, making the sign of benediction. 'I promise to ask the sisters to pray for your son later, at the convent.'

The woman sobbed in gratitude. 'Thank you, holy father . . .'

Several more men and women asked for blessings on the street – they were satisfied with his blessings, none of them insisted on bothering the nuns, who all looked completely focused on communing with the Holy Spirit through the agency of their rosaries.

They turned into the street where the town house stood. Steven allowed himself a moment of delirious hope as they walked half the distance to the door without trouble. Perhaps Master Tisdale was not home. His hopes were dashed just as their small group reached the town house.

'Prior Steven!' Mistress Tisdale's voice reminded the Prior of Evelyn – but whereas Evelyn made up for her personality and shrill tone with other, extremely pleasant attributes, Mistress Tisdale was extremely disagreeable to look upon. Her nose was like a miniature squash, her eyes were a watery filthy grey, and her body, in general, resembled that of a corpulent walrus.

'Mistress Tisdale. Blessings of the Lord unto you.'

Mistress Tisdale nodded impatiently. She was never one for social pleasantries. 'Who are these?' She eyed the women with a peculiar type of fascination – as if they were some kind of a strange animal. 'Nuns!'

'Not quite, Mistress Tisdale. These are novices from Mother Elsbeth's convent. They are going to help me start up the orphanage here . . .'

Mistress Tisdale sniffed. 'Orphans? Here? On this street? Master Tisdale is not going to like that . . . Of course, I have nothing against having an orphanage in Salisbury, Prior Steven. Poor benighted creatures! Of course . . . does it have to be in this street?'

Steven frowned. 'What is wrong with this street?'

'These – "children." They are not from . . . good families, is that right?'

'They are from poor families, Mistress Tisdale, for the most part.'

'That's what I mean, Prior Steven. Couldn't you – couldn't you keep the poor ones in Redfork? Proper young ladies like that Evelyn Wentworth girl have my full support to school themselves under the tutelage of these . . . nuns, of course. These are the teachers?'

'Yes. They are the teachers.' Steven suppressed a frown. This woman seemed to know everything! She even knew Evelyn's name. Of course, calling Evelyn a proper young lady was just a touch more preposterous than calling Heather, Amber and Stacey novices in a convent.

Mistress Tisdale curtsied, an awkward disturbing motion that set the folds of fat on her body rolling. 'I never learned my letters.'

'They are under a vow of silence until classes begin.'

'Oh . . .' Mistress Tisdale looked disappointed.

'I will let you know when the first orphans arrive, Mistress Tisdale.'

'Please . . . Prior, let me send Master Tisdale over to discuss this with you. Does it have to be . . . An orphanage is such a *vulgar* place, isn't it?'

'Blessings of the Lord unto you, Mistress Tisdale.' He opened the door and ushered the 'nuns' in. He shielded the entryway with his body – even so, Mistress Tisdale made a valiant effort to catch a glimpse of the interior. He shut the door, slightly harder than he intended.

Heather lowered her rosary. 'That hag seriously needs to take up knitting or something.'

Steven wiped the sweat from his brow. 'She is a minor irritant compared to her husband. The man is a menace.'

'We need to keep them occupied or we can't play. I bet they are keeping a close eye on the town house.'

Amber frowned. 'Yes. How will we get food and wine and . . . pretty clothes . . . delivered?' She rubbed herself against Steven. 'You want us to look pretty, don't you, Friar Slut?'

Heather giggled. 'I think I can solve that problem, Amber. For now . . . I think Friar Slut deserves a small reward.' She led them into the solar. She sat on the couch and slowly unbuttoned the hidden buttons of her habit, exposing her long slender legs. She parted the fabric, teasing the addled monk with the view of her sex. 'Come here, puppy . . .' she cooed.

Steven's erection was a mindless stiff goad in between his legs. He found himself eagerly moving towards Heather's offering.

'Get on your knees, Friar Slut. Show me how you pray to pussy.'

He dropped to his knees. He felt himself drool as he leaned forward to begin the worship of Heather's brazenly exposed cunt. He felt the hands of Amber and Stacey on his robes, freeing his flesh from the confines of his sacred garment. One of the women began to manipulate his erection as his tongue lovingly explored every nook and cranny of the sultry brunette's womanhood. He moaned as his balls contracted.

'Wait.' Stacey giggled and cruelly halted her manipulation of his member. He groaned with unmet need, the frustration goading him to ever greater effort in between Heather's legs. The brunette writhed, softly moaning.

'Is he good, Heather?'

Heather panted, her legs wrapped around the pussy-crazed monk's face. 'He's had a lot of practice. Yes, he is good.'

'Let's take turns, then. I want him to lick my clit.'

'Me too.'

'Oh . . . all right. You may cum, Friar Slut, after you have pleasured us.' The women sat on the couch, giggling and conversing, while he crawled on his hands and knees in between them, pleasuring them with his tongue.

He carried beeswax candles in each hand. Candles like these were very dear – these were originally procured by Lord Peabody to be used during chapel services. Now, they would light his way as he looked for Stephanie's special drug. The cellar was a dark dank place. He has been here on numerous occasions, seeking the hidden alcove, all to no avail. The town house was large, and the cellar extended underneath the entire building. Heather was counting her steps.

'Seventeen, eighteen, nineteen, twenty . . . Here we go. Stop.'

He looked around with interest. He had been through this corridor before – it was dotted with alcoves, but all of them were empty.

Heather faced the wall. 'Bring the candles over here.'

She carefully examined the stone. 'One, two, three, four, five, six . . . Here it is.' She tapped on a brick. Now that he looked at it closely, it was obvious that this brick was considerably newer – or less dusty – than the other ones. 'Push that brick in, Friar Slut. I don't want to break a nail.'

He dripped some wax on the floor and affixed the candles onto the stone. When he pushed against the brick, it smoothly retracted into the stone and he heard a soft click. The entire stone façade pivoted inward, revealing gloomy darkness beyond. The smell of rotten apples wafted into the corridor.

'Tea or apples are best to cover up the smell.'

Heather motioned for him to go first. He picked up the candles and stepped inside. The only item within the small chamber was a barrel. The smell of apples emanated from there. 'This is it.'

He nodded. 'Yes, this is what Princess said. A barrel of apples. The drug should be inside.'

'It should be. Let's get it out.'

He began to toss apples out onto the stone floor. The apples were withered, but otherwise looked healthy. He raised one to take a bite.

'I wouldn't do that.'

'Why not?'

She simply picked one up and threw it full force against the wall. The fruit exploded on the stone. White maggots wriggled aimlessly on the floor, confused by the air and the light of the candles.

Steven felt a momentary pang of nausea. 'What are they?'

'Just maggots. Old apples.'

He nodded, but kept glancing back towards the disgusting creatures as he worked. To avoid having to touch any of the apples, he tore his robe and wrapped his hands in the coarse wool. Soon almost all of the apples littered the floor, forming a disgusting withered pile of rotten fruit. There was a large jar and a small jar inside the barrel. Strangely, the apples that surrounded it on the sides seemed completely healthy, glistening red and untouched by disease. He tried not to touch any of them. His appetite for apples seemed to have deserted him for life.

The large jar was round and immensely heavy. Lifting it was out of the question.

'Good enough, for now.' Heather reached inside and picked up the small jar. 'This, I will hold on to. You can take the large jar to the castle, to Sylvia.'

'What is in the small jar?'

'The same thing. The seal . . . It doesn't matter. Just get the big jar to Sylvia. She will know what to do.'

Heather knocked on the heavy door. An exhausted-looking boy in faded livery answered the call. He gaped as his mind absorbed the unusual scene before him – three nuns and a monk, with a tray!

'Kindly tell your master we have come to see him. I am Prior Steven of Redfork.'

'Yes, your eminence. I shall summon the Mistress right away.'

Steven glanced at Heather – this was not a part of the plan. He did not bother to correct the boy's confusion about his title. The boy bowed and went upstairs. Steven hissed to Heather. 'What do we do now? He was supposed to –'

'Prior Steven! It is so good of you to call! Such honour . . .' Mistress Tisdale's descending bulk blocked out the feeble sunlight coursing through the stairway. Her piggish eyes travelled from nun to nun, dismissing them. She focused on the tray like a falcon upon a sickly finch. 'What can we do for you, Prior? And . . . what have you brought? Such a pleasant surprise!'

Steven was not at all happy about this turn of events. 'Blessings of the Lord on your family, Mistress Tisdale.'

He tried to come up with a good exit strategy.' I heard – I was told by –'

'We made some sweets for your family. Is your husband home?' Heather's voice was stern, strict, matter of fact.

'Oh! I thought you were under a vow of silence!'

Heather's voice brooked no argument. 'Last night I fulfilled my sacred obligation.'

'Master Tisdale is out today. He will be back very late. Can I be of service?'

'We – I wished to ask him further about his concerns. Perhaps we will come back tomorrow.' Steven turned to face the door.

'I could not possibly let you leave with those sweets, Prior Steven! I insist you at least let me try some, so I can rave about them to my husband!' Mistress Tisdale put her pudgy hand on the tray. After a moment of frozen indecision, Amber let go of it.

Triumphant, Mistress Tisdale shoved a cookie in her mouth. 'MMmmmmph . . .' A single tear of pleasure escaped through the tightly pressed seal of her eyes. 'Heavenly!' she sighed, eyeing the rest of the tray with undisguised longing. 'I will hold on to this until Master Tisdale gets back.'

Steven's smile was strained. He felt like a little mouse inside a hungry weasel's cage. His voice formed an alloy of amusement and alarm. 'We must leave. *Now.*' He shepherded the women out. He did not relax until they were inside the town house and he had locked and barred the reinforced door.

'What happens now?'

Heather shrugged. 'I have no idea. It all depends on how many she eats.'

'What if she eats all of them?'

Amber began to giggle. Heather joined in, then Stacey. Soon, the women were practically rolling on the floor laughing.

'What is it?'

'Well . . . I wouldn't want to be Master Tisdale when he gets back . . .'

Nine

They took a coach to Prince Henry's castle. Molly talked non-stop from the moment they boarded.

'Remember – men like to see a little skin.'

'I know, mother. You've already told me that a hundred times today.'

'Don't you dare talk back to me. You will be properly grateful to your mother for bringing you up like this.'

'Yes . . . I know, mother.'

'Don't you take that tone with me, Little Miss Perfect. I can simply ask Lady Peabody to leave you behind.'

Laura stifled a groan. Suddenly she was Lady Peabody again? Evelyn's mother was an unpleasant disagreeable woman. She did not want her to drive a wedge between her and Evelyn.

'Oh, I would not leave you behind . . .' She smiled at the redhead.

'Thank you, Laura.' Evelyn leaned forward and planted a light kiss on the tall girl's lips.

Laura gasped slightly. She tasted so wonderful . . . All she wanted was to shove her tongue in the tiny redhead's mouth. Somehow, she managed to control the urge. Evelyn giggled, a gloating vapid sound, gently petting her head with a prettily manicured hand. Laura's eyes followed the movement of her fingers with unabashed longing.

Molly pointedly looked out of the coach's window, her lips locked in a condescending sneer. She watched her daughter's reflection in the dirty glass of the coach window. Evelyn smiled at Laura, resting her head on the tall girl's shoulder, whispering in her ear. She cruelly teased the helpless girl with constant insistent caresses. Molly pointedly did not turn around. Evelyn's vapid giggle and Laura's longing sighs were an acceptable price to pay for this golden opportunity.

She watched the reflection of her daughter's expert manipulation of the Peabody heiress. 'Remember what I told you, Evelyn.'

'Yes, mother.'

The driver made good time. By the end of the day, they had made it to the square adjoining the barbican of Prince Henry's castle. Many other coaches stood there. The passengers had already disembarked. Molly made it a point to come 'fashionably late'. The women waited until the bitter terrified old driver opened the doors for them. As Laura exited, she caught a glance of his eyes and she stopped in mid-stride. The man's blue eyes looked a perfect copy of the tiny redhead's. Could he be one of Evelyn's relatives? Perhaps a distant uncle . . . Her musings were cut short as the sheer size and majesty of Prince Henry's castle permeated her consciousness.

'It is enormous!' The redhead's voice lacked its usual shrill note of impatience. She stood before the barbican, jaw agape, gazing up at the cluster of towers, white parapets and countless colourful flying pennants.

'Stop gaping like a country bumpkin! Frederick, get your dau – get Lady Wentworth's things.'

Troubled, Laura opened her mouth to pose a question. Suddenly, Evelyn was in her arms, kissing her softly. She broke away just as it began to get interesting. 'I am so glad we are here . . . Thank you, Laura.'

Lady Peabody could not seem to remember the reason for her puzzlement. She smiled at the little redhead. 'Yes, Evelyn. I am glad I could bring you.'

A guard was looking them over. He had a large bristling moustache and thick black eyebrows. Slowly, he made his way over to them. He stopped when the two young women kissed, acquiring the most peculiar smile as he watched them. When they finished, he spoke: 'Tell your man to take your bags to the east tower. That is where Lady Annabelle's guests lodge. You are here for the ball, aye?'

Molly answered for her. 'Yes. They are here for the ball.'

'Names?'

Molly swallowed, the response squeezing past her lips like a bitter tight-lipped surrender. 'Lady Laura Peabody and . . . companion.'

Laura smiled at the guard. 'I am Lady Laura Peabody. This is my companion, the Lady Wentworth.'

The guard bowed. 'My Lady.' He turned to face Evelyn, that peculiar grin never leaving his face. 'You can find lodgings anywhere in the castle.'

Laura paled. 'I thought she would be allowed to lodge with me.'

The guard shrugged. 'Up to you. Most highborn ladies make do with Prince Henry's servants in the east tower.'

'I am no servant!' Evelyn shrieked, her body shaking with rage.

Molly simply slapped her, which calmed the hysterical redhead into stunned silence. 'Get a hold of yourself, Evelyn. Men don't marry hysterical women.'

Evelyn bit her lip and stared ahead, saying nothing.

Laura nervously smoothed her hair. 'I insist that my . . . Lady Companion be allowed to lodge with me. I am used to her company.'

The guard grinned wickedly. 'As your Ladyship commands. Follow me, then.'

The coachman and the girls followed the guard to the east tower. The old man was wheezing, having trouble with the heavy bags.

'You lazy oaf! Can't you move any faster?' Molly shoved at the coachman's struggling back. There were a lot of bags. To Laura, it seemed Evelyn brought a shoe for every occasion. When she asked her about it, the redhead laughed. 'Exactly. Exactly. I brought a shoe for every occasion. Didn't you?' After that, Laura stopped asking Evelyn about the contents of her heavy bags. Even with the shopping trip to Garode's, her own few dresses and shoes fitted in two modest leather satchels.

They made their way up the stairs, the old man dragging their heavy bags. Molly watched from the courtyard below, screaming out a continuous stream of instructions to the coachman. He tried to obey all of them at the same time, accidentally dropping a shoebox. One of Evelyn's favourite golden dancing shoes fell out onto some filthy rushes.

'You idiot oaf!' screamed Evelyn. 'Go and get it!'

The man's eyes were full of anguish. 'I am sorry, hon –'

'Lady Wentworth to you!'

He sighed and bowed, collecting her shoes. 'I humbly beg your forgiveness, your Ladyship.'

She nodded, satisfied, and giggled. 'That's better. Maybe I will talk to mother to let you eat at the table tonight.'

He thanked her with his eyes downcast.

Laura nervously smiled. Sometimes she thought Evelyn was unkind to others. But how could someone so beautiful be so cruel? Evelyn was just firm, it must be that. She glanced at the tiny redhead. Evelyn was patting down her glorious hair, making sure her elaborate hairdo was perfect before they entered the tower proper.

'You look beautiful.'

'I know,' she replied absently.

Laura lowered her eyes. She wished Evelyn sometimes acknowledged her a little bit more. Was she so ugly as to deserve no compliments at all? 'How do I look?'

'Fine. How are my shoes?'

Lady Peabody sighed. 'They look fine, Evelyn. You look gorgeous.'

'Then let's go in and break some hearts!' Evelyn walked up to the guards standing erect on either side of the tower gate. One of them glanced at Laura and smiled, not unkindly. It was only after she followed Evelyn inside the tower that Laura realised what the smile meant. The guard thought she was Evelyn's servant, and commiserated with her on having a harsh mistress! She sighed and caught up to the redhead. Evelyn was standing impatiently in front of a stern older woman in a nun's habit. The nun gave a perfunctory nod to the young women. 'Ladies. I am Mother Superior Danielle. Perhaps you have heard of me?'

‘I am afraid not, Mother Superior,’ answered Laura dutifully. Evelyn stifled a yawn.

The Mother Superior looked at her sharply. ‘I am responsible for the education of Princess Annabelle. Your names are . . .?’

‘I am Evelyn Wentworth.’

The nun frowned and scanned the parchment. ‘I don’t believe you have been invited to this ball, young lady.’

Laura spoke. ‘I am Lady Laura Peabody. Evelyn is my best friend and companion.’ She squeezed the redhead’s hand.

Mother Superior Danielle nodded curtly. She consulted the parchment. ‘Yes. Lady Peabody. My condolences over the death of your father,’ she sighed. ‘So be it. Keep in mind we keep . . . companions . . . on a short leash here.’ She glowered at Evelyn. ‘Keep your manners proper and your tone courteous at all times, young lady.’

‘Yes, Mother Superior.’ Evelyn’s voice could have frozen water.

The Mother Superior rang a hefty silver bell and in a moment a young woman in a maid’s smock curtsied before them. ‘Colleen will take you to your chambers. Will there be anything else?’

Laura shook her head. ‘No, Mother Superior. Thank you.’

Mother Danielle smiled. She gently petted Laura’s head. ‘Years ago, I knew your father. *You* –’ here she trailed off for a moment to give Evelyn a distrustful dubious eye ‘– look like a proper young lady, a credit to his memory.’

Laura felt herself begin to tear up. ‘Thank you so much.’

Evelyn put her hand on Laura’s. She softly caressed the tall girl’s skin with her fingertips. ‘Can we go to our chambers now?’

Laura’s breath caught in her throat. She blushed. What was she thinking about just now? Stammering, she took her leave of the Mother Superior. ‘Yes. Of course, we must go to our chambers. I am sorry, I am being inconsiderate.’ She hastily curtsied to the Mother Superior. Laura scrambled to catch up to Evelyn’s form as the redhead took the lead in following the maid through the corridors. Evelyn nearly ran into a tall handsome young Lord in a yellow and blue mantle. He was chasing a cat through the corridors. As the animal shot past the corner, he barrelled into Evelyn, knocking her to the ground.

'I am so sorry, Lady . . . Lady . . .'

Evelyn's purr could have come from the cat. She curtsied, bending low, her cleavage exposing her beautiful breasts. 'Evelyn Wentworth.'

The young man's eyes were riveted on the tiny redhead's brazenly displayed charms. He bowed. 'I am Prince George. Forgive me, I am sure we will meet again. I have to find Elizabeth's cat.'

Evelyn's former displeasure seemed to have evaporated as they took possession of their chambers. 'Did you see how he looked at me? I shall be a Lady before this ball is over, I tell you . . .' She picked up an elaborate silk corset and held it up against her body. 'Yes – this one should do just fine for tonight, I think . . .'

'You know he is engaged?'

Evelyn frowned. 'Yes. There is that. And he was chasing his betrothed's cat.' She chewed on her lip. 'I am not worried. Mum said I was too pretty not to turn the head of some rich young Lord. Think of it! Princess Evelyn!' She giggled. 'If George liked me, Henry will like me even more.'

Evelyn's petulant whine cut the silence of the sitting room like a shrill note in a gentle piece of music. 'When is Prince Henry going to visit?'

Laura blushed and lowered her eyes. 'I do not know, Evelyn.'

Princess Annabelle gave a strained but polite smile. 'He may visit later. Let us concentrate on the game, shall we?'

Evelyn looked down on the checkered board and sniffed. Laura looked up in dismay – the sound was an exact duplicate of her mother's. 'This is boring!'

'Well, it isn't like you are playing.' Princess Annabelle's companion, the pretty blonde bride of Prince George, the

Countess Elizabeth, looked at Evelyn with undisguised annoyance. 'If you are so bored, why don't you go somewhere and . . . and play with your dresses and shoes.'

Evelyn turned a pasty white. The sheer extent of pure rage seemed to overpower every attractive aspect of her features. She closed her eyes for a moment and breathed deeply. Very formally, she curtsied to Princess Annabelle. 'With your leave, your Grace.'

Annabelle seemed absorbed in the game. She nodded and waved absently.

Evelyn tugged at Laura's sleeve. Lady Peabody sighed and got ready to stand.

Without looking up from the board, the princess spoke. 'I really must insist you stay, Laura. At the very least, for this game and the next.'

Laura shot a look of desperation at Evelyn. She bowed her head. 'As you command, princess.'

The redhead nearly stomped her foot, then thought better of it. She slipped through the archway, her high-heeled shoes clicking against the stone floor. The moment she was out of sight, the countess exploded with undisguised mirth.

'Where did you find her, Laura?'

'Yes, do tell! Those shoes! And that dress!'

'And those manners! I kept waiting for you to give her a good dressing down.'

'She is a good friend . . . To be honest, she was the one who really wanted to come to your ball, princess. I was still in mourning. This was a way for her to attend.'

Annabelle smiled fondly and put her hand on Laura's arm. 'Please call me Annabelle. I think your servant – I mean lady companion – is only here to tempt eligible men in this castle. Show a man some skin and he loses all common sense.'

'Prince George is not like that.'

Annabelle chuckled. 'You are in love, Elizabeth. Not that there is anything wrong with that, of course. I could not have asked for a better sister-in-law.' She hugged the countess.

Laura smiled. She tried to push Evelyn out of her thoughts. Lately she could not seem to stop thinking about the redhead. Suddenly, Laura saw something previously unnoticed on the board.

'Check!' she cried triumphantly, moving her bishop.

'You are the best player I have ever played against.' Annabelle pondered her next move. 'Tell me, do you read?'

'Yes, of course. I used to have a large library at my father's castle and at the town house in Salisbury.'

'Splendid! Maybe we can go and read some stories later in my room.'

'That would be wonderful!' Laura was beaming. The princess thought she was good company! For the first time in weeks she stopped thinking about Evelyn. She would be able to talk about interesting things with Annabelle – something other than shoes and clothes and men. One day the redhead had caught her hiding in the attic with Homer's *Iliad*, in Greek. Evelyn was livid – she wanted a snack, and here Laura was letting her waste away while she read useless garbage in some stupid foreign tongue. Laura ended up begging for Evelyn's forgiveness and made her a snack, but the book disappeared shortly thereafter. She could not wait to see what books the princess had – now that all the books were sold off by her father's evil widow, she had nothing to think about other than Evelyn.

'Let us finish this game and we can go, then!' They played on – Laura was slightly better than Annabelle. After her second straight defeat, the princess leaned back in her chair and examined the Peabody heir. 'You are the most intelligent young woman I have ever met. Most women at court have no interest other than men and dancing.'

Laura smiled. 'Thank you so much, Princ – Annabelle.'

'My pleasure. I think I shall introduce you to my brother.'

Excited, Elizabeth clapped her hands. 'Oh, Annabelle, you don't think . . .'

'She is of a good family, a virgin, the ward of an honest good man.' Annabelle smiled. 'And she can play chess.'

Laura's face flushed a violent crimson. She lowered her head in shame.

'Do you think Henry will like her?'

'Only one way to tell.'

The princess rose and smartly let her dress brush against the figurines on the board. Her sadly outnumbered forces, along with Laura's superior legions of dark figurines, tumbled off the board.

Annabelle allowed herself a mischievous little titter. 'I suppose we will never know if you would have won this one.'

Laura sighed. 'I suppose not.' Such fool she had been! She could see Prince Henry's handsome loving countenance turn into a mask of disappointment and rage. In her mind, he screamed at her a thousand times, sneering as he turned down the offer of her unworthy sullied sex on their wedding night. Visions of the chopping block danced through her head. The queen, of course, would order her beheaded. She had wasted her irreplaceable purity on the sinful pleasures of a corrupt monk.

Annabelle confused her distress with anxiety. 'Fret later. I will be right back. Remain here and play a game with Elizabeth.'

The princess left the chamber. Laura tentatively stood as well. Anguish mixed with inexperience to create a powerful brew of desperation in her mind. Who could she confide in? Where was Evelyn? She needed to talk to Evelyn. Evelyn was her only friend in this world.

Elizabeth frowned. 'You heard the princess, Laura. Sit down and play! Of course, I am no worthy opponent. Annabelle beats me all the time.'

She smiled, distracted, and helped Elizabeth gather the spilled figurines. They began to play. Laura was so distracted that in no time at all Elizabeth acquired a significant advantage.

'You are trembling! He is not that handsome . . .' Elizabeth giggled. 'Check!'

Annabelle hurried through the doorway. Her face was beaming with pleasure, good-natured excitement shining from her eyes. 'Here they come!'

Henry walked through the door. Laura had seen him before, of course, striding through the hallways with a falcon on his arm. The prince was most fond of falconry. Inevitably, the tide of girlish giggles seemed to follow him around every nook and cranny of the east tower. Laura did not seek his company, but somehow still seemed to see his handsome silhouette nearby on a regular basis. Of course, of late, she had been spending a lot of time with Princess Annabelle – still, his presence had been a nearly unfathomable constant in the background.

He was so handsome! A long tangle of black hair framed a proud yet kind face. And those eyes . . . They were the bluest of blues, stars of the heavens above naturally red lips. Laura found herself smiling, her anguish momentarily forgotten. A tall, just as handsome young man stumbled into the women's chamber behind Prince Henry, similar in stature and countenance, just a touch taller, excited and possessed of a greater degree of youthful exuberance. Laura recognised Prince George. The tall handsome young man scanned the room, looking a touch disappointed. He absently waved to his betrothed, Elizabeth, who smiled back at him.

Princess Annabelle nodded in greeting. 'Laura, allow me to present my brothers, Prince Henry and Prince George. They have too many other names and titles to enumerate, and besides, they are not big on formality.'

Laura curtsied deeply. She smiled at the Prince and saw with pleasure that his face was becoming suffused with a soft crimson hue. He was blushing!

Annabelle noticed as well. 'You look like a fourteen-year-old boy with a crush, Henry.'

The Prince did not say anything. He kept smiling at Laura, his eyes soaking in her image. George rolled his eyes behind him. Annabelle cleared her throat. Finally, Henry bowed, deeply, and with a tone of absolute sincerity, spoke. His voice was heavy with suppressed emotion. 'Lady Peabody. I am very much pleased that you have chosen to accept my invitation and attend my sister's ball. You grace us – you honour me – with your delightful company.'

Had he been practising this? What was happening? Laura glanced at Annabelle – the princess was grinning like a Cheshire cat.

'Evelyn! Evelyn!' Laura burst through the door to their modest chambers.

The redhead sat in a high-backed chair. Her lips were tightly pressed together, locked in a peculiar angry scowl. Evelyn never seemed to do any needlepoint or reading – she was playing around now with a pretty gold bracelet, luxuriating in the play of candlelight on the rich yellow metal. A heavy jug of wine and a goblet stood on the dark oak table. Evelyn still wore the same revealing white lace dress that she wore earlier, while she attended Laura. Her breasts, always prominent, seemed ready to burst out at a moment's notice. With her narrow pretty waist and crushing corset, she was the definition of a perfect, even exaggerated hourglass shape. It was this dress, and Evelyn's customary high-heeled dancing shoes, that was the cause of so much good natured teasing by the princess and her ladies in waiting.

'I am sorry they chased you out, Evelyn. I could not leave, Annabelle ordered me not to go until I met the prince . . .'

She trailed off – if possible, Evelyn paled even more.

The redhead closed her eyes and breathed in deeply. Her voice rose in pitch with each word until she nearly spat out the last of them in shrill fury. 'So you abandoned me to be the laughing stock –' she sobbed '– the laughing stock! – of this castle so you could get your clutches around Prince Henry?'

'I wanted to come after you but the princess commanded me to stay . . .' Laura tried to take Evelyn's hand but the redhead shook off her touch.

'What do you want?'

'I am sorry, Evelyn. I will make it up to you, I promise . . . I am in trouble though and I really need a friend. Please help me!'

Evelyn drained the contents of her goblet and poured some more.

'How can a mere commoner like Evelyn Wentworth serve a great lady such as Lady Laura Peabody?' She drank again.

'Please, Evelyn. I need you! Prince Henry . . . I think Annabelle is trying to set me up with her brother. I think – I think he has taken a fancy to me.'

'Really?' The petulant drunken tone disappeared from Evelyn's voice, to be replaced by one of wakeful calculation.

'Yes . . . He said I honour him with my delightful company.'

'And here I thought he was following *me* around like a besotted puppy.' Evelyn bitterly tasted her cup. The sweet Madeira tasted like ashes in her mouth.

'What do I do, Evelyn? If he courts me . . . on the wedding night . . .' She blushed and finally broke down in tears.

The redhead sniffed loudly. 'Who cares? I can't believe I thought he fancied me . . .'

'I thought I could become a princess!' Great tears were streaming down Laura's face. 'I wanted you by my side, always, Evelyn, believe me! I would have asked the Queen to grant you lands and title, befitting the best and only true friend of her sister-in-law. I had so many stupid fantasies! But I have given it all up for this – for this dress!' Laura tugged at her sleeves in disgust. The delicate lace tore. Laura looked at it in horror and flung herself onto the bed, burying her face in the pillows.

'You would get me a title? And a position at court? Oh, Laura, I am sorry for yelling at you. You are my very best friend. I am sure we can figure something out . . .' Evelyn hopped onto the bed, softly stroking Laura's hair. She raised the brunette's head and moved it into her lap, slowly petting her. 'There . . . there . . . just calm down.'

'How can I be calm? He will know that I am not a virgin . . . And I will be beheaded!'

'Now you are just being silly. What do men know on their wedding night? Just be smart – get him drunk before he gets into bed and he will never know the difference. Men will never admit to not performing on their wedding night. When he wakes up just tell him he was great . . . He will lap it up.'

'How? I do not know what to do, Evelyn. I am no schemer.'

Evelyn giggled. 'Here. You will be Henry, I will be you. Drink this.' She passed her the goblet.

'Are you sure? Can't we just play this out without drinking?'

'You should feel the way he feels. You will be more confident about the whole night if you know just how out of control a drunken man can feel.'

'I suppose so.' She drained the whole goblet in a single motion. The wine was strong, clean, it went down into her belly where it spread quick tentacles of relaxing fire through her veins. 'It is very tasty.'

Evelyn nodded. 'I love Madeira. It is fortified somehow. It is much stronger than normal wine.' She poured more into the goblet. The wine nearly spilled there was so much of it. 'Make sure you overpour. Slip the cupbearer a gold mark and he will do the same before you retire to your bedchamber. That way, if he counts how many he had, he will still have had twice as much as what he can bear.'

'This is . . . Isn't this wrong?'

'You want to marry him, don't you?'

'Well . . . Yes. Who wouldn't?'

'Do as I say, then. Go on, drink up.' Evelyn pushed her goblet-holding hand towards her lips and Laura had to drink or the wine would have spilled.

'It really is tasty,' Laura smiled. She really did feel a lot more relaxed. Maybe she was panicking for no reason.

'So after he's had a few, he will want to feel you up. Don't worry about it – keep his eyes and his mind busy with some skin while you fill his cup.' Evelyn arched her back, exaggerating the swell of her breasts. She pulled down on the white lace until her nipples showed pink at the edge of the fabric.

'Go ahead . . . Prince Henry. Show me how you want to feel Laura's titties.' She giggled cruelly and pressed Laura's hands over the heaving flesh of her breasts. 'Drunk and randy, he will be helpless . . . he will fondle your tits. Go ahead, Laura – I mean, Prince Henry. Don't you want to play with my titties?' Laura felt lightheaded. She was touching her best friend's naked breasts, drunk . . . She had done it before and it was wrong – now she was doing it for her own good. This could not be evil. She began to massage Evelyn's tits.

The redhead smiled encouragingly. 'Now I pour more of the wine . . .' Evelyn poured and raised the cup to Laura's lips, tilting it.

Laura opened her lips, afraid it would spill. She swallowed each drop as the redhead emptied the goblet into her mouth. As if she had not even willed it, her fingers began to play with Evelyn's nipples.

'Yes . . . You are a good little boy . . . Play with pretty Eve – I mean, play with pretty Laura's firm titties.' The lace came undone and her breasts sprang free, filling Laura's hands with firm hot, luscious flesh.

'Now you kiss him . . .' Evelyn leaned forward and softly kissed Laura on the lips. She felt the redhead's tongue push into her mouth.

The wine made it easy to play. She felt herself responding to Evelyn's velvet tongue. Her sex became a wet hot place, eager for attention. She saw her own fingers slide around the redhead's gorgeous nipples, softly teasing, tugging, caressing. Her hands could not seem to stop the adoring finger worship of Evelyn's beautiful breasts.

'You see? He can't stop playing with your titties . . . Now you put his hand over your cunnie, to make him feel how wet you are.' She moved Laura's hand from her breast under her dress. Evelyn was so wet and hot, it felt like Laura had put her hand in a steam bath. 'That's it . . . Now you play with yourself, keep him interested . . .' The redhead leaned back and spread her legs wide, brazenly exposing her femininity. She slowly, softly manipulated her sex with thumb and forefinger. 'If he is not drinking . . . Use your free hand to pour more wine down his throat . . .' She picked up the jar and slowly began to pour it over Laura's head.

The brunette scrambled to catch every drop – she did not want to ruin the expensive dress completely with an ugly stain. Unlike Evelyn, she could not afford to replace it all the time. She did not feel like whoring herself out to the monk every single time she wanted a new dress. She sobbed as she realised she did not catch all of it. Sweet Spanish wine dribbled out of the corner of her mouth, dribbling down her face, staining the delicate white lace. The rest of the wine went down smoothly, warm and fiery at the same time, making her feel relaxed yet aroused.

'Yes, now he should be good and drunk . . .' Evelyn giggled, a vapid cruel sound. 'Now you make him nice and hard with your mouth.' She leaned down and raised Laura's dress until her head disappeared beneath her undergarment.

Laura gasped, all rational thought leaving her mind as the redhead's demanding mouth locked around her pussy lips. She could not stop her legs from moving as far apart from one another as possible, exposing her sex and her vulnerability to the vapid evil slut conducting her corruption. Evelyn's tongue was a skilful, honey-sweet tool of absolute persuasion, a beautiful wet file wearing away the Peabody heir's character.

Just as she was about to climax, the redhead emerged from beneath her dress and smoothly continued her demonstration. 'Once he is hard and unable to think . . . You hop on top of him and ride his cock. He will be too addled to realise you are not a virgin. Yell as if you were in pain and that's it.'

'I have never – never pleasured a man with my mouth.' Laura found it difficult to speak. She was so . . . so drunk, so aroused, so needy for attention *there* . . .

'You are joking. I don't even remember how many . . . Oh well. We will have to find someone for you to practise on.'

'I could never –'

'Do you want to be beheaded?'

'No – No. You really think it is that important?'

'I do.'

'Please . . . Evelyn . . . Can we – can we –'
The redhead smirked. 'Yes, Lady Peabody?'
'Can we finish please?'
'You want me to lick your cunnie, Laura?'
'Yes. Please. Please. I beg of you. Please lick my cunnie.'
'Well, you have to practise you know. I will lick you if you are a good girl and you practise on some cock.'
Laura moaned. The picture of the scene in her mind was so degrading, she never would have considered it sober. Now . . . Now it was not so much that it was wrong, it was that it made her even wetter. She wanted nothing more right then and there than to be Evelyn's debased toy slut.
'Yes. Please. Lick me. I beg of you. I beg of you.'
'Go play with yourself while I find you a playmate, Laura. Keep your eyes closed, I don't want to spoil the surprise.'
Laura obediently closed her eyes. Her hand was an obscene blur of shameless masturbation. The redhead tied a silk scarf around Laura's eyes. 'Now don't cheat . . . I don't want you to cheat, Laura.'
'I will not cheat,' Laura panted.
'Now, you need your hand to finger your cunnie . . . But you don't need both of them.'
Laura felt the redhead tie down her left hand to the headboard. 'What are you doing?'
'I just want to make sure you don't change your mind, sweetie . . . You don't mind, do you?'
'Please just come back quickly . . .' Laura was nearly crying with unmet need. She wanted Evelyn's tongue back on her clit. Her fingers were like dull sticks against her sex, so unlike the redhead's masterful pink instrument of pleasure-filled debasement. Even so, the Peabody heiress came close to cumming several times over the course of the next few minutes. She tugged on the rope binding her left hand – it was loose after a few tugs. She felt better knowing she could get away. A fresh wave of pleasure as her fingers found a new way to pleasure herself pushed thoughts of escape aside.
'Here she is.' Laura's eyes snapped open upon hearing Evelyn's voice, but the blindfold kept her from finding out

the identity of her new visitor. She felt Evelyn's familiar fingers on her clothes. In a moment, her sex was completely exposed. She could feel open air on her skin, mixed with the heat of the fire coming from the hearth. Evelyn's glorious hair brushed up against her stockinged legs as she lowered herself over her sex. The redhead giggled. 'Be a good girl and open your mouth, Lady Peabody.'

Laura was ashamed. Did she really want to do this? Suddenly she felt Evelyn's tongue deftly, insistently resume the manipulation of her sex. She moaned with wave upon wave of excruciating pleasure. Lady Laura Peabody put her free hand against the headboard, shoving her hand into the loose knot around her left hand, trapping herself completely. Her sopping wet sex rewarded her voluntary imprisonment with shuddering waves of intense pleasure. The tall solemn girl had become a writhing moaning vessel for the pleasures of the flesh imparted by the tongue of her harlot seductress. Laura's lips parted and stayed that way. She felt the touch of hot flesh against her lips, stiff, firm.

'Suck on it.' Evelyn's shrill voice was impossible to ignore. She knew the command was an obscene foul directive, but the sensations emanating through her trembling spasming clit made further analysis impossible. She clamped her lips around the shaft until the warm flesh of her mouth had it completely enveloped.

'She is a natural cocksucker.' Laura felt obscenely pleased at hearing the stranger's rough compliment. She moved her tongue up and down the shaft, teasing, caressing the man's flesh. He began to move his hips in response to her efforts, fucking her mouth slowly, then with increasing rapidity. He was breathing heavily.

Evelyn's tongue was replaced by her fingers. She was equally skilled with her hands – the wine-stained cocksucking heiress was no longer able to care what was being done to her, as long as the overwhelming demands of her womanhood were fully satisfied.

Evelyn laughed cruelly, her shrill contralto oozing with triumph. 'I knew I could turn you into a drunken little whore, Laura.' Her fingers continued the thorough manipulation of the girl with consummate skill. Laura felt hot cum fill her mouth just as her pussy spasmed with a mind-altering wave of explosive pleasure. Her lips slid off the man's spent cock and she fell back on the bed, exhausted yet still aroused. Her humiliating treatment by the vapid red-haired little slut only fuelled her sexual excitement.

Evelyn withdrew her finger from her soaked sex and pushed it in between her lips. 'Show me what you have learned, Laura . . .'

Lady Peabody began to suck on the redhead's finger as if it was a man's cock, licking her hand, her manicured useless fingernails, every digit that Evelyn chose to put in range of her questing tongue. Laura could not stop herself. Her sex seemed to have become the centre of her being. If sucking on Evelyn's fingers or a man's cock was the price she had to pay for satisfying her new all-consuming needs, she was willing to pay it.

Laura heard faint whispering. Why were they talking when her pussy was being ignored? She moaned with unmet need.

Lady Peabody heard Evelyn sneer. 'Yes. Bring him too. The more the merrier.'

Laura raised her head to ask what Evelyn meant by that, but the redhead's tongue and fingers swiftly resumed their teasing manipulation. The heiress fell back on the bed, the question a quickly forgotten useless thing amidst all this pleasure. She spread her legs as wide as she could, permitting full access to Evelyn's skilful caresses.

She panted. 'Please . . . Faster.'

'I will give it to you faster if you practise some more . . . You want to marry the prince, don't you?'

'Yes . . . Practise . . . Marry the prince . . .'

Another man's cock slid into the young woman's warm willing mouth. She sucked on the new member with relish, using all her newfound experience to pleasure her latest study subject. Laura felt Evelyn's tongue on her clit resume her debasement, the rewards coming faster, more insistent, more intense. She dutifully swallowed the man's seed when he finished. Almost immediately, another shaft entered her lips.

She curtsied to Annabelle when she entered the salon. The princess was surrounded by many of the ladies who had been invited to the ball. The princess was reading out loud from a book. Some of the ladies looked bored – they looked up with a flicker of interest upon her arrival. The princess finished the passage and realised they had a new visitor. She smiled, pleased, upon seeing Laura. Upon closer examination of her friend, she let out an audible gasp. 'Why, you look exhausted!'

'I am so sorry, princess. Please forgive me.'

'You are being uncharitable, Annabelle.' Elizabeth gently rebuked her friend. 'Her skin is practically glowing!'

The princess begrudgingly nodded. 'Not an entirely lost cause, perhaps.' Suddenly, she grinned. 'The first dance is tonight! I will help you get ready myself. You will have to . . . you have to knock my brother off his feet!' Annabelle was nearly exploding with joy at the prospect of having a sister-in-law of Laura's quality.

With fresh confidence, rooted in hours of fellatio, Laura smiled back. 'I hope so. He is very handsome.'

Steven yawned. It was past noon, but he had just awakened. He had a terrible headache, a reminder of last night's champagne-filled orgy. Was that a knock? Yes, that was definitely a knock on the front door. He sighed and put on his new silk robe. The three women sharing his bed did not move a muscle. Heather's eyes were open.

She yawned and stretched. The satin sheet covering her breasts fell off, exposing her firm pretty breasts. 'When you come back up, bring me some champagne for breakfast, Friar Slut.'

His retort died on his lips as the vision of her delectable naked flesh burned through his eyes. That godforsaken knocking! After a moment's reflection, he picked up the crumpled heap that was his monastic robe and donned it over the cool silk. A deliveryman bringing luxuries would have knocked on the servant's entrance. This may be a messenger from the Bishop. In that case, his breath . . . He picked up an onion from the bowl by the bedside and bit down on it, gagging on the sudden burst of foul taste.

He opened the door a crack, squinting in the sharp sunlight. 'Who is it?'

'Mistress Tisdale, my Lord Prior.' The fat woman from across the street wore a most peculiar expression. It was best described as a mixture of satisfaction and unmet craving.

'Blessings of the Lord upon you, Mistress Tisdale. What – what brings you here today?'

'I just wanted to say I really . . . I mean, we really enjoyed those sweets you brought us the other day.'

'Ah. Yes. Of course. I am . . . I will tell the Sister Heather, she will be so pleased.'

'Is – is Sister Heather in?'

'She is . . .' He searched his mind for a suitable activity. 'She is at Mass.'

They stared at one another. He could see the question forming on her lips. He pre-empted her. 'I am not going to Mass today – not feeling well. I decided to stay in my cell, fasting and praying.'

She sniffed loudly. He was confused for a moment until he realised she was smelling the onion on his breath – the irritating fat nag thought he was breaking his fast with an onion! He nearly chuckled.

'Please tell Sister Heather I loved those sweets.' Her vast bulk shook with unabashed yearning. 'Please tell her we would be – we would be delighted to make a generous contribution to the orphanage if she would . . . Well, just please tell her we liked the sweets.'

'How is Master Tisdale? I have not seen him in a while.'

'He should recover . . . I mean, he is fine.'

Steven suppressed a grin. 'I will have Heather come by with a tray after Mass.'

'Thank you, Prior!'

'Can I have the honour of this dance, my Lady?' Henry bowed deeply. When he straightened up, his face was a scant foot away from her own.

She blushed but managed not to stammer. 'I am honoured, Your Grace.'

'Please – call me Henry.'

She swept past other ladies in waiting. None of them were dancing – they were waiting for the first couple. Laura realised they were waiting on Henry and her! The unusual situation filled her with a sense of power. She smiled at her handsome prince and softly spoke his name. 'Henry. Henry . . .'

He smiled back, enchanted with her obvious relish of his name. 'Laura. Laura . . .' She nearly fainted as he returned her unspoken compliment. When they began to dance, other couples formed up beside them.

'You dance very well, Henry.'

'Mother hired the best tutors from the continent. She said dancing was as important for a gentleman as good manners were for a young lady.'

Laura smiled. As they danced past one of the guards manning the entryway to the great hall, the man's lips twisted into a toothsome grin. Could the man have been staring at her bosom? She was confused for a moment, then dismissed the incident as a trick of her imagination. Henry led her past the archway.

More and more of the eligible ladies were asked to dance by the young men in attendance. Nearly all the young gentry of the neighbouring counties attended the ball. Only a few girls were not attracting attention. There were a few of these at every social event, unfortunately. Laura always felt sorry for them – this time, however, she was just too happy to pay attention to the poor or the untitled.

A subtle, yet powerful circle of repulsion seemed to surround Evelyn. The other ladies did not seek her company, and the men did not ask her to dance, despite the obvious attraction she engendered in a number of them. The most powerful reaction she had been able to observe were in some of the women – they glanced at her cleavage and her shoes and whispered amongst themselves, frequently giggling. She felt like an outcast. After an hour of this torture she tried to catch Laura's eye.

The Peabody heir, with her hair all done up by the princess herself, was dancing the night away with her handsome prince, ignoring the plight of her best friend.

Evelyn sobbed. This was so unfair!

She saw the princess smiling at her brother as he danced past. Annabelle and her cronies, led by that bitch Elizabeth, were hogging the most eligible young men. She could not even get close to them without drawing the baleful eye of that irritating hag in the nun's habit. Mother Superior Danielle seemed to take a special delight in keeping a watchful eye on Evelyn.

She decided she was going to ask the princess straight out if she could join them. It did not matter if she did not speak about stupid things like books or old things. She could just stand there, next to the princess, looking fabulous. Perhaps some of the men would associate her with the other high-born ladies. She felt confident that once one of them developed an interest, she could fan his passion more than adequately. Evelyn faded from Danielle's hawklike gaze into the shadows in the back of the ballroom, and made her way to the cluster of high-born femininity at the other end.

She saw the back of the princess. Elizabeth was talking to her. Evelyn was just about to walk in front of the princess and curtsy, when she froze. Did she just hear her own name? She stepped back and listened carefully.

'Absolutely not, Elizabeth. I love Laura, but I am confident Mother would never accept a common tart like her – not even as a common servant, and definitely not as a lady-in-waiting.'

'I am so pleased you agree with me. The first time I saw that Evelyn woman I was certain she was nothing more than some tramp looking for a good match.'

'It is so unusual for a lady of obvious breeding to keep such a companion.'

'Yes . . . I thought about that. Perhaps she is doing it out of charity.'

Evelyn was mortified – she retreated from the ballroom unseen. When she got to their chamber, she threw herself on the bed, weeping. Slowly but surely her anguish gave way to rage. She began to strike the goosedown pillow with both fists. Her face was a mask of demonic rage.

'Here, I brought you some more wine.' The redhead pressed the jug into her hand, plopping herself down on the bed, next to Laura's exhausted form. Lady Peabody had not deigned to return to their joint chamber until past midnight. She was ecstatic.

'He said he was taken with me! He said I was enchanting!' Laura did not notice the tearful smudges below Evelyn's eyes. 'He said I was the most beautiful maiden he has ever seen!' She twirled around, curtsying to an invisible queen. 'It is an honour just to be here, Your Majesty!'

Evelyn pressed her lips together, smiling as if she had just eaten a lemon. 'I am so very happy for you, Laura.'

This was hours ago. Since then Evelyn had kept the Peabody heir well lubricated. Laura finally passed out around dawn, brought to an exhausted drunken climax by Evelyn's skilful soft lips and tongue.

Laura smiled weakly. She did not feel like drinking. She turned to the bedstand, to point out to Evelyn that she still had a full jug. Lifting the glazed blue pot, she found it empty. Had she drunk it all already?

'You will feel better if you drink some more. It is the only way to keep yourself from getting sick.'

'Thank you, Evelyn. You are such a good friend!' Sobbing, she hugged the redhead. 'I love you!'

Evelyn giggled, petting the confused tipsy heiress. She cooed in her ear as her fingers massaged the tall orphan's shoulders. 'I love you too, sweetie.'

Laura closed her eyes, enjoying the touch of her fingers. She gasped each time Evelyn came near a sensitive area. When the redhead stood, Lady Peabody let out a disappointed moan of frustration.

'Evelyn . . . Please . . . Will you, will you play with me now?'

'You are such an insatiable little slut, Laura.'

'I am so sorry! I – I can't help it.'

'Well, if you practise on some cock first . . . I will think about it. I only have your best interest at heart, you know.'

'If you think so . . .' Laura was uncertain. She felt quite confident she had the skill down pat.

'Just one more time. Go on, drink up . . .' Evelyn put the blindfold on the tipsy Peabody heir. 'Now no peeking!'

'No peeking.'

'I will be right back. Remember, no matter what, you must make him cum.'

'I promise to make him cum.'

Evelyn glanced back at Laura. The drunken lingerie-clad slut on the bed bore little resemblance to the solemn book-loving young lady who had arrived at the castle a few days ago. The first guard had already arrived, grinning at Evelyn as he made his way into their bedchamber. She held out her pretty hand. He gave her a silver penny in the doorway. The tall man was busy already, freeing his erect cock, getting himself ready for his session.

The redheaded little madame tapped him on the shoulder. Her whisper was a warning hiss. 'Remember, you don't know me.'

He nodded, grinning. 'Know who?'

Evelyn glanced into the hallway. More guards were arriving. She softly tongued Laura's quivering, helpless clit until she was confident the Peabody heir was thoroughly infused with lust. The redhead pulled Laura's hand from the headboard to her sex, leading her fingertips to her secret place. 'Go on. Laura. Go on . . . It feels so good to rub yourself. Play with little clitty.'

Laura moaned, obeying her friend. She felt a nameless obscene craving as her clit was stimulated. Every time she was allowed to climax over the last two days, she had a cock in her mouth. She licked her lips, eager for more. She was conditioned to feel pleasure now with each act of fellatio. Laura began to pleasure the first man who stood in the line.

Evelyn found Princess Annabelle in the great hall, playing the harpsichord with Elizabeth. Perfect!

Annabelle looked at her with a mixture of distaste and delight. 'Ah . . . It's you. Evelyn, where is your mistre – I mean, where is Laura? I was hoping for a long talk about the *Iliad*.'

Elizabeth giggled. 'Oh, Annabelle, you really are too much! What will you do when Henry marries her? He might want to be alone with her, once in a while.'

Annabelle smiled at the countess. 'Really, Laura is most delightful company! I so hope Henry will continue to favour her!'

Evelyn squeezed her eyes shut and thought of all the dresses and shoes she was missing out on by not being at the town house, milking the monk. Sure enough, a trickle of tears graced her eyes, startling the high-born ladies, stemming from such unexpected source.

Both of the high ladies exhibited signs of concern and surprise. 'Evelyn, what is wrong?'

'I fear I must do what is right, even though it pains me, both personally and in a dire, more material sense. My very livelihood, I fear, shall be in jeopardy after tonight.'

The princess looked worried, yet intrigued. 'What do you mean? Sit and tell us what troubles you!'

Evelyn broke down in tears. 'I fear my situation with Lady Peabody shall be no more by the end of the day. She will no longer desire my companionship after she learns of my . . . betrayal of her peculiar appetites. I am really at her mercy, both financially and socially. If I had a title as well, of course, this would not be the case . . . I . . .'

'What are you talking about?' Annabelle was simply stunned. 'What do you mean by "peculiar appetites"?'

'I – I know his Grace your brother fancies Lady Peabody. I was hoping she would not act in her . . . customary fashion after learning of his regard, but . . . I am so sorry.'

'I am not sure what you are intimating . . . Peculiar appetites? Customary fashion?' Annabelle shot a perplexed look at Elizabeth. The countess shrugged. She appeared fascinated by the unexpected news, a noble hound suddenly attracted to juicy rotten meat.

'I am sorry – I cannot bear to talk about it. It is a foul, disturbing and obscene . . . thing.' Evelyn flung herself against the princess, burying her face in her skirt. Her voice was a muffled tearful sob. 'I am not even allowed to wear respectable clothes . . . or talk in a manner befitting a lady. Lady Peabody made it clear she would dismiss me if I upstaged her.' Evelyn raised her head, looking terrified. 'I have said too much – what have I done? When she finds out –'

'I can see you find it difficult to talk. If what you intimate – if what I think you intimate – is true, rest assured I will see to securing a proper situation for you.'

Evelyn nodded, smiling sadly. 'I shall be eternally grateful, princess. I cannot bear to stomach the sight of another . . . session. Please come with me. I will stay in the hallway, out of sight, if that would be all right – I have seen her in one of these moods before. If she finds out about my betrayal, my life could be in danger!'

Ten

Heather shook him awake. 'You have a visitor, Friar Slut.'

He gaped. 'Who is it?'

'I am not sure . . . But does a five foot tall slut with blue eyes and long red hair strike a bell?'

Stacey frowned with distaste. 'Look at his cock, Heather. He is practically oozing at the tip. She must be a special friend.'

'You won't forget us, will you, Friar Slut?' Amber wrapped her hand around his cock and tugged on it. 'I don't want you to run off now . . .'

He trembled with impatience. 'No . . . I won't.'

He ran downstairs, putting on his silk slippers and his new brocade robe on the staircase. He hurriedly unbarred the door. A breeze of jasmine scent entered the anteroom, a whirlwind of tiny white flowers.

'Daddy Steven!' Evelyn threw her arms around Steven. She was wearing one of the dresses he bought her at Garode's – the black one with the bare shoulders and the long transparent lace gloves. Her corseted waist was as thin as ever. She arched her feet, displaying new high-heeled dancing shoes. 'You like, Daddy Steven?'

'Uh . . . yes.' With those long red curls down to her bottom and her large, nearly naked tits pushed up in the tightly laced corset, she looked like a tawdry little fuck-doll. He wanted to ride her until she squealed for mercy.

'Lady Evelyn Wentworth,' she giggled. 'I am Lady Evelyn Wentworth!' She performed a full spin, displaying her luxurious blue silk robe in the scant torchlight of the antechamber. 'Will you not ask me to come in?'

'Of course. Please come in.' He opened the door to Lord Peabody's den. He did not want to expose the exquisite little redhead to the coterie of demanding pretty young women servicing him upstairs – at least, not yet. There was a comfortable couch in the den, some books – although Stephanie had sold most of the elaborate library by the time Warener's men evicted her – and his fancy new belt, bulging money purse attached, resting on a peg in the wall. He sat down in the stuffed leather armchair.

'Miss me?' she giggled, looking like she knew the answer but was just asking to be polite.

'Yes,' he said, tightly. 'Where is Laura? What do you mean Lady Evelyn Wentworth?'

'She could not make it,' she giggled. 'I don't think she will be coming by anytime soon to make a claim on her inheritance.'

'What do you mean?'

'Seems she really became obsessed with sucking cock . . .' Evelyn giggled. 'She was caught fornicating with a group of soldiers, just when it looked like Prince Henry really took a shining to her, too. When Princess Annabelle saw her sucking off her personal guard . . .' Evelyn giggled. 'Her brother withdrew his suit. It is such a scandal! The Queen could not possibly allow her son to get involved with a sullied whore like her. They just had to find someone more suitable to assume her title.' She straightened her fingers and studied her long red fingernails.

Steven shook his head to clear away the cobwebs. 'Lady – Lady Evelyn?'

'Lady Evelyn Wentworth!' she sighed happily.

'So where is she now?'

'She has been sent to the continent, to the convent at Saint Denis. Princess Annabelle was practically devastated . . . I told the Laura woman that she should take the sacred vows and become a nun. It is really all she can hope for, now. To think that she was like a sister to me! I've even tried to help her appeal to Prince Henry . . . to think of the damage she may have caused my reputation . . .'

His eyes devoured her perfect little body. She mockingly covered her brazen cleavage with her hands. 'Are you staring at my titties again, Prior Steven? So unbecoming of a man of God such as yourself . . .'

Her voice became needy, petulant. 'Princess Annabelle was duly grateful for saving her brother from a fate worse than death. She and I have become the best of friends! Now, her new wardrobe is so much better than those ugly plain things she used to wear when she was still friends with that slut Elizabeth. The princess is holding a ball for me in a few weeks, to celebrate my entry into society.'

Steven gaped. All this was a little too much to absorb right away. 'Your entry into society?'

'Why, yes, of course. I cannot possibly attend my own ball in these rags, of course. I will also need a suitable coach, footmen . . . Many new dresses . . . I think this new Parisian silk dress should be a good start.' She planted herself in his lap, her cascading red curls a scented tangle over his tonsured head. 'It just arrived at Garode's . . . the red silk really shows off my tits.' She peeled off the top of her dress until her young firm breasts were exposed, right in Steven's face. She smiled cruelly. 'They practically spill out of the red silk, like this. Only fifty gold –'

'I want to stick my cock inside of you,' he said, his dick practically talking with his mouth. He had to have this little bitch no matter the cost.

She pouted. 'We discussed this so many times . . . I can suck on your cock . . .' She moved closer, running her perfect little hand over his erection. 'Daddy Steven likes it when I suck on his big hard cock . . .'

'No,' he gasped. 'Not this time. I want to fuck you.'

She giggled, her greedy eyes locked on his bulging money purse. 'I am a Lady now . . . I have to spend money to befit my station. A hundred gold; but not in the cunnie.'

His heart nearly burst from his chest as he shoved the purse into her demanding hands. His trembling fingers made short work of his robes, baring his more than ready member.

The redhead softly purred, nibbling on his ear. 'Why don't I make your cock nice and wet so you can just slide it into my ass?'

He nodded numbly as she took possession of his manhood and the tattered sullied remnants of his will yet again.

When he could not be any harder, she let go and scrambled onto all fours before him, her ass swaying seductively from side to side. She did not let go of the stuffed money purse, practically fondling the heavy pouch with her pretty fingers. 'Use some of those lubricants. From one of the untouched jars.'

He obeyed her with alacrity, eager to engage in the obscene pleasures he purchased.

When she was satisfied with the level of lubrication, she giggled and wriggled her perfect round bottom. 'Go on, little Stevie. Shove your big fat cock in my pretty tight ass.'

It took several tries – she was indeed as tight as advertised. He nearly fainted with heart palpitations each time his shaft slid into her more and more compliant anus.

Steven sighed. 'Her father would have been so disappointed. Such is the corrupting power of the flesh – even a young woman of . . . *seeming* quality, such as Laura Peabody, is not exempt from the taint.'

John nodded. 'I agree, milord. I even heard she charged for her sessions.'

They were sitting in the Master Merchant's solar. Two jugs of heavy Bordeaux, by now largely empty, adorned the table. The Prior drained his goblet. John politely wet his lips.

Steven broke the silence. 'Now that she has been stripped of the title and is a novice at Saint Denise she is not going to make a claim upon the estate.'

John nodded. 'Highly unlikely, milord.'

'To meet some unexpected expenses of the Priory, I am considering the sale of these assets.'

'I fear an outright sale may not be possible, milord. Technically, she is still within her rights to make a claim, despite her . . . fall from grace.'

Steven was disappointed. He spoke empathetically. 'Yes, of course . . . Then again, her sin was so great – as a man of God I have seen many similar cases – I do not believe true contrition is possible.'

John politely nodded and poured more wine in the monk's goblet. He looked into the dancing flames of the hearth. He smiled gently. 'I may be of service even without an outright sale.'

'Do tell, Master John.' The Prior pulled his chair closer towards the merrily burning hearth and the merchant sitting in front of it, his attention piqued.

'You hold the rights to the income of the castle and the lands, subject to a future claim by the heir. Sell me those. If she never makes a claim, I should have made a very good deal. If she makes a claim, I shall be a pauper and you can laugh in your cups when you think of that poor fool John of Salisbury. Obviously, I cannot offer as much in this manner, but it would still be a very respectable sum.'

John named a figure and left while the Prior pondered the offer. It was indeed a paltry offer for a castle and all that land, but still a huge sum nonetheless. His fingers twitched greedily as he thought of all that gold, all the rewards. The Prior stroked the majestic coin purse, sadly light, empty of treasure. With inevitable finality, the chest of gold from the sale of the Flanders accounts had been exhausted, plundered on luxuries and gifts for the exquisite tiny redhead.

John bowed silently as he set the Priory seal on the parchment. The income from the Peabody castle and lands now belonged to the merchant. Steven grinned as he watched Michael load the huge dark chest of ironwood in the foyer of John's mansion. Sack after sack of gold filled the chest, a sizable fortune. He picked one up, dipping his hands deep inside, luxuriating in the feel of the cold coins against his palm. He poured the soft yellow gold into his empty ever-hungry beautiful purse.

Steven simply asked for Sylvia in the kitchens, describing her ample bosom with his hands. A fat red-faced baker sighed as he nodded in recognition. 'Aye – I know her. She is a handful, she is. I will send her up to your chamber.' He grinned lasciviously.

Sure enough, within the hour she arrived. She wore the colours of the diocese, purple and white. In her hand she carried an empty bucket and a rag. Her livery only seemed to have shrunk during his absence. His eyes shamefully lingered over her delicious breasts.

'Prior Steven.' She curtsied.

'I have something for you.'

She giggled, her tits shaking in her slutty shift. 'Another laundry job?' she asked with an evil smile.

He shook his head, rolling the jar out from underneath the cot. It was just as heavy outside the barrel. She gaped. 'Is that – is that what I think it is?' her eyes were huge.

'Heather seemed to think so.' He stopped to think for a moment. The bitchy brunette did not open the seal on this jar. She took the small jar – why? Was there something special about this pot?

He sighed. 'There is only one way to tell.' He paused with his hand over the wax seal. It was thick hardened red wax with the symbol of a slithering serpent in the centre. He took the crucifix off the wall and pried the seal off, using the Lord's foot and the cross as a lever and a crowbar. The stench of sweet resin filled the small chamber. There was a hundred times more of the sweet stuff – no, maybe a thousand times – than what he had at the convent. He breathed in deeply – his erection throbbed painfully against his robe.

Sylvia whimpered softly, her eyes fixed on the open pot. She put her finger into the thick heavy grease and put her stained digit in between her lips. A soft sob of recognition escaped her mouth. She dropped to her hands and knees. 'Fuck Sylvie,' she begged, her immense tits springing free of the livery's overly tight confinement.

He mounted her. Her pussy was dripping wet. He fucked the serving wench with frantic mindless passion, his erection and his desire mercilessly constant even after his second orgasm. His robe was covered in drops of semen. The air seemed saturated with a cloying insistent sweetness.

'Fucky fucky,' moaned Sylvia. 'More fucky.' She slipped off his member and pushed him on the floor. She sat on his face, grinding her curvy round bottom into his lips while emitting a low obscene moan.

Steven felt her bend down, her huge tits pushing against his stomach as her lips wrapped around his cock. His balls contracted – again – and he finally felt himself soften a touch with his third orgasm. He scrambled out from underneath her moaning thrashing body and covered the sweet stinking jar with Sylvia's bucket. As the sweet smell receded, the desire did not fade – it just became slightly manageable.

She finally managed to sit up. Her eyes were dazed. 'We fuck later?' she asked, her voice pleading.

He wiped the sweat from his forehead. 'Later. Well, we now know this is the stuff, that is for sure.'

Sylvia got off the floor and pulled up her shift. She stuffed her melon-sized tits into the garment, fondling her nipples during the whole process. 'I have to get the Bishop to taste this stuff, at least a couple of times. Does he drink?'

'Boiled water only.'

Sylvia frowned. 'You can't put this in boiled water without making it cloudy and sweet.'

'Wait – before we talk about Warener any further . . . We need to split in half what is in this pot.'

'Split it?' She looked wary. 'Why?'

'I want to send some to the convent. Princess will need it if we – if we fail with Warener . . . and I have someone – maybe more than one – that I can trust who will help her when she arrives.'

'How will we handle this stuff? I really want your cock now, Prior Steven, even with the stuff covered by the bucket.'

He pondered. 'Let's cover our noses and mouths with cloth. I will buy a new robe later – we will use strips of cloth from this one.' He tore long strips from the monastic robe, handing them to the promiscuous serving wench.

She nodded. With practised ease she made herself presentable. 'I will be right back.' Sylvia went into the

Cathedral. She looked around – the nave was empty. She furtively dipped the strips into the baptismal pool. The fresh cum stains on the wool clouded the clear water. She rolled up the strips and hid them in between her breasts. The cloth felt moist and cool against her hot flesh. Her nipples hardened as she luxuriated in the sensation of holy water on her luscious tits.

Steven's wait for Sylvia was pure torture. The air in the small cell was thick with the sweet smell of sin and sex. He desperately wanted to pleasure himself, but someone could come by and he did not want to take the risk. Finally, he heard a furtive knock on the door. Sylvia's whisper came as an immense relief.

She came in brandishing the wet strips. 'Here they are.'

Steven took his time – his eyes roved over the buxom wench's wet tits, her full erect nipples, plainly visible through the thin fabric of her shift. He finally accepted the offered cloth and tied it around his nose and mouth. Sylvia did the same. As an afterthought, they used some of the cloth on their hands as well, impromptu gloves to protect their exposed skin. They heaped roughly half the thick resinous grease into Sylvia's bucket and covered it up with her rag. Even so, he was sorely tempted to fondle Sylvia's tits during the procedure – he could tell she was thinking the same thing as well. 'Take what's in the bucket. I will keep the pot.'

Sylvia nodded. 'I will think of a way to get to Warener.'

'I think we are done, then.'

'Not yet.' She grabbed his hand and shoved it beneath her shift. She was dripping wet. 'Fucky fucky . . .'

Another week passed. Steven was getting extremely concerned. Bougric was still coming and they had not been able to drug the Bishop. The irritating dullard only drank boiled water; he only ate the simplest of foods, without sweeteners of any kind. The Bishop was intensely paranoid about being poisoned, and used a regular food taster as a matter of course. Adding insult to injury, Warener halted the regular confessions. 'She had her chances. Nobody takes a week to confess their sins, regardless of the extent of their wickedness.'

'Yes, my Lord Bishop,' Steven said meekly.

'You say she is contrite, huh?' The Bishop picked up the sketch of the Virgin. 'This is certainly a powerful picture. Well, we will see how much rapture she is in after Bougric is through with her.'

'Yes, my Lord Bishop.'

'Something on your mind? Speak like you have a spine, Prior.' The Bishop frowned. 'I was told when I gained this office that you were a man who could walk on burning coals with your bare feet. Was I misinformed?'

Steven wanted to squeeze the fool's neck until his eyes popped out of his head. 'I thought you agreed not to let Brother Bougric – interrogate her.'

'If I didn't know any better, Prior, I would think you had a soft spot for the wanton harlot.'

Steven said nothing.

'I changed my mind. I want to know exactly what she has been doing, with whom, why, and what she hoped to gain. I will know it, too, if it's the last thing I do. Nobody – I mean nobody – will stand in my way.'

'Yes, my Lord Bishop. Brother Bougric will interrogate her, then, when he arrives?'

'Yes. I assume he will. I fought with Bougric in the holy land – we were both comrades in arms, members of the Order.' His eyes caressed the mighty sword in the corner. 'Those were the days. Every single day there was a pitched battle, it seemed.'

'Is that so?'

Warener's eyes seemed lost in a different time, a different place. 'Oh yes. I remember, one day Bougric made us attack an Arab stronghold in Jerusalem. It turned out to be a bakery. They made good gingerbread there, or some such. He was not much of a man of God back then . . . He told us the Holy Grail was kept there, among the candied dates and the sacks of flour – we attacked the poor devils in force, swords swinging . . . When we got inside he used his dagger to carve a goblet out of gingerbread, just so he would not be considered a liar. He drew a cross on it with the dagger's point.'

Warener laughed. 'We nearly killed him for it – my comrades and I literally waded through an ocean of heathen blood to get him his sweets.'

Steven smiled. 'A very interesting story, my Lord Bishop.'

Stephanie had been in the sordid frightening chamber since dawn. Placed next to the door, and greeting the sight as she entered, was a collection of hideous masks. She recognised a dog's mask, and the face of a giant gruesome turtle with the snout of a goat. The other masks were so fantastic, so frightening in their aspect, she could not even begin to identify the beast that may have inspired them. Were these the beasts of Hell that awaited her? The guards escorting her averted their eyes in trembling fear.

Machines of obvious purpose had been brought by Brother Bougric to assist him in his mission.

There was an odd-looking small vice – Stephanie recognised it as an instrument for splintering the fingers of the heretic. More devices for finger torture littered the room. There was a horrid pair of tongs to help the monk with the tearing out of her tongue – no doubt something he would threaten her with if she lied. There was a collection of iron cords, with a spiked circle at the end of each. She gasped when she saw the shreds of skin and dried blood which still clung to the end of these horrible whips. There were iron cages and numerous shackles and restraints to keep a heretic bound while Brother Bougric's ministrations forced a confession of heresy or of witchcraft. An iron ladle with an extra long handle – no doubt to allow the administration of hot lead – stood next to a cradle full of sharp spikes. An iron-backed armchair was the only piece of furniture not obviously dedicated to pain. The absence of an obvious purpose to the chair made it even more terrifying than the bloodstained barbed clearly identifiable terrors.

Stephanie moved from instrument to instrument, fascinated. Her initial terror faded with each passing hour.

She suspected her long unattended detention inside the torture chamber was intentional, a customary method for breaking the will of the victim even before actual torture was commenced.

She opened a chest – within, a slew of wicked metal implements gleamed with a cruel light. She picked one up – it resembled a foot-long cage with wicked sharp claws of iron facing inward. She could tighten a screw and make the claws longer, or retract them if she turned the screw the other way. She dropped the device back in the chest and quickly lowered the lid. Footsteps were finally approaching the torture chamber.

The monk entered the sordid cell like a haughty prince enters his throne room. He sat in the iron-backed armchair, examining his prisoner with thorough professional care.

She did not feel the least trace of lust in his gaze.

'Blessings of the Lord unto you, wench,' Brother Bougric sneered with undisguised loathing.

'Blessings of the Lor . . .'

Brother Bougric gasped, stunned by her impertinence. 'I did not ask you to respond, woman. Your kind is nothing more than a temptation of blonde hair and stained lips. Women like you should be eradicated, expunged from Heaven and earth. I would never believe your kind would ever make it to the Gates of Heaven, of course – but I am bound to try to wring the truth out of you, so that you can go to Heaven. You will confess – I have never failed. Perhaps the truth will colour your cheeks better than any of your foul powders.'

Stephanie lowered her eyes. The silence was sharp, long, uncomfortable.

'Auto-da-fé. Do you know what that is, wench?'

'No, milord.' Stephanie's purr was a soft tentative rub against the Inquisitor's defences, a feathery sinister probe.

Bougric chuckled. He spoke with undisguised condescension. 'Trying to work your foul spells already, aye? You are not the first to try. Better than you have tried, with even more luscious curves, prettier eyes, prettier faces.'

Stephanie's look was sharp, calculating. So the monk thought she was pretty, did he? This was a beginning, at least.

'I believe I shall tell you of the auto-da-fé. Do you know what that is?'

Stephanie nearly smiled. The fool just repeated himself – he might say she was not affecting him, but his actions spoke louder than words. Her voice was a clever mixture between the terrified cry of a weak maiden and the soft purr of a woman impressed by a man's power. 'No, milord. I am but a humble widow, a victim of sad circumstance. I am but a silly and helpless woman without my poor departed husband.'

Bougric sneered. 'You hoard your lies like a moneylender. Auto-da-fé – Act of Faith. Your lies shall be washed away by the touch of flames, foul creature.'

'I have been convicted already? Are you so certain of my guilt, my Lord?'

'I am. I only needed to catch a single glimpse of your haughty face to know you a fornicating whore, a willing tool of Satan. Repent and I promise you a quick death.'

Stephanie paled. He sounded so certain – and time was not on her side. Rumour had it these interrogations quickly degenerated into old-fashioned torture. She knew she could not stand up to something as brutal as physical pain. 'Quick death? Is that all I can hope for?'

'Death by strangulation. Better than the flames. Repent your witchcraft and I shall personally ensure your execution by a competent craftsman.'

'Is there no hope for contrition? Could I not – could I not join the convent, perhaps?'

Bougric chuckled. It was a cruel cold sound. 'No. I will not permit the foulness of your soul to infect a place dedicated to God. I shall leave you here, tonight, to rest amidst these instruments of contrition. Tomorrow, they shall be put to good use. Do not try to escape – I shall lock this door. The guards are my own men – they have orders to put a blade through you if you even seek to draw them into conversation.'

'Please . . . my Lord . . . I would be so gratefu –'

'Save your breath, whore. I am not interested in your foul flesh.' Bougric stood. 'Prepare your confession, and I shall spare you the touch of fire.'

He bowed deeply, a mocking, condescending gesture. 'Good night, Lady Peabody. May God have mercy upon your soul.'

She collapsed into the chair he had just vacated. Her eyes stared at the door, but they did not focus. For the first time in her life, Stephanie Hayes was afraid.

'Thank you, young woman. This is really most kind of you.'

'Prior Steven heard you like gingerbread, milord.'

'He heard right!' Brother Bougric swallowed hard. Saliva seemed to flood his entire mouth. The scent was wonderful. 'I can't wait to taste them.'

The serving woman, a young, not unappealing wench with light blonde hair in a bun, her large breasts properly covered up in a shapeless gown of rough homespun, curtsied. She walked off, leaving the tray on his cot. He smiled at the tray.

At dawn, the two men who guarded the entrance all night came in. Stephanie looked up from her cooped-up seat in the armchair. She had spent the entire night awake, coming to terms with the possibility that this was the end of the game. Perhaps she had finally met her match – Warener and Bougric may have the final say in the game she had been playing all her life. The guards said nothing – she did not dare to talk to them. One of them held her while the other one expertly tied her down onto a flat cast-iron instrument resembling a narrow metallic bed. They used thin chains and thick leather bands. By the time they were done, all she could do was wriggle. Cold fear rushed into her, the fear of pain. As the minutes trickled away, she began to wish the torture would just begin. Still, it was not until noon that the door opened again. It was Bougric.

'Are you ready to confess, foul witch?' There was a note of anguish in the Inquisitor's voice.

Her fear and physical exhaustion were so great that Stephanie nearly missed the signs of Bougric's particular affliction.

The Inquisitor's eyes were red-rimmed gateways of exhaustion. His hands were trembling. A peculiar sweet scent wafted from his clothes, as if he had been sleeping in a bakery.

Stephanie's last-ditch desperate plea turned into a coy seductive purr. Her body flushed with sudden hope, slowly swaying against her restraints, moving in rhythm with each word. 'I am ready to confess . . . everything, my Lord. Please – please permit me to tell you all that I have done, detail every single act of foul witchcraft.'

'Thank you so much, miss. This gingerbread was heavenly!'

'You are too kind, milord.' The serving woman curtsied, her sweet-smelling blonde hair a tumble of bright golden-yellow locks.

He noticed she was not wearing the shapeless homespun robe today. She wore the livery of the Bishop, purple and white, tight and hugging the luscious curves of her huge inviting breasts. At least she had the good sense to keep her cleavage modest. His gaze lingered over her chest, where other less reputable women would have shown more skin.

'My name is Sylvia. Would you like anything else . . . anything else at all, milord?'

'No . . .' Bougric's voice stumbled. 'No, thank you.'

'I am pleased that I can unburden my soul, my Lord,' Stephanie moaned softly, her long pretty legs straining against the restraints. 'My legs are in so much pain, my Lord. I have done nothing but answer your questions all day. Could I just move my legs a little bit? Please, milord . . .'

Bougric's eyes were riveted to the bound widow's legs. The flawless skin of her thighs was visible through the torn cloth. He moved a little to the side – yes, he could see straight to the swell of her beautiful bottom.

She arched her back, displaying her tempting flesh, permitting his eyes free passage to roam over her buttocks. The expanse of skin revealed by the tear was quite large. 'Please, milord . . . just untie my legs for a few minutes . . . I will be so grateful . . .' Her droning purr was a soft velvet caress, wearing away at his will.

The Inquisitor came closer. His hands reached out as if of their own volition, brushing against the smooth inviting flesh of Stephanie's ankle. Bougric groaned, leaning closer, his crotch pressing against the iron cot, hiding his arousal from his cooing seductive prisoner. The Inquisitor was sweating.

'Please . . . nobody has to know you unbound my legs for just a minute or two, my Lord . . .'

Bougric's deep voice was a shadow of its former self. He croaked without any sense of right or wrong. 'This is true.'

Stephanie purred encouragingly. 'Just slide your finger underneath the knot, my Lord . . . Yes . . . Right there. Just slide your finger right there, and tug on the cord until it comes undone.'

The Inquisitor slid his finger against the harlot widow's skin, feeling the heat of her beautiful body. Her flesh felt like smooth inviting velvet. He could not seem to stop sliding his finger against that flawless skin.

'That's it . . , That's it . . . Just slide your finger until you find the knot. Use your entire hand. Take all the time you need . . . All the time you need . . .'

He picked up a piece of gingerbread from the tray and stuffed it in his mouth. His eyes devoured the luscious body of the serving wench. Her breasts were nearly spilling free from the tight confines of the Bishop's livery. A piece of gingerbread dropped to the floor, landing on a filthy floorboard inside Bougric's cell. He bent low, picking it up, drool dribbling from his lips as he used the opportunity to get a better look at the serving maid's long legs. Sylvia giggled with amused condescension as the Inquisitor pushed the soiled sweet into his drooling mouth.

She laughed triumphantly. 'It looks like you are finally ready for some fucky-fucky . . .' The serving wench pushed the Inquisitor down on the cot, her heavy naked breasts smothering his face. The monk whimpered, emitting an uncharacteristically helpless pathetic moan of lust. Sylvia kept the Inquisitor pinned on the cot. She undid his robe belt. His member sprang free, eager, helpless, desperate for release.

Sylvia softly stroked his shaft with her fingers. 'Now isn't that nice?'

He sobbed as she disgraced him. He struggled weakly against the sinful embrace. 'Call Bishop Warener,' he whispered pathetically.

She giggled. 'You are such a silly little monk . . . He wouldn't understand.' The serving woman sat up on top of the Inquisitor and picked up another piece of gingerbread. She ground the sticky sweet against her nipples. Her soft purr was no longer a suggestion – it was a command of irresistible force. 'Suck on my titties, Inquisitor.'

Eleven

'Fucking my ass felt soooo nice, didn't it, little Stevie?'

Evelyn's bitchy tone once again got him so hard it was hard to think of anything other than the redhead's gorgeous exquisite offering. As always, the instant gratification of his twitching insatiable cock lasted no more than a moment. 'It was nice,' he said, tightly.

She leaned back on his lap until her gorgeous cascading curls completely covered his tonsured head. He was lost in a cloud of flowering jasmine. 'So, so nice . . . my pretty, tight ass completely surrounding your thick long hard cock . . .' She giggled. 'It would be soooo nice if you could stick your erect prick in my beautiful young tight round ass again . . . it would be soooo nice . . .' She slowly caressed his head, her perfect white fingers forming a sharp contrast against his flushed red scalp.

'. . . Yes, it felt very . . . very nice.' The expensive little bitch kept coming back for more. She practically sucked him dry. He wanted to say no, but then she would come by and do this . . . and his prick just took over.

'My tits would look sooooo pretty with that pearl necklace I saw at Ganavarre's . . . they would look so nice with those pearls tumbling up and down over my titties as you fucked my tight pretty ass . . .'

'God, Evelyn. How much?'

'Only two hundred . . .'

'I don't have – I mean –'

She immediately got up and looked at him with smirking contempt. 'You don't have a measly two hundred gold to get me a little present?' She pouted and looked at him petulantly. 'Can't you get it?' She put her tiny hands on his erection. 'Pleeeease . . .'

He gasped as she manipulated his mindless drooling cock. This little bitch was a bigger gold-digger than Stephanie. The huge pile of gold in the ironwood chest was shrinking rapidly. Amber refused to drink anything except French champagne. Heather only allowed him to climax if he brought her an expensive pretty. Of late, they had to be made of gold or jewels. The most expensive obsession of them all, of course, was the tiny redhead. 'I have to be careful . . . that bastard Warener is keeping a close eye on the people at the diocese.'

She frowned. 'Warener?'

'Yes. You know of him?'

She giggled. 'Well, perhaps. Mum told me about a Warener. This one was a handsome young knight. I think he fell in love with her.'

'That's him! Warener was one of the Knights Templar.'

'Can you believe it? Some rich Bishop, in love with Mum! Oh yes . . . I'm sure now that he is rich Mum would love to see him. She told me he was full of energy back then.' She chuckled. 'I am just like her, she often says.'

He stared at her, considering. She caught his eye and shook her head.

'No, Stevie. Mum is no more of a harlot than I am. I am Daddy's child. You really should listen, Steven. I am just like Mum. She guarded her virtue too, and at the time Daddy was a lot richer than a poor little Knight Templar. No cunnie for him.' She giggled and slowly bent over, wiggling her ass. 'No cunnie for you either, Prior Steven. Now . . . I think I should have that pearl necklace . . .' She smoothly shoved herself against his raging erection and ground her rear against Steven's cock. 'Play your cards right and you can give me two of them . . .' She giggled.

'You agree with Prior Steven?' Bishop Warener's voice was completely incredulous.

'Yes, my Lord Bishop.' Bougric's voice was a deep grating well. 'The woman repented her crimes completely. I recommend releasing her to Mother Superior Elsbeth's custody.'

'Tell me what you learned of her crimes. Has she admitted to trying to seduce a man of God?'

Bougric took another healthy bite of his gigantic slice of gingerbread. 'No. She has not tried to seduce a man of God.' There was no doubt in Bougric's voice.

'Could I be mistaken?' Warener whispered to himself.

Bougric shrugged. 'Anything is possible, God willing.'

'You interrogated that wanton slut for an entire week!'

'I had to make sure she was . . . truly contrite.'

'You told me after the first day that she was the most foul corrupt creature that ever walked without hooves!'

'Sometimes – sometimes we make mistakes.' Bougric stared at the gingerbread in his hand, his nostrils twitching with need. He bit into the sweet, wolfing it down.

'Very well . . . I will release her to Elsbeth. How is your stay in Salisbury? I was hoping you would stay with me in the palace. I wanted to spend more time with you, talk of old times . . .'

Bougric's head turned a bright shade of crimson. 'Prior Steven was kind enough to let me stay at the Peabody town house.'

Bishop Warener stared at his comrade's tonsured head in fascination. 'Are you blushing, man?'

'Brother Bougric is fond of the gingerbread made by the . . . orphan cook at the town house. He is, perhaps, ashamed of his taste for sweets, such treats being a needless luxury,' Steven offered.

'Yes. That's it.' Bougric laughed with hearty relief. 'I must seek absolution for the sin of gluttony, my Lord Bishop.'

'Hmm. Perhaps so.' Warener did not look pleased. 'Orphan cook?' He faced Steven. 'You are extending the orphanage, truly?' He looked a little bit happier. 'That is indeed most charitable. I must come and inspect your preparations. Of course, it will have to be after my trip to Elsbeth's convent.'

'You are visiting the convent, my Lord Bishop?' asked Steven.

'I want to drop off our penitent whore myself. Make sure she looks and acts like a penitent, if you know what I mean. I want to be there when her head is shaved and I want to see her put in the penitent's robe of rough homespun. I want to watch her collect acorns in the woods with the pigs so she has food for dinner . . . Why the sudden silence?'

'Nothing, my Lord Bishop. You paint a vivid picture, that's all.'

'Thank you, Brother Bougric.' Warener frowned as he glanced at Steven. 'And I will continue on to the monastery from the convent. I will reclaim my horse and audit your books.'

'Audit my books?' Steven looked stunned.

'My right as head of the diocese. I will audit your books, check the numbers, see what you have done with the Peabody estate – I hear you have a good man overseeing your finances.'

'Yes; Sub-Prior Anders.'

'His mother was my second cousin. Good stock! I can't wait to meet him.'

'I am – I am sure Sub-Prior Anders can't wait to meet you.'

'Splendid! I am looking forward to a trip in the woods, out of this cesspool of filth. Maybe we can do a bit of hunting, aye Brother Bougric? I mean . . . maybe we can have a long ride in the woods . . .' Bishop Warener grinned.

'Sounds wonderful, my Lord Bishop.'

'It's settled then. Let's ship this wench off to Elsbeth's tender mercies.'

It had been three days since the messenger from Salisbury came and Anders still had not been able to glean any information from Sister Patricia or Mother Elsbeth about his mission. He had the distinct feeling that neither of the women appreciated his curiosity. Sister Patricia cornered him, and – once again – in fact, every single night since the messenger's arrival – ordered Novice Mary to confess her sins in elaborate vivid detail to the Sub-Prior. She was not to leave anything out. Anders sat in the Chamber of Penitence – he had no idea such a room existed until now – with an expression of helpless fascination. The corrupt little slut in the nun's habit exuded filthy story after filthy story. Every night seemed a special torture. Each passing moment in Patricia's company was a burning firebrand of unfulfilled desire, accented by a more and more insistent raw lust for the buxom brunette. Tonight was no exception.

'I had to touch myself . . . I was thinking what it looked like on a man . . . a man's penis . . . how hard and warm it would be, sliding in between my thighs . . . I was thinking of you, Sub-Prior Anders . . . and how you must have a really nice one. I really wanted to see it. I couldn't stop thinking about what it would be like to have your cock in my cunnie . . . and then I thought of Mistress Patricia's long pretty legs, and how beautiful she looks when she bathes, naked, in the sacred pool on Mount Eleanor. I thought of what her beautiful blonde . . . you know, what it looks like when she is naked. And I thought of your cock sliding into my pussy and I thought of Mistress Patricia's pretty blonde pussy and – and – it made me soooo hot . . .' Mary writhed on the floor, her hands slowly pulling up her habit around her waist, exposing a freshly shaved, glistening pink slit. 'Then I thought, it would be soooo much nicer to have a shaved cunt for you to fuck, Sub-Prior Anders . . .'

'Shameless evil slut!' screamed Patricia. 'How dare you tempt Sub-Prior Anders with your unworthy cunt? As if a mere woman could tempt someone so in touch with the Holy Spirit as Sub-Prior Anders!' She fondly caressed Anders's cheek. 'You are a man of iron principles and duty, Sub-Prior.'

Anders closed his eyes. This was pure hell. He was not sure if his sinful erect member would permit him to get up, ever. 'Thank you, Sister Patricia,' he mumbled.

'Sister Mary – I should not even call you Sister, of course, you are just a novice – you are a harlot masquerading as a Bride of the Lord. You have no right to that habit. The habit is a sign of a nun's total consecration to the Lord. It is a reminder that nuns are all one family in the Lord. A habit is an expression of the poverty and penance of our lives.' She touched the rosary on her belt, seeking inspiration. 'Strip, at once. I shall bring you appropriate clothing for you to contemplate your sins in.' She turned to Anders, flashing him that devastating green-eyed smile. 'Please keep an eye on her, Sub-Prior, while I am away. Do not allow her to engage in shameless self-degradation.'

Anders opened his mouth to respond – but no sound came out. He whirled around to face Mary as the door clicked shut behind Patricia's departing footsteps.

Mary was, indeed, stripping as ordered. Her body was luscious, curvaceous, practically bursting with the rosy glow of youth. The moment she was completely nude, he saw she was, as predicted, already engaging in shameless self-degradation. Her impudent sparkling dark eyes locked with those of the Sub-Prior. She licked her luscious full lips. 'I can suck your balls dry before she gets back . . .' she purred seductively. Her finger was busily circling her special place.

Anders could not speak at all. His erection felt like a stiff fleshy compass, its point unwaveringly pointing towards the seductive temptress before him.

Mary giggled and got on all fours. She crawled in front of him.

He watched her tangled brown hair disappear beneath his robe, nearly fainting when her luscious full lips wrapped around his cock. He had never felt anything like this in his entire life. The Sub-Prior suddenly felt her lithe fingers around his balls, caressing, fondling, manipulating him in a way that felt utterly filthy yet completely pleasurable. A loud moan escaped his lips and he closed his eyes, leaning back – and his head bumped into the wool of Patricia's habit, her statuesque tall body a tightly wound wall of rage towering over his pleasure-dazed head.

Anders's eyes snapped open, horrified. He scrambled a few feet away from his seductress, only to reveal Mary's grinning, shameless, completely naked body beneath his robe. The novice giggled and licked her lips.

Patricia's face was a mask of fury. 'Sub-Prior Anders! You are a shameless fornicator! How dare you tempt a womanchild of this convent into sin?!'

Anders opened his mouth to protest, but she cut him off.

'I know what you are about to say, Sub-Prior, and I simply *do not care*! What will Prior Steven say when I tell him how you stuck your stiff cock in between those innocent young lips?'

'Please . . . can't we . . . can't I serve penance here?' Anything but Prior Steven's judgement! There would be no way for him to succeed the Prior if his transgression became public knowledge.

Patricia seemed to consider. 'You wish to perform your penance here? Are you certain you feel true contrition?'

'Yes. Yes, Sister.' He avoided looking at the gorgeous luscious bundle of tempting femininity lying naked on the floor.

Patricia seemed to arrive at a decision. She tossed the heavy bundle in her arms on the floor. 'Both of you shall serve penance!' Her voice brooked no argument.

'But –'

'Silence!' she thundered. 'You will confess all your foul filthy cravings within this chamber, before the object of your unholy lust!'

He glanced into Patricia's emerald eyes within that gorgeous perfect face and blushed. 'Yes, Sister Patricia.'

'You are not a Sub-Prior anymore, not while you serve your penance, is that understood?'

'Yes, Sister Patricia,' he said, meekly.

'You are one of my novices while you are here. If you are still a Sub-Prior, I am not empowered to levy punishment. Your status while within this chamber is that of novice.'

'Yes . . . Mistress.'

'Good. Agreed, then. Obviously, your sin is that of the

flesh. You have been tempted, and you have been found wanting.'

Anders nodded, ashamed.

'True contrition only has value before God if it is tested in the cauldron of temptation. As I said before I left the two of you here to begin your unholy fornication, Mary no longer deserves to wear the sacred garments of a nun, not even those of a novice.'

She pointed at the bundle on the floor. 'Open it up, harlot.'

Mary shook the contents of the bundle to the stone floor. White dancing shoes and high-heeled red pumps, the kind whores in town wear, fell out first. Shimmering silk and lace lingerie, white, black, pink, red, they spilled forth in a torrent. A small but heavy box tumbled out last.

'Make yourself into a true test of Novice Anders's devotion to the Lord, slut.'

Mary opened the box first. It was full of rouge, powders and paints of the whore's profession. She applied the paints and powders with surprising skill. She outlined her eyes with kohl – they looked huge in the candlelight. She then put on silk stockings and a garter belt, a brazen cutout bra that left her large breasts completely exposed, and finally the red stiletto pumps. She looked like a gorgeous fresh young whore, rather than a chosen Bride of the Lord.

Anders could not seem to look away. His eyes drank in the scene of the torrid transformation.

'Slut!' Patricia's slap stung his cheeks. 'You can't tear your eyes away from her flesh. All you care about is your cock. Let's see if you desire that young slut's flesh.'

'What – what is it you want me to do?' he asked.

'Take off your robe. When wanton lust truly leaves your heart, it will be evident to my eyes.'

'That's – that's true,' he said, troubled. 'Can Mary put on her . . .' he trailed off because Patricia simply slapped him again.

'Mistress Patricia, novice!'

'Yes, Mistress Patricia.' He swallowed.

Slowly his trembling fingers undid his triple-knotted rope belt and his robe fell to the ground. He took off his plain undergarment as well. His cock was a thick throbbing finger of accusation in between his legs.

'I must get my . . . instruments. I am warning you, novice, to keep your foul member away from that Bride of the Lord.' Patricia gathered his robe and her habit in her hands and left the cell with a last look of warning.

As soon as Patricia left the cell Mary stood up and walked towards Anders. Her six-inch heels click-clicked on the stone floor. Her gait was sinuous, like a serpent's. 'Touch me . . .' she cooed as she approached him.

He turned to flee, reaching the heavy oak door and about to wrench it open, but suddenly he realised he was naked. He whirled to face his insatiable pretty seductress. Backing up, his bare buttocks contacted the cold wood of the oak door and he was suddenly out of room to flee. He tried to avoid touching her breasts as he was pushing her away, but only succeeded in allowing her to close in. She pressed her young body against his, her firm luscious breasts pushing against his skin. She traced her hand against his body, stroking him here and there. It felt like he was on fire anywhere she touched him.

'Where were we?' She giggled cruelly and dropped to her knees, her rouge-stained lips wrapping around Anders's oozing virgin cock.

He feebly tried to push her away. His flailing hands kept immersing themselves in her unruly silky dark hair. The soft wet machinations of her mouth and tongue made resistance impossible. He slowly slumped against the wall, sliding all the way down into a passive supine heap against the cold stone.

Mary moaned with anticipation as his cock pumped pre-cum into her mouth.

The door opened. His eyes flickered open to focus on Patricia's beautiful furious face. She carried a bag in her left hand. In her right hand, she held the riding crop he was so familiar with.

'How dare you!' she hissed as he scrambled upright. Mary's insistent warm lips kept their grip on his cock, rising with him as he stood. She was giving him lurid pink-lipped fellatio in plain view of the Mistress of Novices. He heard the giggling of nuns outside – have any others seen him? – panicked, he scrambled away from the open door, the brunette novice latched on his member like some parasite of fornication. Patricia swung the riding crop, the wicked stroke leaving a long pink welt on Mary's gorgeous naked bottom. The brunette gasped in pain, her lips slipping off his cock. He heard the hissing sound of Patricia's anger and he felt a violent stinging pain on his own buttocks, the intense sensation somehow mixing with the obscene pleasures of his twitching abused member. With an inarticulate gasp, he ejaculated all over Mary's pretty young face.

'Fornicating sinner.' Patricia reached out with her hand and grabbed his twitching spent cock in her fingers. 'Sub-Prior Anders . . .' She said his name with such contempt he nearly broke down in tears. To his horror, his cock responded in her hand and stiffened again. Patricia sneered and let go of his member. 'I see Mary is not the only one who must be taught a lesson. You will either cooperate or I will call Mother Elsbeth to witness this spectacle.' She pointed at the cum-covered novice in the stiletto heels and torrid lingerie.

'No . . . Please.' He remembered too late. 'Mistress!' he cried in pain as the riding crop abused his rear again.

'Get on top of the cot and lie on your stomach.'

He did as she commanded. Was she going to whip him? The thought was strangely alluring. She used the restraints in her bag to tie him up against the cot. The wooden rails of the cot seemed tailor-made for this operation. His hands were completely immobile against a wooden rail, as were his legs. His bottom was propped high in the air. She stood behind his trussed up body, by the window.

'Fornicating sinner,' she said, again. 'Tell me what filth you have been thinking about me.'

'I have not been –' His cry of pain was sharp and loud. It felt as if a hot iron had been laid on his ass.

'Mary – tell me what filth you've been thinking about me.'

'Yes, Mistress. I have been thinking of kissing your soft warm lips.'

'You are a common little slut, Mary.'

'Yes, Mistress.'

'Novice Anders, tell me what filth you've been thinking about me.'

'I have not been . . . please don't . . .' His voice rose in pitch as the riding crop swished through the air. Breathless, he spoke rapidly. 'I have been – I have been thinking about kissing you too . . . about touching you.'

'You are a disgusting little pig, novice Anders. At least Mary has not been thinking about touching me. Is that right, Mary?'

Mary sobbed and did not answer.

'I think you should be tied up as well next to the disgusting little pig.'

Anders felt hot naked flesh press against his left. Mary's ankles were tied up to the head rail next to his head. A deadly stiletto heel nearly poked him in the cheek as Patricia promptly trussed her up as well. Mary's curvaceous bottom was propped high up in the air.

'Mary – tell me what filth you've been thinking about me.'

'Yes, Mistress. I have been thinking of touching your cunnie and ass with my fingers . . . and with my . . . toy.'

'Now we are getting somewhere. You can't repent until you admit your sin. Cunnie *and* ass. You are a disgusting sinful creature, novice Mary. Now – what toy are you talking about, novice Mary?'

'It is under the cot, Mistress.'

Patricia leaned low and took out a piece of shaped wood wrapped in smooth leather. 'Did you carve this, novice Mary?'

'Yes, Mistress.'

'Tell me, novice Mary, what is this supposed to be?'

'It's supposed to be a man's member, Mistress.'

'Did you model it on a real man's cock, novice Mary?'

'No, Mistress. It is what I imagined Sub-Prior Anders's cock looks like.'

Patricia's hand casually reached in between Anders's legs and examined his raging erection. 'Not a bad likeness, novice Mary. Of course, novice Anders is not a man. Men can't be Brides of the Lord. Have you showed your filthy cock to this innocent, novice Anders?'

'No . . . no, Mistress.'

'Novice Anders, I find it difficult to forget that you are a man. If you are a man, I cannot discipline you. Instead, I must report you to Prior Steven.'

'Please . . . please don't report me to Prior Steven, Mistress.'

'Novice Anders, I must do something about your garb to help me not think of you as a man. What can I do to think of you as a woman, novice Anders?'

'I – I don't know, Mistress.'

The sharp pain of the riding crop was excruciating. 'You should think harder, novice.'

'I – I could talk in a higher pitch, Mistress.' He tried to make himself sound as girly as possible.

'Hmm. That helps, a little bit. But I am still reminded by your discarded garments of your sex and your office.'

'I could . . . change, Mistress?'

She whipped his bottom, with cruel perfect precision. 'You are a perverted filthy creature, novice Anders. You want to put on frilly lace panties and dancing shoes, don't you?'

He sobbed with the injustice of it – but he could not stop himself from being obscenely, intensely aroused. His arousal was completely obvious to his harsh disciplinarian.

'I will momentarily untie your legs. If you struggle, this session is at an end and I shall summon Mother Elsbeth before a formal complaint is made to the Priory and Bishop Warener.'

Anders swallowed hard. The idea of a formal inquiry nearly made him nauseous. 'I will . . . I will not struggle.' He felt Patricia unbind his legs. In a moment, the cool touch of light lace touched his skin. Patricia pulled the sleazy crotchless lace panties over his aching cock, his manhood an all too apparent sceptre of lust in the centre of the frippery fabric.

Patricia moved away to the other end of the cot. 'Does this look like a woman's cunt, novice Mary?'

'No, Mistress.'

'I agree, Slut Mary.'

Anders could not see what they were talking about. He did not dare to turn his head too far in any direction. All he could see were Mary's high-heeled shoes and naked brazen flesh immediately to his left. The tempting vision combined with the cool touch of lace over his member, fuelling his arousal. He could not even begin to guess when his erection would subside – if ever. The telltale symbol of his pervasive need was on blatant display, surrounded by frilly lace.

'You look almost like a woman now, novice Anders. Tell me, novice Anders, why I should not report the filthy perversions of a man of the cloth to Prior Steven.'

'I – I am not a . . . man, Mistress?'

'Very good, novice Anders. What are you, then?'

'I am a novice.'

Patricia rained blows on his lace-clad ass. 'You dare call yourself a future Bride of the Lord, you filthy little slut?' She was enraged.

'I – I am sorry, Mistress.'

'What are you, then?'

'I am a – I am a woman?'

'No, novice Anders, you are a debased slut. What are you, then?'

Voice trembling with fear, Anders replied: 'I am a debased slut, Mistress.'

Patricia stiffly marched back to his end of the cot. In the identical tone she used earlier, she posed her question, again. 'Tell me, novice Anders, what filth you've been thinking about me.'

'I just wanted to kiss you and touch your face . . .' The pain was excruciating. It did not stop with a single stroke, either. After a few minutes of intense painful whipping, she calmly resumed his interrogation. 'Tell me, piglet Anders, what filth you've been thinking about me.'

Great salty tears were running down Anders's face. 'I –

I've been thinking about fondling your bottom . . . and . . . your bosom . . . and your long beautiful legs . . .'

'*Show* me what unspeakable filth you wanted to do to me, novice Mary.'

'I – I can't . . .' Mary's voice was hoarse. 'I can't reach you, Mistress Patricia. My legs are all tied up.'

'Your hands are not tied up, novice Mary. Show me how you want to play with my ass, novice Mary.' Patricia handed the pretty brunette her own handcrafted dildo.

Mary stared at the gorgeous cruel blonde with the riding crop. 'How? I can't reach you . . .'

She cried with fear and anguish as Patricia literally lined her ass with fresh red welts.

'Why do *I* have to play the part of your filthy play puppet? Now, show me how you want to play with my ass, novice Mary.'

Tears in her eyes, Mary tried to force the dildo into her own anus. She couldn't seem to get it in. 'I can't do it all tied up . . . it's too big . . .' She halted her efforts in utter terror as Patricia raised the riding crop.

'Novice Mary, I did not ask to witness yet another bout of obscene masturbation. I can watch you do that every single night. I asked you to show me how you want to play with my ass.'

Understanding finally dawned in Mary's tear-drenched eyes.

Anders began to squeal, fully deserving of his new title, as Mary showed the Mistress of Novices what exactly she had in mind.

'Can you get away for a week or so? I could tell your father you wish to study Latin at the convent.'

She playfully slapped him. 'Why would I go to a silly place like the convent?'

'If you come . . . you can have another pearl necklace . . . and the ruby one as well.'

She gasped. 'What ruby one?'

'Ganaverre thinks I am his best customer. He had it brought over from his shop in London.' He reached into his pocket and pulled out the glittering blood-red and gold masterpiece.

For a change, Evelyn was speechless. 'I want . . .' she finally whined, caressing his cheek and slowly rubbing her bottom against his rock-hard erection.

'All yours . . . if you come with us when we leave for Saint Eleanor's.'

Twelve

'I want no trace of evil to mar these proceedings.' Warener's tone was utterly serious. Some priests did not really believe in the devil. The Bishop was not one of them. 'Satan walks among the living, tempting, corrupting, destroying the lives of the righteous.'

Steven nodded. 'I cannot agree more. However repentant, this woman has stolen from the church and corrupted a man of fine character and godly virtue. Surely not calling her a concubine of the devil is only a technicality.'

Warener looked at him sharply. 'Under normal circumstances I would trust Brother Bougric's judgement in these sorts of matters, but –' he trailed off with obvious unhappiness. 'Do *you* think she is a witch?'

Steven did not have to pretend doubt. 'I do not know. It is too late to allege such without attracting charges of fabrication.'

Warener slammed his fist down on the altar. 'I do not wish to desecrate this chapel with her presence if she is a witch.'

Steven sighed and looked out across the nave. His eyes chanced upon a metal vessel suspended on three chains about two feet long. There were twelve small bells on the chains, signifying the voices of the twelve Disciples. The picture of the censer was like a seed in his mind, the seed of a powerful evil flower, germinating in the fertile cesspool of his soul.

He turned to face the Bishop. 'We must purify the church for the ceremony.'

Warener considered. 'What exactly did you have in mind?'

Steven closed his eyes and recited in a hushed reverent tone: 'An angel came and stood at the altar, with a golden censer; and he was given much incense to mingle with the prayers of the saints upon the golden Altar before the Throne of God; and the smoke of the incense rose with the prayers of the Saints from the hand of the angel before God.'

Warener made the sign of the cross. 'Amen,' he whispered. It was obvious Steven was divinely inspired. 'Prior Steven, you believe we should purify the church with sacred incense?'

Without opening his eyes, Steven nodded and continued his recitation: 'Then flew one of the Seraphim to me, having in his hand a burning coal which he had taken with tongs from the Altar. And he touched my mouth, and said: 'Behold, this has touched your lips: your guilt is taken away, and your sins forgiven".'

Warener asked Elsbeth to have two nuns walk back and forth across the nave twelve times, the number of the apostles, carrying burning censers. The smoke lay heavy in the small chapel.

Steven glanced at Sylvia with some concern. 'How much did you put in them?'

'Nearly all of it. You want this to work, right?'

'Yes, of course . . . but . . . won't the stuff affect everyone the same way?'

'Well . . . of course. But so what? All we really care about is Warener, anyway. The rest of them are already ours.'

Steven nodded. This had to work, of course. It was literally impossible to drug Warener. They had tried everything. Whenever he tasted something unusual, he spat it out. His food tasters were as paranoid as he was, and refused him access to anything that tasted out of the ordinary. He didn't eat any sweets.

* * *

The congregation, mostly the nuns of the convent and the Bishop's retinue, including Brother Bougric, stood before the altar. They were all paying close attention. Some of them coughed, despite all efforts to the contrary. The smoke in the chapel was still incredibly dense. It was an all-out effort to smoke out the devil, and none of the nuns wanted to appear as if the cloud adversely affected them. Bishop Warener's sermon reached a passionate fervent crescendo:

'I want to talk about the sin of fornication. Lust is the most evil of the tools of the devil. It takes the dignity, the virtue, the good character of a man or a maiden, and sullies it until the Kingdom of Heaven is no more. Hellfire! Hellfire awaits those who give in to the foul lure of the flesh. None who succumb can hope for more than slithering serpents in a pit of fire, trapped for time eternal within the circles of Hell. Repent, sinner!' Bishop Warener's powerful deep voice boomed around the chapel. His eyes were trained squarely on the widow's solitary figure standing before the altar. 'Your foul fornicating days are at an end, Stephanie Peabody. This is the time for contrition . . . And penance. As you accept this Host from my hand, lower your head and pray for forgiveness. Sister Patricia shall shave your head. Mother Superior Elsbeth shall dress you in your new penitent robe of homespun. Rejoice in the coarse fibres of your new garment, for it is the livery of the Host of Heaven.'

Bishop Warener raised the Host in the air and lowered it in his hand. With infinite care, he placed the Host on his tongue. The wafer dissolved in his mouth. Certainly tastes sweet – he thought. He drank from the wine. It was as sweet, at least, as the wafer. He wished he had more of the Host for himself. That was the sweetest wafer he had ever tasted. He eyed the tray greedily. No wonder Bougric liked his gingerbread so much! With some regret, he turned around to face the congregation as the women of the convent came up to partake of the Host.

The nuns came up to the pulpit, one at a time, and took a wafer from his hands. Some of them kissed his ring. One of the novices, Mary, kissed his ring a couple of times, smiling at him in a most disconcerting manner. Her lips were so red, so luscious. He felt an odd forgotten tingle below his belt. All these nuns looked . . . they looked so young and pretty. The penitent came up last. Stephanie's face was completely expressionless. She kissed his ring and took the wafer, placing it on her tongue. She looked at him searchingly for a moment before walking away. Was that a look of disappointment on her proud pretty face? He halted in mid-stride as he realised he had called her pretty within the privacy of his mind. That figure was certainly something that could tempt a man into sinful thoughts. He pushed away the impulse to engage in some himself.

He addressed the tall statuesque Mistress of Novices. 'Sister Patricia, step forth and shave the head of the penitent.'

Patricia stepped forward. She walked slowly to face Stephanie in the centre of the nave. Very slowly, deliberately, she stared into Warener's eyes and lowered her lips over Stephanie's.

The two women's tongues intertwined in a vulgar display of naked lust. Both of their eyes were open – emerald-green and vapid greedy blue, impudent, torrid stares, a vulgar calculated display intended to stoke the furnace of lust within him while they engaged in their drawn-out filthy kiss. Warener's jaw dropped. He stared at the foul obscene display for an infinitely long moment. The sweet tingle in his mouth seemed to travel down his body directly into his member. He felt himself becoming more and more aroused.

'Stop this foul madness!' he bellowed. 'Mother Superior, do something!'

Mother Superior Elsbeth nodded – she emitted a soft helpless moan and allowed her habit to slide to the ground. Beneath, she wore a sleazy tight black corset with matching garters and hose. Her thighs and shaved pussy displayed the smudged imprints of painted lips, pink, red, lavender, kisses of adoring fornication by the corrupted lips of her flock. The needy lust-crazed nun dropped to her knees before the nearest nun – a young brunette named Sister Gladys – and raised her habit to busy her tongue over her similarly shaved sex. All over the congregation similar scenes played themselves out. Nun after nun shed her holy garments to reveal the sleaziest silk or lace lingerie and engage in the lewdest form of unholy coupling.

Stephanie emitted a frustrated moan as her fingers fumbled with the buttons keeping Patricia's habit shut. Her lust did not have any patience left; she simply tore the holy garment off. The gorgeous tall blonde Mistress of Novices was completely naked below the habit, her beautiful young body flushed with the excitement of the orgy.

The pretty widow looked upon her with open desire. 'I will lick your clit until all you can do is moan.' She slid to her knees before the Mistress of Novices.

Sub-Prior Anders was happily lost below six corrupted horny nuns. Sister Lisa – or, as she liked to be called of late, Little Bitch – was fighting two other nuns and a novice for the privilege of riding his cock. Two others were brazenly kissing each other over his face, occasionally leaning lower to kiss him as well. Yet another was seductively rubbing her small firm tits against his chest, her lips parted slightly to display a questing glistening red tongue.

Another pile of naked moaning fornicating women began pouring hot wax on each other's bodies using the consecrated candle of the Mass. Every time the wax dripped over exposed skin, the woman in question would squeal and scream for mercy – and fondle her womanhood at the same time. Sister Susan finally could not deal with it anymore, and slowly inserted the candle into her drenched wet cunt. The others looked at her with petulant envy – until they noticed Brother Bougric. The Inquisitor was masturbating, his hand a blur around his engorged cock. His eyes were locked on Patricia and Stephanie in the centre of the nave. The nuns literally swallowed Bougric up in an avalanche of naked lust-crazed flesh.

The only participant in the Mass who was not yet fornicating was Bishop Warener.

* * *

His cock was a raging iron-hard goad, an evil hook of the devil inside his soul. Warener stared at the unholy spectacle before him for a long, long moment. He wanted to spear his member into every single fallen angel, each shameless corrupt whore who had demeaned, sullied and degraded the name of God.

He did not just want to merely fornicate with them, he wanted to fuck them until they were covered in his cum. Those sluts!

Stephanie's gorgeous blonde locks were shielding the view of her wanton tonguing of Patricia's pussy. The pretty blonde Mistress of Novices held the widow's head in both of her hands, surrendering her clit completely to her skilful ministrations.

Warener hurried out of the chapel. His need was so great, he was worried he might succumb to temptation. He practically ran all the way to his chambers.

A young woman with pretty red hair saw him approach. She bent over, raising her habit up to expose her trimmed red pussy. 'Fuck me, Bishop . . .' she begged. 'Please fuck me.'

His cock twitched with desire – it nearly pulled him in her direction. She was almost exactly his ideal woman as far as looks were concerned, just a touch too tall, a touch too tan, a touch too subservient. He tore his gaze from her luscious ass. 'I know what happened to you now, Brother Bougric,' he muttered to himself. He rushed past the pine gates of the convent on his right. The visitor's lodge was immediately ahead. By divine providence, it seemed to lack the presence of the corrupted nuns. He reached his private chamber, breathing heavily. Once inside, he barred the door. He gazed upon the signet ring on his hand, the Cross a sacred reminder of his duty. A cross – a cross of a different sort reminded him of a different time – a time when there was no ambiguity in his life, when temptation was never a continuous insistent corrosive seeping through his soul. He faced the corner, the most powerful reminder of that past right there for his hand, as always, faithful and ready to serve. Slowly, he put his hands around the hilt of his two-handed sword.

'This is your doing, Stephanie Hayes.' He smiled a dark smile, a Templar smile. The sound of steel rasping free of the scabbard was louder than the sound of the trumpet on the last day. 'We shall see how you work your foul witchcraft . . . without a head.'

Prior Steven looked around with concern bordering on panic. Where was the Bishop? He had already cum twice – once inside Heather, looking delectable in sleazy white lace underneath her custom-made easily shed habit, and once on the lips of the convent librarian, an illiterate but comely young nun with the ability to make Elsbeth moan like a bitch on heat. If Warener got away this could get bloody – there might be some burnings, even.

Finally! He saw Warener's purple vestments through the haze of incense. Something was wrong, however. Why wasn't the Bishop engaging in shameless fornication? Suddenly, he knew his concern was not misplaced. The Bishop was holding his monstrous Templar sword, cutting the silhouette of a terrifying figure with a grim dark smile on his humourless lips. He was walking with steady purpose. His steps were dignified, unhurried, unwavering and directly on course towards Stephanie's writhing body. The widow was lost inside Patricia.

The Mistress of Novices had her eyes shut, shaking, her fingers buried in Stephanie's pretty golden hair, grinding her quivering needy clit unto Stephanie's merciless tongue.

Steven looked around in desperation. How could he stop Warener? He was no warrior. He could not allow him to kill Princess. He had to have Princess. He had to stick his dick inside Stephanie. It was just something he had to do. Warener had to be stopped. Desperate, he scanned the crowd for inspiration.

Warener approached the two harlots in the centre of the nave. He raised his sword, about to strike, when he heard a voice call out his name. The voice – the voice was somehow familiar.

'Bishop Warener . . .' The shrill manipulative whiny contralto seemed to touch a heretofore unsullied portion of

Warener's soul. His cock, already iron-hard from the stimulation of the unholy orgy around him, twitched beneath his vestments. His eyes focused on the small figure in the very back of the church. She stood next to Prior Steven. The girl was naked except for golden dancing shoes, the kind with the very high heels, and a rich yellow gold necklace with sparkling red rubies over her bosom. She was tiny, exquisite, with long, lustrous ringlets of red hair cascading all the way down to a round perfect white bottom. The beautiful red-haired slut was holding one of the censers in her hand, the vessel still emitting great clouds of sweet-scented smoke. Despite her diminutive size, the girl's breasts were large and firm, the nipples stiff little daggers digging into his soul. Her pussy was covered in a soft silky carpet of red hair. He heard himself address the seductive little vision, speaking the name of the woman who tore his heart out so many years ago. 'Molly?'

She giggled – my god, he thought, that voice! – it is her! – and she began to walk towards him, her stiletto heels clicking on the chapel floor. He lowered his sword, his mission forgotten.

'Molly? Is that really you?'

'Mum never had tits like mine . . .' giggled the redheaded harlot before him. 'Don't you think?' She was swinging the censer as if she was chasing away the devil, the cloud of incense a shadowy haze, a dark aura surrounding her.

He found it difficult to breathe. His skin tingled. Every time he took a breath his cock twitched, oozing at the tip with unholy lust. He wanted to fuck every single one of the corrupted Brides of the Lord he passed by, he wanted to fuck them until they squealed for mercy . . . But more than anything in this world, more than salvation, more than God, more than the honour of his sword or his order, he wanted to fuck the little redheaded bitch in front of him.

She was coming closer, shepherding her cloud of smoke. Her appearance only improved with less distance. He was staring at the gorgeous temptress with his mouth agape, drawing great gulps of sweet-scented smoke-tainted air. His fingers weakened and the sword clattered to the floor.

The sound was sharp, metallic, coldly different from the moans of fornication that filled the small church. He felt skilful fingers disrobe him from behind, long pink- and red-tipped fingernails stroking his addled flesh from all sides as they stripped the vestments of his office and his calling. He numbly stepped inside Evelyn's cloud of smoke.

'Bishops are rich . . .' giggled Evelyn, and wrapped her exquisite manicured fingers around Warener's member.

The leading publisher of fetish and adult fiction

TELL US WHAT YOU THINK!

Readers' ideas and opinions matter to us. Take a few minutes to fill in the questionnaire below and you'll be entered into a prize draw to win a year's worth of Nexus books (36 titles)

Terms and conditions apply – see end of questionnaire.

1. **Sex:** Are you male ☐ female ☐ a couple ☐?

2. **Age:** Under 21 ☐ 21–30 ☐ 31–40 ☐ 41–50 ☐ 51–60 ☐ over 60 ☐

3. **Where do you buy your Nexus books from?**

☐ A chain book shop. If so, which one(s)?

____

☐ An independent book shop. If so, which one(s)?

____

☐ A used book shop/charity shop

☐ Online book store. If so, which one(s)?

____

4. **How did you find out about Nexus books?**

☐ Browsing in a book shop

☐ A review in a magazine

☐ Online

☐ Recommendation

☐ Other ____________________________________

5. **In terms of settings, which do you prefer? (Tick as many as you like)**

☐ Down to earth and as realistic as possible

☐ Historical settings. If so, which period do you prefer?

____

☐ Fantasy settings – barbarian worlds

☐ Completely escapist/surreal fantasy
☐ Institutional or secret academy
☐ Futuristic/sci fi
☐ Escapist but still believable
☐ Any settings you dislike?

____

☐ Where would you like to see an adult novel set?

____

6. In terms of storylines, would you prefer:

☐ Simple stories that concentrate on adult interests?
☐ More plot and character-driven stories with less explicit adult activity?
☐ We value your ideas, so give us your opinion of this book:

____

____

____

7. In terms of your adult interests, what do you like to read about? (Tick as many as you like)

☐ Traditional corporal punishment (CP)
☐ Modern corporal punishment
☐ Spanking
☐ Restraint/bondage
☐ Rope bondage
☐ Latex/rubber
☐ Leather
☐ Female domination and male submission
☐ Female domination and female submission
☐ Male domination and female submission
☐ Willing captivity
☐ Uniforms
☐ Lingerie/underwear/hosiery/footwear (boots and high heels)
☐ Sex rituals
☐ Vanilla sex
☐ Swinging
☐ Cross-dressing/TV

☐ Enforced feminisation
☐ Others – tell us what you don't see enough of in adult fiction:

____

____

____

8. Would you prefer books with a more specialised approach to your interests, i.e. a novel specifically about uniforms? If so, which subject(s) would you like to read a Nexus novel about?

____

____

____

9. Would you like to read true stories in Nexus books? For instance, the true story of a submissive woman, or a male slave? Tell us which true revelations you would most like to read about:

____

____

____

10. What do you like best about Nexus books?

____

____

11. What do you like least about Nexus books?

____

____

12. Which are your favourite titles?

____

____

13. Who are your favourite authors?

____

____

14. **Which covers do you prefer? Those featuring: (tick as many as you like)**

- ☐ Fetish outfits
- ☐ More nudity
- ☐ Two models
- ☐ Unusual models or settings
- ☐ Classic erotic photography
- ☐ More contemporary images and poses
- ☐ A blank/non-erotic cover
- ☐ What would your ideal cover look like?

____

15. **Describe your ideal Nexus novel in the space provided:**

____

____

____

____

16. **Which celebrity would feature in one of your Nexus-style fantasies? We'll post the best suggestions on our website – anonymously!**

____

THANKS FOR YOUR TIME

Now simply write the title of this book in the space below and cut out the questionnaire pages. Post to: Nexus, Marketing Dept., Thames Wharf Studios, Rainville Rd, London W6 9HA

Book title: ____________________________________

TERMS AND CONDITIONS

1. The competition is open to UK residents only, excluding employees of Nexus and Virgin, their families, agents and anyone connected with the promotion of the competition. 2. Entrants must be aged 18 years or over. 3. Closing date for receipt of entries is 31 December 2006. 4. The first entry drawn on 7 January 2007 will be declared the winner and notified by Nexus. 5. The decision of the judges is final. No correspondence will be entered into. 6. No purchase necessary. Entries restricted to one per household. 7. The prize is non-transferable and non-refundable and no alternatives can be substituted. 8. Nexus reserves the right to amend or terminate any part of the promotion without prior notice. 9. No responsibility is accepted for fraudulent, damaged, illegible or incomplete entries. Proof of sending is not proof of receipt. 10. The winner's name will be available from the above address from 9 January 2007.

Promoter: Nexus, Thames Wharf Studios, Rainville Road, London, W6 9HA

NEXUS NEW BOOKS

To be published in November 2006

STRIP GIRL
Aishling Morgan

Shy, self-conscious Sarah is all too used to attracting male attention to her ample bust and well-formed bottom, despite never really knowing what to do about it. Offered her dream job as a cartoonist, she is willing to sacrifice a little of her own dignity by drawing cartoons for men's magazines. Unfortunately, the job also means sacrificing every last scrape of propriety for Sarah's heroine, the exquisite Celeste du Musigny, which has unforeseen repercussions, ensuring that Sarah comes to live out every last detail of her darkest and most secret fantasies.

£6.99 ISBN 0 352 34077 0

SLAVE OF THE SPARTANS
Yolanda Celbridge

Ben Fraunce goes up to Oxford to read classics, and is sucked into the Society of Spartans: a cult of female domination specialising in the cruel punishment of innocent males, by bare-bottom flogging, and humiliating cross-dressing. When he is allowed by the Spartan dommes to spend his summer vacations on their Greek island, toiling as a naked slave, under their whips, or with his young skirted body used to satisfy their most lustful and decadent desires, he at last understands that no male is ever innocent.

£6.99 ISBN 0 352 34078 9

OVER THE KNEE
Fiona Locke

This is the life story of a girl addicted to the sensual pleasures of spanking. A girl who feels compelled to manipulate and engineer situations in which older authority figures punish her, over their knees.

And as *Nexus Enthusiast* publishes convincing and exciting literature, written by the devotee of a single fetish for the large number of enthusiasts of that same kink, the author is fully qualified, as an adult corporal punishment film star, and active participant of the S&M scene.

£6.99 ISBN 0 352 34079 7

This information is correct at time of printing. For up-to-date information, please visit our website at www.nexus-books.co.uk

All books are priced at £6.99 unless another price is given.

ABANDONED ALICE	Adriana Arden 0 352 33969 1	☐
ALICE IN CHAINS	Adriana Arden 0 352 33908 X	☐
AMAZON SLAVE	Lisette Ashton 0 352 33916 0	☐
ANGEL	Lindsay Gordon 0 352 34009 6	☐
AQUA DOMINATION	William Doughty 0 352 34020 7	☐
THE ART OF CORRECTION	Tara Black 0 352 33895 4	☐
THE ART OF SURRENDER	Madeline Bastinado 0 352 34013 4	☐
AT THE END OF HER TETHER	G.C. Scott 0 352 33857 1	☐
BELINDA BARES UP	Yolanda Celbridge 0 352 33926 8	☐
BENCH MARKS	Tara Black 0 352 33797 4	☐
BIDDING TO SIN	Rosita Varón 0 352 34063 0	☐
BINDING PROMISES	G.C. Scott 0 352 34014 2	☐
THE BLACK GARTER	Lisette Ashton 0 352 33919 5	☐
THE BLACK MASQUE	Lisette Ashton 0 352 33977 2	☐
THE BLACK ROOM	Lisette Ashton 0 352 33914 4	☐
THE BLACK WIDOW	Lisette Ashton 0 352 33973 X	☐
THE BOND	Lindsay Gordon 0 352 33996 9	☐

THE BOOK OF PUNISHMENT	Cat Scarlett 0 352 33975 6	☐
BRUSH STROKES	Penny Birch 0 352 34072 X	☐
BUSTY	Tom King 0 352 34032 0	☐
CAGED [£5.99]	Yolanda Celbridge 0 352 33650 1	☐
CALLED TO THE WILD	Angel Blake 0 352 34067 3	☐
CAPTIVES OF CHEYNER CLOSE	Adriana Arden 0 352 34028 2	☐
CARNAL POSSESSION	Yvonne Strickland 0 352 34062 2	☐
CHERRI CHASTISED	Yolanda Celbridge 0 352 33707 9	☐
COLLEGE GIRLS	Cat Scarlett 0 352 33942 X	☐
COMPANY OF SLAVES	Christina Shelly 0 352 33887 3	☐
CONCEIT AND CONSEQUENCE	Aishling Morgan 0 352 33965 9	☐
CONFESSIONS OF AN ENGLISH SLAVE	Yolanda Celbridge 0 352 33861 X	☐
CORRUPTION	Virginia Crowley 0 352 34073 8	☐
DARK MISCHIEF	Lady Alice McCloud 0 352 33998 5	☐
DEPTHS OF DEPRAVATION	Ray Gordon 0 352 33995 0	☐
DERRIÈRE	Julius Culdrose 0 352 34024 X	☐
DICE WITH DOMINATION	P.S. Brett 0 352 34023 1	☐
DISCIPLINE OF THE PRIVATE HOUSE	Esme Ombreux 0 352 33709 5	☐
DOMINANT	Felix Baron 0 352 34044 4	☐
THE DOMINO ENIGMA	Cyrian Amberlake 0 352 34064 9	☐
THE DOMINO QUEEN	Cyrian Amberlake 0 352 34074 6	☐

THE DOMINO TATTOO	Cyrian Amberlake 0 352 34037 1	☐
DOMINATION DOLLS	Lindsay Gordon 0 352 33891 1	☐
EMMA ENSLAVED	Hilary James 0 352 33883 0	☐
EMMA'S HUMILIATION	Hilary James 0 352 33910 1	☐
EMMA'S SECRET DOMINATION	Hilary James 0 352 34000 2	☐
EMMA'S SUBMISSION	Hilary James 0 352 33906 3	☐
EXPOSÉ	Laura Bowen 0 352 34035 5	☐
FAIRGROUND ATTRACTION	Lisette Ashton 0 352 33927 6	☐
FORBIDDEN READING	Lisette Ashton 0 352 34022 3	☐
FRESH FLESH	Wendy Swanscombe 0 352 34041 X	☐
THE GOVERNESS ABROAD	Yolanda Celbridge 0 352 33735 4	☐
HOT PURSUIT	Lisette Ashton 0 352 33878 4	☐
THE INDECENCIES OF ISABELLE	Penny Birch (writing as Cruella) 0 352 33989 6	☐
THE INDISCRETIONS OF ISABELLE	Penny Birch (writing as Cruella) 0 352 33882 2	☐
IN HER SERVICE	Lindsay Gordon 0 352 33968 3	☐
THE INSTITUTE	Maria Del Rey 0 352 33352 9	☐
JULIA C	Laura Bowen 0 352 33852 0	☐
KNICKERS AND BOOTS	Penny Birch 0 352 33853 9	☐
LACING LISBETH	Yolanda Celbridge 0 352 33912 8	☐
LEG LOVER	L.G. Denier 0 352 34016 9	☐

LICKED CLEAN	Yolanda Celbridge 0 352 33999 3	☐
NON FICTION: LESBIAN SEX SECRETS FOR MEN	Jamie Goddard and Kurt Brungard 0 352 33724 9	☐
LESSONS IN OBEDIENCE	Lucy Golden 0 352 33892 X	☐
LOVE JUICE	Donna Exeter 0 352 33913 6	☐
MANSLAVE	J.D. Jensen 0 352 34040 1	☐
THE MASTER OF CASTLELEIGH [£5.99]	Jacqueline Bellevois 0 352 33644 7	☐
MISS RATAN'S LESSON	Yolanda Celbridge 0 352 33791 5	☐
NAUGHTY NAUGHTY	Penny Birch 0 352 33974 4	☐
NEW EROTICA 5	Various 0 352 33956 X	☐
NEW EROTICA 6	Various 0 352 33751 6	☐
THE NEXUS LETTERS	Various 0 352 33955 1	☐
NIGHTS IN WHITE COTTON	Penny Birch 0 352 34008 8	☐
NO PAIN, NO GAIN	James Baron 0 352 33966 7	☐
NURSE'S ORDERS	Penny Birch 0 352 33739 7	☐
THE OLD PERVERSITY SHOP	Aishling Morgan 0 352 34007 X	☐
ONE WEEK IN THE PRIVATE HOUSE	Esme Ombreux 0 352 33706 0	☐
ORIGINAL SINS	Lisette Ashton 0 352 33804 0	☐
THE PALACE OF PLEASURES	Christobel Coleridge 0 352 33801 6	☐
PALE PLEASURES	Wendy Swanscombe 0 352 33702 8	☐
PENNY PIECES [£5.99]	Penny Birch 0 352 33631 5	☐

PETTING GIRLS	Penny Birch 0 352 33957 8	☐
PET TRAINING IN THE PRIVATE HOUSE [£5.99]	Esme Ombreux 0 352 33655 2	☐
THE PLAYER	Cat Scarlett 0 352 33894 6	☐
PLAYTHING	Penny Birch 0 352 33967 5	☐
PLEASING THEM	William Doughty 0 352 34015 0	☐
PRIZE OF PAIN	Wendy Swanscombe 0 352 33890 3	☐
THE PRIESTESS	Jacqueline Bellevois 0 352 33905 5	☐
PUNISHED IN PINK	Yolanda Celbridge 0 352 34003 7	☐
THE PUNISHMENT CAMP	Jacqueline Masterson 0 352 33940 3	☐
THE PUNISHMENT CLUB	Jacqueline Masterson 0 352 33862 8	☐
RITES OF OBEDIENCE	Lindsay Gordon 0 352 34005 3	☐
SCARLET VICE	Aishling Morgan 0 352 33988 8	☐
SCHOOLED FOR SERVICE	Lady Alice McCloud 0 352 33918 7	☐
SCHOOL FOR STINGERS	Yolanda Celbridge 0 352 33994 2	☐
THE SECRET SELF	Christina Shelly 0 352 34069 X	☐
SERVING TIME	Sarah Veitch 0 352 33509 2	☐
SEXUAL HEELING	Wendy Swanscombe 0 352 33921 7	☐
SILKEN SERVITUDE	Christina Shelly 0 352 34004 5	☐
SINS APPRENTICE	Aishling Morgan 0 352 33909 8	☐
SLAVE ACTS	Jennifer Jane Pope 0 352 33665 X	☐
SLAVE GENESIS [£5.99]	Jennifer Jane Pope 0 352 33503 3	☐

THE SMARTING OF SELINA	Yolanda Celbridge 0 352 33872 5	☐
STRIPING KAYLA	Yvonne Marshall 0 352 33881 4	☐
STRIPPED BARE	Angel Blake 0 352 33971 3	☐
THE SUBMISSION GALLERY [£5.99]	Lindsay Gordon 0 352 33370 7	☐
THE SUBMISSION OF STELLA	Yolanda Celbridge 0 352 33854 7	☐
THE TAMING OF TRUDI	Yolanda Celbridge 0 352 33673 0	☐
TASTING CANDY	Ray Gordon 0 352 33925 X	☐
TEMPTING THE GODDESS	Aishling Morgan 0 352 33972 1	☐
THAI HONEY	Kit McCann 0 352 34068 1	☐
TICKLE TORTURE	Penny Birch 0 352 33904 7	☐
TIE AND TEASE	Penny Birch 0 352 33987 X	☐
TIGHT WHITE COTTON	Penny Birch 0 352 33970 5	☐
TOKYO BOUND	Sachi 0 352 34019 3	☐
TORMENT INCORPORATED	Murilee Martin 0 352 33943 8	☐
THE TRAINING GROUNDS	Sarah Veitch 0 352 33526 2	☐
UNDER MY MASTER'S WINGS	Lauren Wissot 0 352 34042 8	☐
UNEARTHLY DESIRES	Ray Gordon 0 352 34036 3	☐
UNIFORM DOLL	Penny Birch 0 352 33698 6	☐
VELVET SKIN [£5.99]	Aishling Morgan 0 352 33660 9	☐
WENCHES WITCHES AND STRUMPETS	Aishling Morgan 0 352 33733 8	☐
WHAT HAPPENS TO BAD GIRLS	Penny Birch 0 352 34031 2	☐

- - - - - - ✂ -

Please send me the books I have ticked above.

Name ....

Address ....

....

....

.... Post code ....

Send to: **Virgin Books Cash Sales, Thames Wharf Studios, Rainville Road, London W6 9HA**

US customers: for prices and details of how to order books for delivery by mail, call 888-330-8477.

Please enclose a cheque or postal order, made payable to **Nexus Books Ltd**, to the value of the books you have ordered plus postage and packing costs as follows:

UK and BFPO – £1.00 for the first book, 50p for each subsequent book.

Overseas (including Republic of Ireland) – £2.00 for the first book, £1.00 for each subsequent book.

If you would prefer to pay by VISA, ACCESS/MASTERCARD, AMEX, DINERS CLUB or SWITCH, please write your card number and expiry date here:

....

Please allow up to 28 days for delivery.

Signature ....

Our privacy policy

We will not disclose information you supply us to any other parties. We will not disclose any information which identifies you personally to any person without your express consent.

From time to time we may send out information about Nexus books and special offers. Please tick here if you do *not* wish to receive Nexus information. ☐

- - - - - - ✂ -